IN THE CHERRY TREE

IN THE CHERRY TREE

DAN POPE

picador NEW YORK

 For information, address Picador, 175 Fifth Avenue, New York, N.Y. 10010.

Picador® is a U.S. registered trademark and is used by St. Martin's Press under license from Pan Books Limited.

www.picadorusa.com

Book design by Jonathan Bennett

Library of Congress Cataloging-in-Publication Data

Pope, Dan.
In the cherry tree / Dan Pope.—1st ed.
p. cm.
ISBN 0-312-42236-9
1. Boys—Fiction. 2. Suburban life—Fiction. 3. Connecticut—Fiction.
I. Title.

PS3616.O6515 2003
813'.6—dc21

2003049893

First Edition: October 2003

10 9 8 7 6 5 4 3 2 1

ACKNOWLEDGMENTS

I wish to express my gratitude to Glenn Schaeffer and the International Institute of Modern Letters for the Glenn Schaeffer Award;

and to my agent, Esmond Harmsworth, and editor, Josh Kendall, for their extraordinary support.

IN THE CHERRY TREE

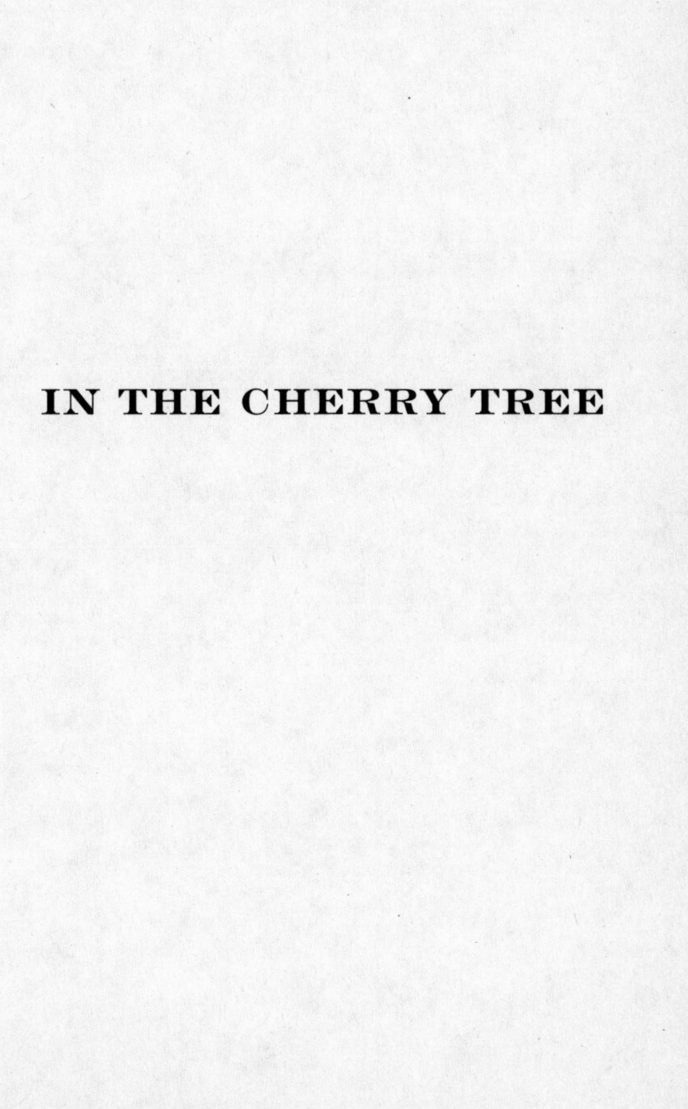

1.
APPLE HILL ROAD

Summer days began without a plan. You got up. You had a bowl of cereal. You went outside. A lawn mower hummed. Ducks passed overhead in perfect V formation like World War Two bombers. A dog barked, and another dog barked back. Somebody was hammering nails into a roof. Somebody was bouncing a basketball two streets away. You heard the sound, then the echo. A cat crept across the grass and disappeared beneath a hedge. It was hot. The sun was strong. The crickets made a seething noise. A sprinkler came on and made a quiet rain sound when the water hit the grass and then a louder rain sound when the water hit the street.

"Let's do something."

"Like what?"

"I don't know."

"Crab apple fight?"

"Nah."

We thought it over. After a while someone got an idea, and we did something.

Our street before it was a street used to be an apple orchard. The apple trees were planted in neat rows that went up the hill as far as you could see. The Dad told us about the apple trees. He remembered them from when he was a boy. He used to come out to the country for picnics with his family in his father's car, which was called a Graham Paige, and they would get a drink of apple cider at the farmhouse and walk around the apple orchards.

That was a long time ago.

When they built our street the builders cut down most of the apple trees and sawed up the logs and dragged the branches away. The builders left some of the apple trees for looks. Every house had one in the front yard, giving off shade and dropping crab apples into the grass. Everyone kicked or swept the crab apples into the street, where they got smashed and worm-eaten and smelled like rot. The crab apples were not good to eat. They were sour. Mik Cosgrove ate them but no one else did. We threw the crab apples at cars and squirrels, at telephone poles and each other. Once I nailed Albert in the middle of his forehead with a rotten crab apple, which exploded. The Dad saw it from the kitchen window and came outside and said, "That's a good way to take someone's eye out."

All the houses on our street looked the same except for the farmhouse. The houses were white, split-level houses with flat roofs. Some of the front doors were painted different colors. On every stoop was a gray milk box. Each house had a sign above the front door that said something like "Welcome," or "Home Sweet Home," or "Bless This House." The sign above our door said "35."

We lived at number thirty-five. Stev lived directly across the street from us. Tiger lived next to Stev. Mik Cosgrove lived next to Tiger. Franky DiLorenzo lived across the street from Mik Cosgrove. The Estabrooks lived next to us. At night Diana Estabrook kissed boys on her porch swing while Albert and I watched from our bedroom window. All the boys liked to kiss Diana Estabrook.

The farmhouse was located at the bottom of the street. The farmhouse was built in 1805, according to the little sign on the front door. A brook ran through the backyard of the farmhouse. There was a well in the yard with a pump and a bucket which no one used anymore. The well was for looks. It had no water. The sign on the farmhouse mailbox said "Geo. W. Sage," but nobody by that name lived in the farmhouse. An old lady lived there, but the lights were always off. The old lady had never been seen. She lived her whole life in the farmhouse and never came out. She was like a rare butterfly. If you could just catch a glimpse of her with your binoculars, your life would be special. But it never happened, not once.

2.
THE GROUNDHOG ARRIVES

That summer, a groundhog invaded our backyard. The groundhog arrived in the middle of June, after school had ended. The groundhog made a tunnel in the backyard that went around and around, making ridges in the grass like a pencil doodle. The tunnel ended underneath the back porch.

The Mom said, "I'll call the humane society. They'll know what to do."

The Dad said, "Don't bother. I'll take care of it. Come on, Timmy."

The Mom said, "What are you going to do?"

He got into the Mark IV, drove very slowly onto the lawn and steered around to the backyard, making tread marks in the grass. He stopped next to the back porch and got out. The car looked strange sitting on the lawn.

The Mom came out onto the back porch. She said, "What in God's name are you doing?"

"Watch and learn," said The Dad.

He taped the black garden hose with duct tape to the exhaust pipe, then stuck the other end of the hose down the groundhog hole and filled in the hole with dirt. Then he got back into the car and gunned the motor. Approximately five seconds later smoke started pouring out of three separate holes in the backyard.

The Dad said to me, "You see him?"

"No. You?"

"No."

"Maybe we got him."

"Maybe. Or maybe he's got some holes that we don't know about. Maybe there's more than one groundhog. Maybe there's a bunch of them."

"What's a bunch of groundhogs called?"

"I don't know. A family?"

After a couple of minutes of gunning the motor, the backyard smelled like car exhaust.

The Mom said, "Stop that this instant. What are the neighbors going to think? I've never been so embarrassed in my entire life." She went inside and slammed the door.

The Dad said, "Okay. That's enough."

He unwrapped the hose, and we drove around the side of the house and parked in the garage.

The Dad looked like Rock Hudson with a gob of Brylcreem in his hair, which was black and thick and low on his forehead. The Mark IV was his pride and joy. He used to own a Mark III, but he traded it in for the Mark IV the day the new model came out. The Mark IV was dark blue and had a V-8 engine with maximum horsepower. The Dad washed and simonized the Mark IV regularly, rubbing and buffing it with a terry cloth. He had a special compound to take out scratches. As soon as he was done washing and waxing he immediately put the car in the garage and closed the overhead door. The Dad acted like a big shot when operating the Mark IV. He'd wheel into a restaurant parking lot, push down the tinted windows and tell the car jockey, "Park it in a safe spot, kid. I'll make it worth your while." Or he'd tell the package store clerk, "Get me a case of your best champagne. I don't care what it costs. Put it in the trunk of my car. The Mark IV." The Dad disliked foreign cars. He often told Stev's Dad, "Do yourself a favor. Get rid of that German car before it burns a hole in your pocket. Get yourself a Continental."

Sometimes The Dad let Albert drive the Mark IV around the driveway. Albert would recline the seat as far as it would go, so that he was practically lying down. He'd drive to the end of the driveway and back, switching the gearshift lever from *D* for Drive to *R* for Reverse. Sometimes he backed into Stev's driveway or went all the way around the block, but generally he stayed in our driveway, going back and forth. I would sit in the passenger seat, adjusting the dials on the radio. I did not drive because my feet did not touch the pedals, even with the seat pushed all the way forward.

Tiger's Brother was standing at the end of our driveway. He said, "What's going on?"

The Dad said, "Got a groundhog here."

I said, "We're smoking him out."

Tiger's Brother said, "You think that'll work?"

The Dad said, "Should."

Tiger's Brother said, "Bob. I got one for you. Listen to this."

Tiger's Brother stood very close to The Dad. Tiger's Brother always stood close to you when he talked, sometimes within inches of your face, so that you could smell his cabbage breath. He talked in a tone of voice like someone telling you a secret. He said to The Dad in his secretive voice: "Three guys go into a bar. A Jew. A guinea. And a Polack."

I couldn't hear the rest of the joke.

The Dad said, "Heh."

Tiger's Brother said, "Did you like that one?"

The Dad said, "Heh heh."

We went inside. The Mom looked up from the kitchen sink, where she was cleaning dishes. She said, "What did he want?"

The Dad said, "Who?"

"You know very well who."

"He told me a joke. I've never known anyone who knows so many jokes. He must write them down."

"Did he see you driving on the lawn?"

"No."

I said, "Yes, he did."

The Dad said to me, "Don't be a squeal."

"Don't yell at him for telling the truth. He's not a liar like his father."

"You call me a liar in front of the kids?"

"You know what that person is like. He'll tell his mother. She'll tell everyone in town."

"Tell them what? What is there to tell, for Christsake? That we got a groundhog?"

"Do you think it's normal driving on the lawn in the middle of the day with everyone watching? Is that what you call normal behavior?"

"Who the hell cares what they think."

"I wanted to call the humane society, but no, you had to do it your way. That's what I get for marrying a Front Street wop."

"Don't start that wop business."

"I'll start any business I like."

"Call the boys wops while you're calling names."

"These boys are Scottish through and through."

"They're half Italian. That makes 'em half wops. Isn't that right, Timmy?"

I said, "I'm a wop. Wop wop wop."

The Mom said, "Don't say that. You're no such thing. You take after me. Anyone can see that."

The Dad said, "Sure, he does. He's a perfect little Scotsman with his black hair and brown eyes."

"Have you been drinking? Is that why you drove the car on the lawn?"

Albert walked into the kitchen and said, "Could you shut up, please?"

The Dad said, "Don't tell your mother to shut up."

Albert said, "Why not?"

The Dad said, "Because I say so, that's why."

The Mom said, "Leave him alone."

I said, "I have hazel eyes. Not brown."

The Dad said, "You hear that? Hazel eyes. Goddamn right you do, just like me. What color are your mother's eyes?"

I said, "I don't know."

The Dad said, "She's got gray eyes like an owl and thin lips. Never get involved with a thin-lipped woman. You boys remember that when you get older."

I said, "Why?"

The Dad said, "Nothing as cold as a thin-lipped woman."

The Mom said, "I wish you would die. I really do."

The Dad said, "Keep wishing."

The next day there were new groundhog tracks in the backyard.

3.
CHERRIES

Stev was my best friend. He and I grew up together. There were family pictures of Stev and Albert and me in each other's playpens, wearing diapers. Stev was always smiling, sitting next to us. His real name was Steve but we called him Stev because we had a rule against having an *e* at the end of your first name. *E*'s were not allowed. Therefore we called Steve Stev and Mike Cosgrove Mik Cosgrove. Stev was fourteen, two years older than me and one year older than Albert. He was going into the tenth grade in the fall. He went to a different school. He and I were the same height even though Stev was older. I was fast but Stev was faster. He could run faster than anyone we knew.

Stev and I liked the same things. We liked badminton, which we played in his backyard in games to 500. We liked eating cherries off the tree. We liked asking each other TV questions. I would ask, "Where does Joe Friday live?" and Stev would answer, "At home with his mother," and I would say, "Correct." We liked keeping lists of our favorite movies and records and TV shows. We liked listening to WDRC's "Top 30 Songs of the Week Based on Sales and Requests in Big D Country." We liked Chicago and Todd Rundgren and Harry Chapin and last but definitely not least Elton John, whose real name was Reg Dwight. Stev and I had every Elton John album ever made. If Elton John came on TV, I would immediately telephone Stev and tell him: "Turn on the Wolfman. Quick. Elton's on." Sometimes the phone was busy when I called Stev because he was trying to call me and tell me the same thing.

The cherry tree was located on the high side of our front lawn. Some of the branches hung over the driveway approximately twenty feet in the air. That did not bother Stev. Stev was fearless. He climbed to the highest branch, which bent slightly when he sat on it. A crow landed on a branch next to Stev and squawked. A crow was a despicable creature that liked cherries. Stev spat three cherry pits at the crow and it looked at him and pecked a cherry and flew away. We counted the cherries as we ate them. The final tally was not available until approximately two hours later. The results were as follows: Stev ate 308 cherries. I ate 251. Taken together, it was the single greatest day of cherry eating in history.

Tiger walked up the driveway while we were picking cherries. Stev and I sat silently watching him. He had no clue that we were on the branches above his head. Stev spat a cherry pit at Tiger. The cherry pit landed on the driveway and made a sound. Tiger stopped and looked behind and saw nothing and scratched his head. He went up the steps to the front door and knocked the knocker and asked The Mom, "Is Timmy home?"

The Mom said, "They're in the tree, Anthony."

Stev and I yelled, "Hi, I'm Tony the Tiger and I've got a purple splotch on my neck. Hi, I'm Tony the Tiger and I'm a spaz. Hi, I'm Tony the Tiger and I'm number two on the all-time-spaz list behind Mik Cosgrove."

The Mom said, "Don't eat too many cherries boys or you'll get sick."

Tiger said, "Can I have some?" He stepped on the precious lower branch and tried to climb the sacred route.

Stev told him, "You're not allowed until you pass the test."

"What test?"

We climbed down and went into the backyard. The test took place underneath the back porch.

Stev said, "Pull down your pants."

Tiger got on the ground and pulled down his shorts. "Don't give me a wedgie," he said.

Stev got behind Tiger and sat on his legs and stuck the end of the little green garden hose in his butt. He dropped three pebbles one by one into the hose. The pebbles rattled and clanked. He poured a handful of dirt into the hose. The dirt sifted and slid.

Tiger yelled, "Hey, cut it out, Steve. That hurts."

Stev said, "Demerit."

"Confirmed," said I.

Tiger got up and went into the corner and bent over and made a face.

Stev said, "The greatest line from *Night Gallery* is 'You got my Charlie flat out on a slab.' "

I said, " 'As ye rip, ye shall be ripped.' "

Stev said, "*Hawaii Five-O*."

"Correct," said I.

Tiger said, "Why did I get a demerit?"

Stev told Tiger, "You said Steve. Steve is wrong. The name is Stev. No one calls me Steve."

Tiger said, "Why not?"

Stev said, "Rule number one. Never have an *e* at the end of your name."

Tiger said, "Can I go up the tree now?"

Stev told him, "You got a demerit. A demerit means you have to pass test number two."

"What's test number two?"

"Do you know what the best song is?"

"No."

"The best song is 'The Night Chicago Died.' "

"So?"

"Do you know what the best movie is?"

"No."

"The best movie is *Killdozer*."

"So?"

Stev picked up the bicycle pump that we kept underneath the back porch and showed it to Tiger. "Do you know what this is?"

Tiger said, "Bicycle pump."

Stev said, "Wrong. This is the most unbelievable farting machine ever created."

I said, "You won't believe it."

Stev said, "This is the best."

I said, "It's unbelievable."

Stev said, "Bend over."

Tiger pulled down his pants and bent over. Stev took the end of the bicycle pump and stuck it in his butt.

"Stay still," I said.

I started pumping. I pumped and Tiger started giggling and I pumped and he grabbed his stomach and giggled and I pumped and Tiger said, "That's enough," and I pumped until it got hard to push down the lever and Tiger reached around and pulled out the end of the bicycle pump and cut the single greatest fart in the history of farting. He farted one long fart that didn't change in pitch or volume but just kept going and going and Tiger held his stomach, which was puffed up, and said, "Make it go down." Stev and I hit the dirt. We rolled in the dirt and laughed the soundless laugh.

Stev and I wrote everything down. Our records were meticulous. If someone dropped a neutron bomb on Apple Hill Road and killed all the people but left the houses intact, the knowledge would survive. Future generations would not be mystified by our existence. Everything you needed to know was contained in seven bright blue spiral-bound notebooks, which were located in my room in the bottom drawer of my desk.

Stev said, "Quiz me."

I said, "What subject?"

"*Big Valley.*"

I turned to the page of the notebook entitled "The Big Valley" and asked Stev the following questions:

"What is the name of the Barkleys' youngest son who is always away at college? Which of the Barkleys is a counselor-at-law? What is the name of Victoria Barkley's husband, who is now deceased? Which Barkley don't take nothing from nobody? What is the nearest town to the Barkley Ranch?"

Stev answered all the questions correctly except for the first, which was Eugene.

After I told him, Stev said, "I knew that. I just couldn't remember it."

I said, "Tough luck." I waited for a moment then said in my cowboy voice, "You Barkleys think you're so high and mighty."

Stev said, "Give me another."

"*Happy Days*. Are you ready?"

"Begin. I dare you to begin."

I said, "What is Potsie's real name, first and last? Who is the basketball star of the Cunningham family? What is the name of the head waitress at Arnold's? Richie goes to what high school? What musical instrument does Ralph Malph play?"

Stev said, "Difficult. But not difficult enough."

He answered every question correctly, and I recorded his score in "The TV Testament" and made a notation of the time and date.

I said, "What do you want to do?"

Stev said, "Watch TV."

We went into the den and turned on the TV. *It Takes a Thief* was playing, starring Robert Wagner as Alexander Munday. We watched the episode entitled "The Day of the Duchess." After the show was over we ruled that "The Day of the Duchess" was the third greatest *It Takes a Thief* episode of all time, behind "Project X" and "The Beautiful People." Stev said that the best line was: "Call Ryker. Tell him the world ends in twenty minutes."

"Confirmed," said I.

We began to watch *The Andromeda Strain* but did not finish because Stev got the runs and had to go home.

After dinner, I went to Stev's house. The Myra was sitting on the couch in the den smoking a Pall Mall and watching the *CBS Evening News with Walter Cronkite*. She said, "Hello, Timothy."

I said, "Hi, I'm Walter Cronkite and I have bad breath. Hi, I'm Walter Cronkite and that's the way it was June 15, 1974. Hi, I'm Walter Cronkite and the big story tonight is, Where's Stev?"

The Myra said, "He's lying down. He's nauseous. His tongue was bright red when he came home and he made in his pants because he couldn't help it. I want you to promise me to stay out of the cherry tree for two days. Promise me, Timmy. Promise me that you won't let Steven go up the cherry tree."

"I can't."

"Why not?"

"Because he might climb the tree when I'm not around. He might pick cherries in the morning when I'm sleeping. I'd never know unless he told me."

"Are you being precious?"

"I'm answering your question."

"I'm serious. Steven is as sick as a dog. Go up and see him if you don't believe me."

I went upstairs and opened the door to Stev's room. Stev was lying on his bed listening with his headphones to Elton John's double album, *Goodbye Yellow Brick Road,* which was number one on the list of the All-Time Top 100 Albums. There was no noise except for Stev's breathing and the faint strains of "Funeral for a Friend," which sounded tinny and far away. Stev nodded when he saw me. I sat on the bed across from his bed. Stev said very loudly although he thought he was speaking normally, "Call Ryker. Tell him the world ends in twenty minutes."

There was a plate on the night table filled with orange peels. I opened the side window and tossed one of the orange peels toward Tony the Tiger's house. The orange peel landed in the bushes. I wound up and threw another. It bounced off the side of the house. Stev removed the headphones and picked up an orange peel and hurled it. The orange peel bounced off Tony the Tiger's den window. I whipped an orange peel and it landed in the bushes. Stev threw an orange peel and it hit the window. I threw an orange peel and it hit the window. There were no more orange peels.

A few minutes later the doorbell rang and we looked out the front window and saw Tony the Tiger's Mother standing on the doorstep with a pile of orange peels in her hand.

We went into Stev's closet and closed the door and pulled the rope to make the ladder come down and climbed the ladder into the attic and crawled into the crawl space beside the attic window where no one I repeat absolutely no one could possibly find us no matter how long they looked, especially not Tony the Tiger's Fat Ass Mother and her stinky orange peels.

Stev said, "I got the runs but it was worth it. Three hundred and eight cherries, a new all-time record."

Later that night a raccoon went up the cherry tree. The raccoon climbed to the top of the tree and went onto the branch that leaned out over the driveway and held on with its sharp fingers and ate tons of cherries that we had seen and wanted but could not reach. The raccoon ran away when I shined the flashlight in its rotten eyes.

4.
ORANGE PEELS

The next morning the doorbell woke me. I got dressed and went down to the kitchen. This was a serious mistake. Simultaneously The Mom and Tiger's Mother got up from the kitchen table and looked at me. The Mom said, "Mrs. Papadakis wants to speak to you."

Tiger's Mother opened her purse and took out a brown paper bag and emptied it onto the kitchen table. The bag was filled with orange peels. She spread the orange peels on the table like magic cards. She said, "I would like an explanation."

I stared at the orange peels.

The Mom said, "Answer her, Timothy."

I said, "We threw them out the window."

"Do you know that you scared me half to death?" said Tiger's Mother. "That I nearly called the police? Do you know what that means? That means they would have arrested you and taken you to jail."

The Mom said, "I can't imagine they would have done that."

Tiger's Mother said, "I thought someone was trying to break in. I thought a burglar was trying to smash the window. That's what I thought."

The Mom said, "Gracious."

Tiger's Mother said, "Why not throw rocks? Why not batteries? Why not just break the window with a hammer?"

She leaned her face close to mine. I had never been so close to her face before. Her eyebrows were black and thick. She had a double chin that wobbled while she scolded me. She said, "Do you have anything to say for yourself?"

I said, "No."

She said, "No?"

I said, "I'm sorry."

She said, "Sorry's not good enough. Anyone can say I'm sorry."

She loaded the orange peels back into the brown paper bag and stuffed the bag into her purse.

"I'm going to keep these," she said.

Tiger's house was always being painted. They had ladders, paint cans, scraping tools, brushes, drop cloths. Tiger's Brother did the work himself, up the ladder. By the time he painted the back of the house it was time to start the front again, like the Golden Gate Bridge. He didn't work very often. Usually the ladder stood against the house with no one on it. Tiger's Brother was older. He had a thick beard and wore gym shorts and flip-flops all the time, even when it was cold. He spent most of his time in the driveway, working on hot rods. He could fix any car in the world. People came from all over to bring their cars to Tiger's Brother. That was his job, along with painting the house. The Mom said the ladders were just an excuse to keep watch. Watching was his hobby. Whenever anyone walked or drove by, he stopped what he was doing and watched. Simultaneously, Tiger's Mother pulled aside the curtain from the bay window in their living room and watched. The whole family watched. There was nothing that went on that they didn't know. They talked to everyone. They asked questions. They told people what they learned. According to The Mom, they were gossips.

The Mom showed Tiger's Mother to the door. She said, "Thank you for coming over, Stella."

Tiger's Mother said, "You should keep an eye on him."

"I'm sure that's my affair."

"Of course it is."

"Yes. It is," said The Mom.

Tiger's Mother looked around the hallway like the lady in the commercial with the white glove checking to see that everything was spic-and-span. She said, "They should play nicely."

The Mom said, "They will. From now on, they will. I promise you that."

"Anthony's not like them. He's a sensitive boy."

"I'm sure he is."

"They shouldn't call him that name. Tiger."

"They don't mean anything by it."

"I don't like it."

Tiger's Mother stepped outside. The Mom waited a long moment. Then she closed the door and said to me, "Go to your room."

I said, "Why?"

She said, "Don't ask why. Just go to your room and wait for your father to come home. Just you wait."

I went to my room and waited.

The Mom called herself a WASP. She disliked anyone who was rude or talked dirty or said "ain't" or ate with his mouth open or was nosy, like Tiger's Mother. The Mom was born on a farm in Nova Scotia. She was the baby of the family, like me. She had many brothers and sisters. One of her brothers died before she was born. The other brothers lived in Nova Scotia and New Brunswick and Ontario. Canada was a long way away. We went to visit once in the Station Wagon. We drove a long time and stayed in motels and visited The Mom's brothers and their families. We kept driving and visiting new relatives, all of whom had red hair and liked to shake hands. The air was fresh and clean, and then the air smelled very bad. "That's the paper factory," said The Mom. "That means we're getting close to Pictou." Pictou was a town by the sea near the farm where The Mom grew up. Some of her relatives still lived in the town, but no one lived on the farm anymore. We stopped by the side of the road and walked around the property where the farmhouse used to be. The field had soft grass spots where deer slept. The farmhouse had burned down a long time ago. There was nothing left except a stone foundation and a barn without a roof.

"None of us girls wanted to spend our life on the farm," said The Mom. Her sisters moved to America as soon as they turned eighteen. Aunt Mabel went to Boston. Aunt Sadie went to Seattle. Aunt Ethel went to Cranston, Rhode Island. The Mom went to Springfield, Massachusetts. She studied to be a secretary at a junior college and taught people how to dance the rumba, the fox-trot, and the samba at the Arthur Murray Dance Studio. After two months of living in Springfield, Massachusetts, The Mom went to a friend's wedding and met The Dad. The Mom had never met anyone like The Dad before. The Dad was an Italian. There were no Italians in Nova Scotia, only Scottish people. Before The Mom got married, she'd had suitors. One of the suitors was a man named Donald Grant, who was a pilot for TWA. Whenever The Dad did something that aggravated The Mom she would say, "To think I could have married Donald Grant. A perfect gentleman. A man who carried a handkerchief in his breast pocket and placed it on the park bench before I sat down." The Dad would say, "I wish to God you had." The Mom would say, "Instead I married a bricklayer, a peasant."

When The Dad came home I tiptoed into the hallway and listened.

The Mom said, "Take off your belt. You have to discipline Timothy."

The Dad said, "For what?"

"For throwing orange peels at the Papadakis house."

"For doing what?"

"You heard me."

"Did he break anything?"

"He scared Stella Papadakis half to death. She went outside in her nightdress to see what was going on."

"That must have been a sight."

"It's no joking matter. She nearly called the police."

"Call the police on my son? Are you serious?"

"That's what she said."

"To hell with her."

"You have to set an example."

"I won't hit him for that."

There was a silence followed by the sound of ice cubes landing in a glass, a splash of water and the uncorking of the half gallon of J&B. The Dad kept the bottle of J&B in the lower cabinet next to the refrigerator. The J&B had a twist-off cap, but The Dad always discarded the cap after opening the bottle and thereafter used a cork to stop up the opening, for quick and easy access. The cork made a musical sound when being pulled out of the bottle.

The Mom said, "I don't want that woman coming over and talking to me like that. I don't want her in my house."

"Who says you have to talk to her?"

"What am I supposed to do?"

"Give her the bum's rush, that's what."

"Be serious."

"I am serious. Grab her by the ass and throw her out the door."

"I can't very well do that."

"Why not? They're Greek. They're used to it."

The Mom made a short laugh, which was a good sign.

5.
THE AMMO BOX

The Dad was a construction engineer and general contractor. He had big fingers with cracked skin from using hammers, trowels, chisels and pinch bars. He and Uncle Sal owned a construction company that built industrial warehouses on a street called Locust Street in the City of Hartford. The buildings they built were square-shaped with few windows. That was the only design they used. Whenever The Dad left for work in the morning he said either, "I'm going to the job on Locust Street," or "I'm going to the office."

The office was located in the center of town. The sign on the door read "Madison Realty." The Dad and Uncle Sal rented the first floor of a small house set back from the street, surrounded by shrubs and flowers. A foot doctor occupied the second floor. Uncle Sal drove a red Mark III. The Dad drove a blue Mark IV. They parked their cars in the rear parking lot, always in the same slots. The slots had signs in front of them that read "Reserved for Madison Realty."

Whenever Albert and I rode our bikes to the center of town we would stop to visit him. We'd barge in and find The Dad and Uncle Sal sitting side by side at their identical white Formica desks. If they were talking on the phone we had to be quiet. Talking on the phone was the only work they ever did. Usually they just sat in their swivel chairs with their feet up on their desks, discussing stocks they should have bought and property they shouldn't have sold.

Uncle Sal was ten years older than The Dad. He had an extremely large, bald head. For that reason Albert and I called him The Head, which was the name of the evil mastermind in the Dick Tracy cartoon. Uncle Sal liked giving us math problems involving sums of money. He would ask: "What would you boys rather have, a million dollars or a penny that doubled in value every day for a month? Don't give me your answer now. Go home and figure out what's better. The million dollars or the magic penny. Then come back next time and tell me."

Every once in a while, on rainy weekend afternoons, The Dad would drive Albert and me to his office for the purpose of taking naps. He'd wink at us and say, "We've got to finish up that job we started last weekend," and The Mom would say, "What job?" and Albert and I would say, "Construction job." The office had a kitchenette, a bathroom and a back room that looked like someone's den, with two easy chairs and the saggy couch that used to be in our living room before we got a new one. The only sounds you heard were faraway voices of people going by on the sidewalk or the motor of some passing car. We'd lie down on the couch and easy chairs and listen to the rain and go immediately to sleep. After a while we'd wake up and The Dad would yawn and say, "Come on, boys, or else your mother will have the cops after us."

Before long The Mom found out about our naps. Albert squealed. He sang like a canary. You couldn't blame him, though, because The Mom had Kreskin-like ways of getting information once she realized you were trying to keep a secret. According to The Mom, weekends were for chores around the house, not slumber parties. After that she didn't let The Dad out of her sight on Saturday or Sunday afternoons. She'd follow him from room to room, making sure he was doing what she'd told him to do, which usually involved mowing the lawn, cleaning out the garage, sweeping the driveway, clearing the gutters and so forth. If she found him hiding in the boiler room listening to a baseball game on the transistor radio, she'd say something like, "Do you expect me to cut the grass in addition to everything else?"

The Dad came into my room and handed me an old green wooden box with a leather strap attached to the top. He said, "Here's to you, jellybean."

I said, "What is it?"

"It's a World War Two ammo box. Do you see how it's shaped?

That's because the bullets come out the top like a conveyor belt to the guy with the machine gun. Thirty-caliber bullets. Big ones. Bu-bu-bu-bu-bu-bu-bu-bu-bu-bu-bu. Like that."

"What's it for?"

"It's for you to keep stuff. Your mother doesn't have to know. It'll be our secret. Do whatever you want with it. Hide it. Bury it in the ground if you like. This box is watertight. It's solid. See?" The Dad knocked on the side of the ammo box with his knuckles. "I've had this box since 1942. You take care of it."

"Sure, Dad."

The Dad went to the door. He said, "Your mother tells me you were throwing orange peels at the Greeks. Is that true?"

I shrugged.

"Gave the old witch a scare, huh?"

"I guess."

The Dad nodded. He said, "Do me a favor. If you're going to do something stupid like that, don't get caught. Then it doesn't matter."

"Okay."

After The Dad left, I looked inside the ammo box, which was empty. I cleaned and polished it and put it under my bed.

The Dad had nightmares. When he took naps, Albert and I sometimes went into his bedroom to watch him twitch and jerk. If you woke him out of a deep sleep, he would yell in a high voice and punch the air with his right hand. The Dad was a lieutenant in World War Two. He had a photo album filled with black-and-white pictures. In most of the pictures he was standing beside a bridge over a river. The bridges were called pontoon bridges, Bailey bridges and fixed bridges. The Dad was a combat engineer. His job was building bridges. His other job was clearing mines called Bouncing Bettys. The Germans laid minefields everywhere. You couldn't step ten feet off the road without entering a minefield in Italy. One time The Dad stepped on a Bouncing Betty in a grass field near the place where his father was born. The mine shot up into the air and fizzled and smoked, but it didn't go off. Therefore The Dad didn't get killed. A lot of guys stepped on mines and blew their legs off. When that happened, The Dad had to write a letter to the guy's family telling them that the guy was dead. Other guys got shot with machine-gun bullets or run over by trucks or died of fever but not The Dad. The Dad made it. He was a Lucky Bastard. He came home after the war to the City of Hartford and started a construction business with his brother and met The Mom at somebody's wedding and married her and moved to Apple Hill Road and built our house and had three babies who grew up to be Daphne, Albert and, last but not least, me.

I said, "How many Germans did you kill? As many as this?"

We were playing Stratego. The Dad was blue. I was red. I moved my marshall recklessly and mowed down everything in its path. The marshall was invincible. Only two things could kill the marshall: the spy and a bomb. I mowed down the blue soldiers and piled the dead in a heap: a major, two captains, two sergeants, a miner, three scouts.

The Dad said, "I don't want to talk about it."

"Why not?"

"It's nothing to be proud of."

"Did they scream when you shot 'em?"

"Didn't I just tell you I don't want to talk about it?"

"I bet they screamed and cried like babies. Stinking Krauts."

"Do you want to play or not?"

Before long, The Dad stumbled upon my line of defense. He said, "Scout."

I said, "Bomb."

He said, "Miner."

I said, "Bomb."

He said, "Miner."

I said, "Flag."

The Dad threw up his hands. "You put your flag in the second row? What kind of strategy is that?"

I said, "Want to play again?"

He pushed the board away. "All you do is hang around and watch TV. Why don't you go to the movies?"

"What movie?"

"Any movie. Just get out of the house for one night."

I thought it over. "*The Poseidon Adventure*'s pretty good. That's still playing."

The Dad said, "I'll call Mrs. Mandelbaum. She'll take you and Albert and Steven in the station wagon. It'll be fun. Right?"

"Sure, Dad. Real fun."

We went to the Elm Theater to see *The Poseidon Adventure* starring Gene Hackman, Ernest Borgnine, Red Buttons, Shelley Winters, Stella Stevens, Roddy McDowall, Carol Lynley, Pamela Sue Martin and featuring Leslie Nielsen as the captain. Stev's Mom, otherwise known as Mrs. Mandelbaum, henceforth called The Myra, drove us. She pointed her long red fingernails at the back door of the Elm Theater and said, "I'll meet you right there after the movie. Don't go anywhere else."

We piled out of the Station Wagon and went inside. Each of us had seen *The Poseidon Adventure* at least once. Stev had seen it three times. *The Poseidon Adventure* was about a cruise ship that gets capsized by a tidal wave. Everything is upside down. The passengers try to escape to the bottom of the ship, while all around them the water rises.

Our favorite character was Mike Rogo, the loudmouthed cop played by Ernest Borgnine, who had a face like a Halloween mask. You could imitate the Ernest Borgnine face by bulging your eyes and contorting your features like a hurricane wind was blowing directly at you.

Our favorite line, which we said as often as possible, was: "We're following the purser."

We waited in line and doled out our coins. The lady behind the counter said, "Down the hall to your right."

Stev said, "Where?"

The lady said, "Down the hall to your right."

Stev said, "We're following the purser."

The lady said, "You're following who?"

Stev said, "The purser."

The lady said, "Who's he?"

Stev ordered popcorn. I ordered popcorn. Albert ordered popcorn. The guy behind the popcorn counter said, "Do you want to get all that stuff for free? All you have to do is stay afterward and clean up popcorn boxes and paper cups and bubble gum wrappers and jujubes. That's not asking much for three free popcorns, is it? Meet me right here, okay?"

We said, "Okay."

Stev said to me, "The guy is a total sex maniac."

"Confirmed," said I.

At the end of the movie we went out the back door. He was waiting for us in the parking lot. He said, "You ready to work?"

Stev said, "We're following the purser."

The guy said, "What?"

I said, "The steel hull is two inches thick in the bow but only one inch thick in the stern. Nowhere is the hull thinner. Don't you understand?"

The Myra honked the horn and we piled into the Station Wagon. She said, "Who was that man?"

Stev said, "Sex maniac."

The Myra said, "Lord save us."

We drove home and got out of the car. The Mom and The Dad were fighting in the kitchen. We could hear them yelling and screaming from the end of the driveway. We stood outside, listening.

The Mom said, "Don't ever try anything like that again. I will call the police and have you arrested. Is that clear?"

The Dad said, “There are such things as grounds for divorce.”

“You go ahead and try, mister. Oh, how I wish you would. What a story I would tell.”

“I’d like to hear it. I’m going to sit down here in this chair and you’re going to tell me your story. Go ahead. Tell me with a straight face. I’m all ears.”

“You go to hell.”

“I don’t have to go anywhere. I’m already there. Hell would be an improvement. Hell would be a walk in the park.”

“I wish you could see yourself. Look in the mirror with your red face and your red eyes and tell me what you see.”

“I don’t need any goddamn mirror.”

“You goddamn wop.”

“So I’m a goddamn wop?”

“To think I married a wop bricklayer. Isn’t that funny? Don’t you think that’s funny?”

“I don’t find anything funny about it.”

“No, I suppose you wouldn’t.”

We opened the front door. The Mom and The Dad stared at us. The Dad took a drink from his glass and set it on the table. The glass was half-filled with J&B scotch, which was The Dad’s favorite. The Mom adjusted her hair and said, “How was the movie?”

Later that night, Albert woke me. He turned on the flashlight and shined the beam in my eyes and said, “Look what I found.” He was pointing to something on the desk. I poked the thing with my finger. It was slimy and shapeless like a jellyfish.

I said, “What is it?”

“Guess.”

“Balloon?”

“Nope.”

“I give up.”

"It's a rubber," said Albert. "You put your boner inside."

"Get out of here."

"That's what it's for."

"Where did you find it?"

"Bathroom," said Albert. "Look at it. It's all stretched out."

"Do you think this is what they were fighting about?"

"Affirmative."

"What should we do with it?"

By way of answer, Albert picked up the rubber with the tips of two fingers, opened the ammo box and dropped it inside.

The next day, The Mom came into the kitchen and placed the grocery bags on the table. She unpacked milk, cheese, bread, eggs, bologna, macaroni, hamburger, Rice-a-Roni. I reached into one of the brown bags and removed *Screen Stars* magazine. Elizabeth Taylor was on the cover. I turned to the last couple of pages and located the Mark Eden Developer and Bustline Contouring Course advertisement. The advertisement read:

> *"Mark Eden is the World's Most Successful Bustline Developer. The Mark Eden Method is not a cream, not an artificial stimulator. It is an exerciser that employs special techniques in enlarging, shaping and firming the bustline to the loveliest proportions. Here is Sandra Wilder, just one of the many thousands of women who are reporting amazing results."*

The Mom said, "What are you reading?"

I said, "Nothing."

Albert and I showed the ammo box to Stev, Tiger and Mik Cosgrove. The showing took place underneath the back porch, which was dark and cool and damp. Sunlight came between the wooden slats. The ceiling above our heads was five feet high, which sloped lower as you neared the rear. The area underneath the back porch was filled with old tools, sleds, steel buckets, paint cans, broken machines and furniture that no one used anymore. Instead of throwing out a piece of broken machinery or furniture, The Dad would stuff it underneath the back porch for later use, and the junk piled up and got pushed farther and farther to the rear.

Albert unveiled the ammo box, and everyone crowded around.

Stev said, "Are the bullets inside?"

Albert said, "Check and see."

Stev opened the ammo box and reached inside and took out the rubber. He held it up, put two fingers inside and moved them around. He stretched the rubber and snapped it like a rubber band. He put the rubber to his mouth and blew it up.

Albert said, "It's a rubber. It goes over your boner."

Stev said, "Cool."

Tiger said, "Gross."

Mik Cosgrove said, "Big deal. My father's got a whole drawer if you want more. They come wrapped up in little packets like mints."

Stev said, "Why does he have so many?"

Mik Cosgrove said, "Duh. Why do you think?"

Stev said, "Use 'em on your mother."

Mik Cosgrove said, "Use 'em on your mother's more like it. Her and her pointy tits."

Stev said, "Use 'em on your sister."

Mik Cosgrove pretended to laugh, then he jumped Stev and put him in a full nelson and pushed his face in the dirt.

Stev said, "Hi, I'm Mik Cosgrove and my father's got a lot of rubbers, do you want some?"

Mik Cosgrove said, "Say uncle."

Stev said, "Rule number one. Never say uncle."

Albert picked up the rubber and put it back inside the ammo box. He grabbed a shovel and said, "Follow me."

We followed Albert into the woods behind the backyard. He dug a hole in the dirt and buried the ammo box and placed a flat rock on top of the ground and marked the rock with an X. He said, "Don't move the rock or else we won't be able to find it. No one's allowed to dig up the ammo box unless we're all here. Is everyone agreed?"

Stev and Tiger and Mik Cosgrove and I said, "Agreed."

When they were gone I dug up the ammo box and took out the rubber and fitted it over my boner. The rubber was cold and slimy.

The Mom and The Dad were sitting in the den watching the Boston Red Sox play baseball on TV. I took *Screen Stars* off the kitchen counter and went downstairs to the laundry room. I turned to the appropriate page. There were two pictures of Sandra Wilder. Picture number one was entitled "Before Her Mark Eden Course, Bust 36 Inches." Picture number two was entitled "After Her Mark Eden Course, a Full 41 Inches." Said Sandra Wilder:

> "*I always wanted fuller and shapelier bosoms, but I didn't think it was possible. With the remarkable product called the Mark Eden Developer, I actually saw an improvement in size, firmness and shape every time I used it. In just six weeks my bustline went from 36 to 40. I felt that 41 inches would be the perfect bust measurement for my height and bone structure, so I continued with the program for another week and quite easily reached that measurement. A full 41 inches!*"

The laundry room was situated directly beneath the den. I could hear Ken Coleman clearly. Ken Coleman said, "Stepping up to the plate, number eight, Carl Yastrzemski." The crowd cheered, as they always did when Carl Yastrzemski came to the plate and waved his bat over his head. The crowd chanted, "Yaz Yaz Yaz." Sandra Wilder's boobs were white like giant eggs. Her boobs turned up like a ski jump. Her bikini top barely contained them. I looked around the laundry room. On one of the shelves was the battery-operated handheld vibrator otherwise known as the Swedish Massager henceforth called the Device which The Dad used for his bad back. I picked up the Device and flipped the On switch. Then I unzipped and placed the Device against my boner to see what it would feel like. I held the Device against my boner for approximately two to three minutes. Then without trying to and utterly to my surprise I made the Ernest Borgnine face and my knees buckled and I reared back and shot white bullets like a machine gun. Bu-bu-bu-bu-bu-bu-bu-bu. Like that.

After recovering, I went upstairs and returned *Screen Stars* magazine to the kitchen counter and walked into the den.

The Mom said, "What were you doing in the laundry room?"

The Dad said, "Say something. Answer your mother."

The Mom said, "Is something the matter, honey?"

I said, "What would you do if I died?"

During the six-month trial period, we didn't have to go to catechism. Instead we went to the Bridge, which was the name of the Christian youth group that held meetings in a classroom in the rear of the First Church of Christ. The choir practiced at the same time our meetings were held. We could hear the organ blaring and women singing in their high voices and a man with a bass voice booming solos so loud that we had to practically yell in order to hear each other. During the meetings we sat in a circle. Sometimes the minister asked us to hold hands with the persons sitting on either side of us. The minister wore regular clothes, like a schoolteacher. He smiled and nodded, and after someone spoke he usually said something like "I hear where you're coming from," or "I dig it," or "I'm hip to that." One time the minister asked each of us to express our feelings about the Bridge. When it came my turn, I said, "It's better than catechism. You don't have to memorize anything." Albert was sitting next to me. He said, "Yeah. No memorizing." The minister turned toward Daphne. He said, "What about you, Daphne? How do you feel about the Bridge?" All the kids in the Christian youth group looked at her and waited for her to say something. She thought for a long time. Finally she said, "I'd like everyone to know that I'm really glad to be here. I don't know if you know what I mean, but I'm just glad to be here with everyone today. Really, really glad. Do you know what I mean?" The minister said, "Thanks, Daphne. We know what you mean." After that day, Albert and I repeated the Daphne monologue approximately one thousand times. Albert had a way of saying the words "really glad to be here" that drove Daphne insane. He could imitate her perfectly. She would say, "Please stop saying that." And Albert would say, "I'm really glad to be here, really, really glad," until Daphne ran out of the room, yelling, "I hate you, I hate you so much."

After the six-month trial period, The Mom and The Dad called a family meeting. We gathered in the den.

The Mom said, "Well? What have you decided?"

The Dad said, "Tell her, kids. Tell her you'd rather come to St. Anthony's with me, like always. Go on. Tell her how much better it is my way."

The Mom said, "You shut your mouth. Don't try to influence them. It's entirely up to the children. They can be Catholic if they want or they can be Protestant. Which is it, children? Which do you prefer?"

We, the children, looked at each other and gave our prearranged response. We said, "Neither."

From that day onward we quit being Catholics and Protestants. The Mom and The Dad gave up. They stopped threatening, bribing and nagging us. They blamed each other. The Dad said, "They were good Catholics until you got involved. They never complained." The Mom said, "After all that rigmarole they learned in catechism it's no wonder they rebelled. Who wouldn't?"

After that, Daphne went to church if The Mom or The Dad asked her to go, but Albert and I refused any and all further forms of religious training or observance except Good Friday, Easter and Christmas Eve, which were mandatory. Albert and I did not get out of bed for nine o'clock mass, like we used to. We did not go to catechism or the Bridge. We slept late. We stayed in bed Sunday mornings, dreaming morning dreams and drooling morning sleep.

Some kids made fun of Tiger because he had a purple splotch down the right side of his face and neck. Some kids said that the splotch covered Tiger's entire body. That was not true. The splotch barely touched his shoulder. The splotch was something you got used to very quickly. Tiger did not call it a splotch. He called it a birthmark. One time a kid at school said, "Tiger's got a splotch on his peter." Everyone laughed. Tiger blushed. He did not answer back. I said to the kid who cracked the joke, whose name was J.C., "Smile, Jenny, you're dead," and punched him in the stomach. J.C. said, "You hit me in the solar plexus. That's dangerous. That's how they killed Houdini. What'd you do that for, Timmy?" I said, "Don't make fun of Tony." J.C. said, "Why not? You make fun of him." I said, "I'm his best friend. I'm allowed."

Tiger handed me a pencil and pad. He said, "Here's what we'll do. I'll work the record player. You write down the words. Tell me when you want me to stop it."

I said, "Okay."

He picked up the needle and started the record. The music began with guitar notes that sounded like raindrops. After a while Harry Chapin began singing.

I said, "Stop it."

Tiger stopped it.

I wrote down the following words: "It was raining hard in Frisco."

I said, "Okay. Start it."

Tiger put down the needle.

I said, "Stop it."

Tiger stopped it.

Then I wrote: "I needed one more fare to make my night."

We continued this procedure. Tiger became skilled at lifting the needle off the record and replacing it in the exact spot without causing a skip. The procedure was working perfectly until we reached the point halfway through the song when someone who was not Harry

Chapin began singing in a very high voice. We listened to the high-voice part of the song approximately ten times. Neither of us could figure out what the high-voiced singer was saying. The words did not make sense. The only word that was clear was "crying."

"Do it again," I said.

Tiger dropped the needle at the precise spot where the high-voiced singer began.

I said, "I think I got it."

At that moment, Tiger's Mother burst into the room and said, "No. That's too much. This game is over."

She went over to the record player and hit the lever and the music stopped. She said to me, "You have to go home now."

I handed the pad to Tiger and went home.

8.
THE GIRL NEXT DOOR

Diana Estabrook lived in the house next to ours. She was sixteen years old and had long blonde hair, bright white teeth and apple cheeks. She wore a bra but it didn't do much good. Her boobs bounced up and down at the slightest movement. There was a constant stream of boys coming to the Estabrook house. They came in cars and honked their horns, and shortly thereafter Diana Estabrook would come running out of the house. Or the boys shuffled up the path to the front door with their hands in their front pockets and rang the bell. Late at night they sat on the porch swing. Albert and I could see everything from our bedroom window. The porch swing was better than TV. It was like having *Kansas City Bomber* playing nearly every night of the week. We turned out the lights, opened the window and watched Diana Estabrook and her boyfriend talk and make out. We could not hear everything they said. Mostly we heard her laughing and the squeaking of the porch swing while the boyfriend felt her up. All the boys went to second base with Diana Estabrook. Frequently it looked like there were two or three puppies moving around underneath her T-shirt trying to get out. As far as we could tell, given our vantage point, no one got any further than second base. Perhaps someone got to third base. This could have occurred without us knowing. But no one, we were certain, went to Home Base. There was no way we could have missed that. Albert and I agreed on this point.

Whenever Diana Estabrook walked up the street with her golden retriever, Albert and I went on full alert status.

"Alert. We have an alert. Attention, all hands."

"Please identify."

"Twelve o'clock."

I put down my bologna and cheese sandwich and pointed. She was wearing cutoff blue jeans and a tank top. Sonny was pulling against the leash and she was laughing, trying to hold him back.

"Nice boobs," said Albert.

"Confirmed," said I.

The Mom said, "Must you use that word?"

Albert said, "What word?"

"You know very well what word."

"Boobs?" said I. "Is that the word by any chance?"

The Mom said, "Those are mammary glands. You might as well get used to them. It is perfectly natural for a girl to have mammary glands. It is not something to gawk at. Men have been gawking at women's mammary glands for centuries and for what reason?"

We stood at the window gawking at Diana Estabrook's mammary glands until she went out of view.

Albert said, "Excellent mammaries."

"Confirmed," said I.

9.
FANNY TRANNY

The Dad and I rolled out of the driveway in the Mark IV. We were heading to the hardware store to get smoke bombs to blow out the groundhog. Franky DiLorenzo was walking down the middle of the street, smoking a cigarette. He moved to the side. As we rolled by, he leaned back and launched a goober onto the trunk of the Mark IV. The Dad put on the brakes, pushed down the electric window, put his left arm out the window and pointed at Franky DiLorenzo.

Franky DiLorenzo came over to the window and said, "What?"

The Dad said, "Did you spit on the car?"

Franky DiLorenzo said, "No."

"Don't lie to me."

"Big deal. It's just water."

"Go around the back and wipe it off with your shirtsleeve."

Franky DiLorenzo looked at the asphalt.

The Dad said, "Don't make me get out of the car." He stared at Franky DiLorenzo for approximately ten seconds, after which time Franky DiLorenzo went around to the back of the car and wiped the goober off the trunk with his shirtsleeve.

We drove off.

I told The Dad, "He talks back to his mother. He swears at her."

The Dad said, "That kid's a delinquent."

"He's adopted."

"He'll get his one day. I knew guys like him in the army. Sooner or later they got theirs. You can count on it."

"Are you going to tell his mother?"

"No."

"What are you going to do?"

"Nothing. Stay out of it."

"You always say that."

"In the army you learn three things. Never volunteer. Stay to the rear. And keep your mouth shut."

Franky DiLorenzo's father was a salesman. He came home once in a while, but you hardly ever saw him. He didn't mow his lawn, trim his hedges or sweep his driveway like everyone else did. He hired people to do those things. Franky DiLorenzo's father was older than the other fathers. He had white hair and wire-rim glasses. He was tall and stooped and very thin. He was much taller and much older than Mrs. DiLorenzo. Mrs. DiLorenzo had lots of curly black hair and moles on her face. She was short and pear-shaped. She looked like a short, pear-shaped man who had lots of curly black hair, moles and a breast shelf. The Mom called her poor Mrs. DiLorenzo because she had a rotten adopted kid who yelled at her and because she was homely. That was The Mom's word. A normal person would call her ugly. Stev called her fugly, which meant fucking ugly.

Tiger's Brother was standing in the street outside the DiLorenzos' house. Stev and I walked over and stood next to him.

Stev said, "What are you doing?"

Tiger's Brother said, "Shhh."

Stev said, "Why?"

Tiger's Brother said, "Listen."

Inside the house, Mrs. DiLorenzo and Franky DiLorenzo were yelling nonstop. There was no way that either person could hear what the other was saying. Franky DiLorenzo's sister was crying. She was adopted, like Franky. They didn't look anything like each other. She was in the same class as Daphne. She hardly said anything. She was one of Daphne's friends, although not one of her pretty friends. She came over to our house once in a while to play records. Her favorite record was *Tapestry* by Carole King. She and Daphne would sing along with the songs. Daphne had a voice like a foghorn, but Franky DiLorenzo's sister had a nice voice. She sang words like "Stayed in bed all morning just to pass the time," and she sounded just like Carole King. Whenever Franky DiLorenzo yelled at his mother, his sister would cry hysterically, like someone had killed her dog, though she didn't have a dog. The DiLorenzos had no dogs or cats like normal people. Dogs were extremely important. Our dog was named Monty. Stev's dog was named Sebastian. Tiger's dog was named Babo. Mik Cosgrove's dog was named Gidget. The Estabrooks' dog was named Sonny. The DiLorenzos had no dog.

Stev said, "What a crybaby. Listen to her cry."

Tiger's Brother said, "Shhh."

The screaming inside the house got louder. Then Franky DiLorenzo smashed the picture window with a baseball bat and the glass exploded in a thousand tiny pieces. Suddenly you could see Mrs. DiLorenzo and Franky DiLorenzo's sister standing in the kitchen with nothing between them and the outside. Both of them had their hands in front of their mouths. They were completely silent. Shortly thereafter, Franky DiLorenzo came out the front door, tossed the baseball bat into the backseat of his car, started the motor and peeled out. The car was a red LeMans. Franky DiLorenzo called the car The Betsy. He burned rubber going down the street and peeled around the corner.

Tiger's Brother said, "That's a good way to drop a tranny."

Stev said, "Rule number one. Never use the word 'tranny.' "

"Why not?"

"It sounds stupid. It sounds like 'fanny.' Tranny fanny. Fanny tranny. See? It's stupid."

"What's wrong with you?" said Tiger's Brother.

Stev said, "What do you mean?"

Tiger's Brother shook his head. He went up his driveway, took a tool out of his back pocket and began tinkering under the hood of some hot rod.

10.
BULLIES

Stev liked torturing insects and amphibians. He devised numerous techniques, like tying beetles, caterpillars and grasshoppers to the clothesline with fishing twine and burning them with a magnifying glass. He dug earthworms out of the garden and kept them in a bucket, where they coiled around each other like intestines. When we rode our bikes to the brook, he liked to catch frogs and kill them. His favorite method was throwing the frogs at point-blank range against a large rock. The frogs exploded and sprayed frog blood and guts in many directions. The reptile bodies piled up on the ground, a mess of green and purple slop.

Stev said, "You try."

I said, "I don't feel like it."

"Do it."

The brook was filled with frogs. They were easy to catch. I picked a big bullfrog out of the water and threw him against the rock. The frog splattered and slid down the side of the rock. He landed in the shallow water and twitched three times. Then he didn't move at all.

Stev said, "See?"

"This is stupid. Let's go."

"Just one more."

I walked up the embankment and got on my bike, knowing that Stev would follow.

The junior high school was empty in summertime. The fields were overgrown and the buildings were locked. We wheeled our bikes around the playground and the baseball diamond and the long jump pits. Stev got off his bike and took a drink from the water fountain outside the gym. Two kids rode up. One got off his bike and came over to the fountain.

He said, "Look who's here. It's Mandelbaum. Hi ya, Mandelbaum."

Stev said, "Hi, Scully."

Scully said to the other kid, "Say hi to the twerp."

The other kid said, "Hi, twerp."

Stev started to walk past Scully but Scully held out his arm. He said, "Wait a minute, twerp. I want to show you something."

Stev said, "What?"

Scully took a balloon out of his pocket, held it over the water fountain and filled it with water, then tied the end in a knot. He tossed the balloon up and down in one hand like a wobbly softball. He said, "Know what I'm going to do?"

Stev said, "No."

Scully said, "I'm going to hit you in the head with this thing."

He wound up and threw the water balloon, but Stev ducked at the last moment. The water balloon hit the brick wall above Stev's head and splashed.

Scully said, "Who told you to duck, twerp?"

Stev said, "Cut it out."

Scully said, "You gonna make me? Huh, twerp? Go ahead and make me."

Stev tried to walk past Scully but Scully grabbed him and put him in a headlock and punched him in the forehead eight times. The punches made the same sound as rapping your knuckles against a desk. The other kid laughed and said, "Cream him, Scully. Cream the little faggot."

Scully let him go, and Stev got on his bike. His forehead was red like an Indian burn. He said, "Come on."

I said, "Do you want to go home?"

"No."

We looked back, but they were not following.

Stev said, "He should be in the tenth grade but he stayed back because his father is a retard and his brothers are retards and his whole family are retards. Everyone knows it."

I looked at Stev. He was crying but not making any noise.

He said, "Are you going to tell?"

I said, "No."

"Swear on it."

"I swear."

We took the shortcut through the field of tall grass and emerged by the old farm on Flagg Road, where cows stood by the fence with their heads lowered, munching grass and swishing their tails in the afternoon sun. I yelled, "Moo," and the cows raised their heads in unison and looked at us as we rode by.

At the edge of the farmland we walked our bikes through the hole in the fence and went across the grass field to the log cabin. We looked through the broken windows. The log cabin had not been occupied for many years. The log cabin was empty except for newspapers and empty beer bottles scattered across the floor. The door of the log cabin was nailed shut with a plank. The following words were written in pen and spray paint on the door and walls by various different people:

Private Property.

Keep Out.

Fuck You.

Kilroy was here.

Wake up to find out that you are the eyes of the world.

Kilroy is a fag.

I slept in the cabin. My name is Martin. I got a big dick.

A life-sized girl was drawn on the wall. She had boobs as big as Chesty Morgan and she was lying on her back with her legs open. "I need a good fuck," read the words written above the drawing.

Stev tried the door. It was locked. I could tell by the way he was walking that he had crapped his pants. Stev walked a certain way when he crapped his pants, like a geisha girl. I could always tell when he was carrying a load by those short, quick steps. Stev had a weak stomach. He crapped his pants easily, whenever he ate too much fruit or ice cream, or whenever he got nervous. Some days he came home early from school with a note from the teacher. The teachers thought Stev was too old to be crapping his pants all the time. For that reason, Stev's dad had decided to send him to a new school in the fall. Stev always said the same thing whenever he crapped his pants. He said, "I gotta go home now."

We climbed onto our bikes. Stev was riding with his butt raised off the seat.

I said, "You want to go home?"

Stev said, "Yeah."

Halfway through *Mike Douglas* The Mom came into the den and stood in front of the screen. She turned down the volume and said, "I want to talk to you."

I said, "What about?"

She said, "Mrs. Mandelbaum says that Steven came home with lumps on his head but he won't tell her how it happened. Did he fall off his bike?"

"No."

"Tell me what happened."

"Scully beat him up outside of school."

"Who's Scully?"

"Bad kid."

"Did he hurt you?"

"No."

"Are you sure?"

" 'Course I'm sure. He put Stev in a headlock and punched him in the forehead eight times."

"Why?"

"No reason."

"That boy should be arrested. I don't want you going near him. If you see him, run in the other direction. Do you understand?"

The Mom turned up the sound and started to leave the room.

I said, "Can we keep a bullfrog in the fish tank? Can he live in there?"

She said, "We have enough pets in this house already. Besides, bullfrogs belong outside."

"Stev likes to kill them. He smashes them against rocks and makes them explode."

"That's terrible. That's cruelty to God's creatures. Why would he do such a thing?"

"He likes to see their guts splatter. He kills lots of them. Other animals too. He ties them to the clothesline and tortures them and sets them on fire with a magnifying glass."

"I'm very upset with Steven to hear that he would do something like that."

"He does it all the time. It's practically his hobby."

"You would never do anything like that. You would never hurt innocent creatures, would you?"

"No."

"Good," said The Mom.

11.
TIME BOMB

The Dad went golfing all the time, even when he was supposed to be at work. Sometimes on weekends, Albert and I went with him. We liked washing the ball in the ball-washing machine and driving the cart, which we were allowed to do only out of sight of the clubhouse, but otherwise golfing bored us. The Dad's golfing friends were named Pinky, Carabello, and Joe Bologna. They were a foursome. They wore brightly colored slacks and short-sleeved shirts and cleats that clomped against the walkways. They played eighteen holes. This took a long time. The Dad's friends said things like "Sliced the bastard," or "Goddamn bunker," or "Did you see where it went?" or "What's taking them sons of bitches so long on the green? You'd think they were having a coffee klatch." Albert and I were the caddies. We doled out the clubs when they asked for clubs and drank icy-cold Coca-Colas from the cooler in the back of the cart. Pinky liked beer. He drank one bottle of Schlitz for every hole he played. Before he hit his tee shot with the driver, which he called the War Club or the One, he would snap open a Schlitz and drink the entire bottle in one glug and put the empty bottle back in the cooler. At the end of the day Pinky's face was bright red. Once Pinky gave Albert and me a twenty-dollar bill. The Dad said, "That's too much, Pink." Pinky said, "I don't know what you're talking about, Bob. I didn't give 'em a red cent. Where'd you get the double sawbuck, kid?"

The Mom did not approve of The Dad's hobby. She said he was squandering our college education. She would telephone his office to see if he was there, and if he wasn't, she would get into the Station Wagon and go looking for him at the country club. If she came across the Mark IV in the parking lot, she would get out of her car and wait for him in the patio bar called the Nineteenth Hole. While waiting, she would drink sidecars, and Albert and I would guzzle icy-cold

Coca-Colas and watch the golfers on the eighteenth green. After a while, The Dad and Pinky and Carabello and Joe Bologna would come bombing up toward the green in golf carts, wearing their brightly-colored slacks and short-sleeved shirts. "Look who's here," The Dad would say, while the others cleared their throats and looked at their shoes.

One day, instead of waiting for him at the patio bar, The Mom sabotaged the Mark IV. She got into the driver's seat and turned every knob on the dashboard to On, including the windshield wipers, the heater, the directional signal, the high beams, the hazard lights and the radio, which she set to the highest volume. The Mark IV was a time bomb. Havoc would ensue whenever anyone turned the ignition.

She said, "Your father's in for a big surprise."

Albert said, "Aren't we going to wait for him at the Nineteenth Hole?"

"Not today," said The Mom.

She drove to the center of town, where all the best stores were located, and handed Albert and me ten dollars each. Ten dollars was exactly twice the amount of our normal allowance.

"Meet me back here in an hour," she said.

Albert and I went to Extra Nice, a coin and stamp shop located on the second floor above the army and navy store. To get into the shop, you had to climb a back staircase, as if you were entering someone's house. Albert collected Liberty Head silver dollars. I collected Indian Head nickels and Lincoln pennies. There was only one Lincoln penny worth anything, the 1955 double die. I looked for the 1955 double die every time a store clerk or lunch lady gave me a penny. I looked for the 1955 double die in The Dad's coffee can, where he kept hundreds of pennies, until I saw double and every penny I picked up looked like a double die. I did not find it. Every slot in my penny book was filled except the spot where the 1955 double die should have been.

The owner of Extra Nice was an old man who had a wart the size of a thimble growing out of his neck. Albert and I discussed this wart on many occasions. The Wart was bumpy and knobby. It was impossible not to look at the Wart while in his presence. We wanted to take a picture of the Wart and frame it and hang it on the wall in our room. We imagined making a movie called *The Wart* where the Wart grows bigger and bigger and starts killing everyone like *The Blob*, or gets smarter and smarter and starts killing everyone like the rat in *Willard*, which was the fifth greatest movie of all time.

The rare coins were kept in locked glass cabinets. The owner watched us browsing. He said, "Which one will it be, boys? Choose wisely. You will never regret purchasing a rare coin. The value can only increase. They will not be making any more of them. Remember that." As he spoke, we watched the Wart jiggle around on his neck.

Albert bought a Liberty Head silver dollar. I bought an Indian Head nickel. When we came back to the car with our coins, The Mom was wearing a fur stole the color of a fox wrapped around her shoulders even though it was hot.

She said, "Well? How do I look?"

After we came home, I went up to my room to listen to WDRC. All the DJ's on WDRC had high-pitched voices. They all sounded the same. It might have been the same guy talking all day long but pretending to be different people with different names. After playing a song, the DJ would tell the title of the song and the name of the singer. Sometimes the DJ would play three or four songs in a row and then say the names of the songs very quickly in a high-pitched voice. He talked about as fast as I could say, "I'm not a fig plucker's son but I'll pluck figs till the fig plucker comes." Every week WDRC published the Big D Sound Survey, which was a list of the "Top 30 Songs of the Week Based on Sales and Requests in Big D Country." The list was distributed free of charge at The Lodge and other record stores. Stev and I collected the surveys and kept them in the bright blue spiral-bound notebook marked "The Music Testament." We did not always agree with WDRC's top thirty picks of the week. I kept a pad and pencil by the radio and wrote down the names of the songs that WDRC played. I gave each song a rating from one to ten with ten being the highest score. Stev did the same thing at his house, and at the end of the week we compared notes and compiled our own list of the top songs of the week.

WDRC was playing "One Tin Soldier" by Coven.

"One Tin Soldier" was the theme song to the movie entitled *Billy Jack*, starring Tom Laughlin, which was the sequel to *The Born Losers* and the prequel to *The Trial of Billy Jack*, also starring Tom Laughlin. The best scene in *The Trial of Billy Jack* was when the cops searched the hippie girls with long blonde hair and the Indian girls with long black hair leaning against the bus with their butts sticking out. During the course of the search the cops squeezed the girls all over, including their boobs. The song "One Tin Soldier" had nothing to do with the movie *Billy Jack*. The song was a fairy tale about the Mountain People and the Valley People. The Mountain People were peaceful. The Valley People were violent. In the end they killed each other.

"One Tin Soldier" ended.

A new song came on. The new song was "The Lord's Prayer" by Sister Janet Meade. The lyrics to "The Lord's Prayer" were not original. In fact, the lyrics were exactly the same thing they made us recite in church. The lyrics went: "Our Father who art in Heaven," etc. The singer of "The Lord's Prayer" was a nun. Nuns were married to God. They were virgins. They did not have sex. This was a serious mistake. If every girl in the world became a nun, it would be impossible to have sex. This fact should be explained to every girl who attended catechism, where Sister Dolores told the girls to keep their legs crossed to protect their pocketbooks and not to French kiss. However, Sister Janet Meade had one thing going for her. She played a fuzz bass during the start of "The Lord's Prayer," which was pretty cool for a nun.

"The Lord's Prayer" ended.

A new song came on. The new song was "I Love" by Tom T. Hall. In this song, Tom T. Hall recited all the things he loved. That idea was fine. I had nothing against that idea in theory. The idea could have had the makings of a great song. You could sing, for instance, "I love Raquel Welch." Or, "I love Carl Yastrzemski." Or, "I love *Kung Fu.*" Or, "I love the movie *Killdozer.*" Granted, these words do not rhyme. But you could make it so that they did. You could sing, "I love Raquel Welch and making a big belch." In any event, Tom T. Hall did not love normal things that everyone else loved. He did not love Raquel Welch. Rather, he loved, and I quote, "Little baby ducks and trucks."

"I Love" ended.

A new song came on. The new song was "The Streak" by Ray Stevens. Musicwise, "The Streak" was stupid. It was almost as stupid as "I Love" by Tom T. Hall. However, this song was not merely a song. It was a craze. It had a direct influence on people's behavior. Specifically, this song instructed girls to take off their clothes and run around naked in public. Obviously, any song that instructed girls to take their clothes off and run around naked should be played over and over and over. Unfortunately, this song also made guys take off their clothes and run around naked, particularly at baseball games and award ceremonies, which was very disturbing.

The music stopped.

The DJ said, "Coming up next: the latest developments in the Watergate scandal."

I turned down the volume and waited.

The Myra came over to look at The Mom's fur. The Myra lived directly across the street from our house. She and The Mom were best friends. They told each other everything. The Myra came over at least once every afternoon to smoke cigarettes, drink J&B and talk. She stayed until her husband, Mr. Mandelbaum, otherwise known as Stev's Dad, called on the telephone and said, "Where's Myra? Is she over there?" If anything important occurred, such as the purchase of a fur stole, The Mom immediately informed The Myra.

She said, "Betty, it's lovely. Absolutely lovely."

The Mom said, "Do you like it?"

"I love it. There's nothing like mink. There's chinchilla but it doesn't compare. Nothing compares to mink." The Myra petted the fur stole and said, "Can I try it on?"

The Mom nodded, and The Myra put the stole across her shoulders and strolled around the kitchen. She said while strolling, "Wearing mink makes you feel like Sophia Loren. You walk into a restaurant and every eye turns toward you."

The Mom said, "Of course it's not full length, like yours. It's just a stole."

The Myra said, "Next time you get the full length. For now, this is lovely."

All the mothers in our neighborhood had furs except for Tiger's Mother, who wore a mackinaw. Furs were very important to them, even though they didn't wear them more than a few times per year. Everyone knew what kind of fur everyone else had. They put on the furs for special occasions, like the theater or expensive dining. Wearing their furs, they sized each other up, like dogs in the park.

I looked at the fur and said, "What's so great about a stinking fur?"

The Myra stopped strolling and stared at me like she was trying to solve a math problem and I had the answer written across my forehead. She said, "Come here."

I said, "Why?"

The Mom said, "Don't be smart, Timothy."

The Myra said, "Don't be precious, Timothy. Don't be a nebbish."

I came over and stood next to The Myra. She said, "I want you to do something for me. I want you to put out your right hand and look at your fingernails."

"Why?"

"You're always asking questions," said The Myra. "Just do something without asking for once."

I stuck out my right hand and looked at my fingernails. I did so by bending my fingers inward like I was making a fist.

The Myra said, "Did you see what he did, Betty?"

The Mom said, "I saw."

The Myra said, "It's foolproof. It works every time. You have nothing to worry about with this one."

I said, "What did I do?"

The Myra said, "You passed the test."

"Any retard can pass that test."

The Mom said, "Don't use that word."

I said, "What word?"

"You know very well what word. Stop showing off. Every time Mrs. Mandelbaum comes over you show off."

The Myra said, "Look. He's blushing. Isn't that precious?"

The Myra had black hair, which she wore in a bun. Her boobs were located high on her chest, practically underneath her chin. She wore tight, fuzzy sweaters and she always had a cigarette in her mouth. Sometimes the ashes landed on her sweater. When that happened, she flicked the ashes away with her hand and in the process touched her boobs, which did not bounce. The Myra's boobs never bounced. They were like highway cones. They stayed in the same place, pointing at you, no matter what she was doing.

The Myra said, "It's not a test to see how smart you are. It's a test to see what kind of person you are."

I said, "I don't get it."

The Myra said, "Think about it. There are two ways you can look at your fingernails."

"What's the other way?"

"The girly way. Like this." The Myra demonstrated by putting her hand out and pointing her long shiny red fingernails like a German soldier doing a *Heil, Hitler.* "It's a test to see whether you like girls or not."

"Everyone likes girls after the sixth grade."

"Some boys don't. Some boys never like them. Do you know what I'm talking about?"

"Yes."

"What am I talking about?"

"Homos."

The Myra laughed and took a sip of J&B. Then without warning and for no apparent reason she grabbed me and pulled me against her chest and hugged me. She smelled like smoke and her boobs pressed against my neck. It was like getting jabbed with someone's elbow. She said, "Precious. What a precious little nebbish you are."

The Mom said, "Go upstairs and get ready for dinner, Timothy. We're eating early tonight."

I climbed the stairs and went into the bathroom, even though I did not have to go number one or number two or wash my face or do anything that a normal person might do in the bathroom. Instead I reached into my pocket and squeezed my boner through my Fruit of the Looms. Getting poked in the neck with The Myra's boobs had given it to me. I assumed that if I squeezed long enough my boner would go away. After approximately one minute of squeezing, the same thing occurred in my underwear as before. Bu-bu-bu-bu. I looked inside. The white stuff was everywhere. It was clumpy like curdled cream and smelled like ammonia. I hid my Fruit of the Looms at the bottom of the hamper, then went into my room and got a new pair out of the dresser. I decided that something was seriously wrong with me. There was no telling what the ailment might be, but cancer was a distinct possibility, and I would probably be dead before my thirteenth birthday.

The Dad came home wearing work clothes stained with dirt and paint and tar. He was sweaty, red in the face, and he needed a shave. He looked at The Mom, who was clearing the plates off the table, and said, "You finished eating already? At five-thirty like the factory workers?"

The Mom said, "Where have you been?"

"Look at me, will ya? Where do you think I've been? We got a big job going on Locust Street."

"I see. A big job."

"Got any leftovers? I'm as hungry as a stevedore."

"There are no leftovers. I threw your dinner down the disposal."

"Just what the hell is going on here?"

The Mom crossed her arms in front of her chest. She said, "Did you have any problems with the car?"

"The car?" Then he exhaled and said, "Son of a bitch. I should have guessed."

The Mom started yelling and waving the dishrag. "Here I am, slaving all day cleaning the house and feeding the children and doing the laundry and food shopping and a thousand other things you know nothing about while you're out gallivanting on the golf course, chasing a little white ball. Is that what you call a big job?"

The Dad said, "There is a big job. I was there all morning."

"How dare you lie to my face? I suppose that wasn't your car in the country club parking lot? I suppose you weren't driving it?"

"I said I was on the job all morning. Not all afternoon. The Sheetrock guy didn't show, okay?"

"No. It's not okay. It's criminal. To go golfing every day of the week is criminal. No one would believe it."

"You expect me to hang around Locust Street in eighty-degree heat for no reason?"

"There are other things you could be doing. You could be out making money, not throwing it away. I see the bills. I know how much you spend. Membership dues. Guest fees. Lunches. Dinners. Cocktails. The pro shop alone nearly bankrupts this family. Two hundred dollars for a set of golf clubs, when you already had a perfectly good set. Not to mention the card games. God only knows how much money you lose playing gin rummy with those hooligans smoking their cigars while the bills around here go unpaid."

"Those are business expenses."

"Don't give me that."

"That's where the deals are made, lady. In the clubhouse. Not in the office. You would know that if you weren't so goddamn—"

"So goddamn what?"

"Did you have to throw my dinner down the disposal?"

"What do I care about your dinner?"

"Ten minutes to eat in peace. That's all I ask."

"Oh, for God's sake. Get the hell out of my house and go someplace else to eat and don't come back if you do."

"You're hysterical," said The Dad.

"Don't you dare call me hysterical after what you've done."

The Dad turned and went upstairs into the bathroom and turned on the shower. The Mom stood at the kitchen sink with the faucet running, allegedly washing the dishes but mostly just banging them against each other.

Approximately one minute later the front door opened and The Myra stepped into the kitchen and said, "What in God's name is going on? I heard you all the way from my backyard."

The Mom said, "I'm sick to death of his lies. I tell you, Myra, I'm sick of it."

The Myra said, "Calm down. Pour yourself a drink."

The Dad grew up during the Depression. Back then people had to scrounge around for food. If someone brought home a turkey the whole family would jump up and down and celebrate. You could get beaten to death for taking someone's dinner from them. That was what The Dad told us about the Depression. He told us, "I hit Mushy Cohen in the eye with my lunch box one day because he tried to steal a bite out of my sandwich." I said, "Who's Mushy Cohen?" The Dad said, "Mushy

Cohen and Izzy Cohen were my best friends. They lived in the apartment across the hall. There were seven kids in that family, all of them boys except for Rosa, who went on to be a showgirl like Sophie Tucker. Later that night Label Cohen knocked on our door and asked to speak to my father and my father called me into the room and Label Cohen told me that I had done the right thing by hitting Mushy in the eye with my lunch box. That he deserved it. Do you understand? I nearly took out Mushy Cohen's eye with a lunch box. He had to wear a gauze pad over his eye for a week. But it was the right thing to do. Never play with someone else's food. That's what Label Cohen told me." I said, "Who's Label Cohen?" He said, "Aren't you listening? Label Cohen was Mushy Cohen's father. His job was delivering coal. A fifty-five-year-old man lugging one-hundred-pound sacks of coal all over Hartford for three dollars a day." I said, "Three dollars is nothing. Pinky gave us twenty for caddying." The Dad said, "Back then guys would sell out their own brother to get a job like that." I said, "Did you sell out your brother?" The Dad said, "Of course not. But that's not the point."

There were two times of day that were important to The Dad: dinnertime and anytime he was reading the newspaper. At such times, The Dad wanted to be left in peace. If someone talked to him while he was reading the newspaper, he would say, "Can't you see I'm reading the paper? Never bother a man when he's reading the paper. You could get killed for less than that in the army." If someone bothered The Dad while he was eating dinner, he would say, "Ten minutes a day, that's all I ask. Can't you leave me in peace for a lousy, stinking ten minutes while I eat my dinner?" The Dad said these words so often that whenever he started to do so, Albert and I would join in and say them along with him. Our favorite line was "Ten minutes a day, that's all I ask."

I went upstairs and opened the bathroom door and stuck my head inside. The Dad was taking a shower behind the shower curtain. I said, "Hey, Dad. What did you think when you started the car?"

He said, "Scared me half to death. Thought a fuse blew."

"Was the radio loud?"

"Turned up all the way. I jumped halfway out of the seat."

"Ha."

"Did you do that?"

"Nah. Mom did."

"What's she doing now? Is she cooking?"

"No."

I closed the door and went downstairs. The kitchen was silent. The Mom was sitting at the kitchen table. The Myra was standing by the window looking out toward her house.

The Myra said, "Hello, Timothy, and what do you have to say for yourself?"

I said, "Ten minutes a day, that's all I ask. A lousy, stinking ten minutes."

She said, "Ten minutes for what? To go number two?"

From her vantage point, The Myra could see the upstairs hallway, which was exactly where she was looking when The Dad opened the bathroom door and came out dripping wet without any clothes on and reached into the linen closet for a towel. Without his glasses, which were Clark Kent glasses, The Dad could not see. The Dad had glaucoma and cataracts. He had numerous eye operations. When he came home from the hospital he wore a black patch for a month over one eye like a pirate. After that, he couldn't drive at night or see three feet in front of his face without his glasses. In addition to glasses, he had to wear a contact lens on his left eye, which he called his bad eye. Each night he removed the contact lens, and in doing so he sometimes dropped the lens into the sink. When this happened he would yell, "Emergency, emergency," and everyone would run upstairs. If we could not find the contact lens on the bathroom floor or in the sink or thereabouts, The Dad would say, "Check my eye." It seemed impossible for the contact lens, which was hard and nearly as big as a dime, to slide around to the rear of The Dad's eyeball, but that was exactly what happened on frequent occasions. When this occurred, The Dad handed over the little plunger and rolled his eyes back into his head like Master Po and said, "Dig it out of there."

The Dad stood in front of the linen closet, touching sheets and pillowcases with the hope of finding a towel. He could not see what he was reaching for, nor could he see the Myra standing in the kitchen approximately fifteen feet away, looking directly at him.

The Myra said, "Dear God in heaven."

The Dad said, "Who the hell is that? Is that Myra?"

The Myra said, "I'm in shock."

The Dad said, "For Christsake. Can't someone tell me when we have company around here?"

The Dad grabbed a towel and went off toward the bedroom.

The Myra said, "Betty. You never told me."

The Mom said, "Myra, please. I have no idea what you're talking about."

"I suppose you get used to it. I don't see how."

"I won't continue this line of talk," said The Mom, and she took off her apron, opened the back door and went out onto the back porch, slamming the door behind her.

The Myra said to me, "What did I say?"

"You said, 'Dear God in heaven.' You said, 'Betty, I'm in shock.' "

The Myra said, "This is a crazy house. I'm going home."

But she did not leave.

There were chimes on the back porch that rang when the wind blew. You could hear them through the open window. The Myra stood by the window, listening to the chimes with her head bent to one side like a dog. After a while she walked out the front door and went across the street and disappeared inside her house.

Albert and I called The Dad's dick the Snub Nose. Whenever we caught a glimpse of it, when he was getting dressed for work, for instance, we yelled, "Aaaagh, the Snub Nose." The Dad's dick had no normal dick-like qualities, so far as we could tell. It did not have a German helmet on the end of it, like our dicks did. The Snub Nose looked more like a fat old knackwurst or a Polish kielbasa that someone had gnawed and left out overnight. The circumference of the Snub Nose was not normal for a dick. It was a circumference in extreme condition. When we took showers at the country club with The Dad, one of his golfing partners always made a dick joke, such as, "Holy mackerel, you got a license to carry that thing?" or, "Let me get you a stool for your joint, Bob."

The Mom hated snakes. She was afraid of them. If a snake came on the screen during a TV show, The Mom would give out a bloodcurdling scream and cover her eyes and run out of the den. Even cartoon snakes caused The Mom to go berserk. For fun, we would cut pictures of snakes from magazines and place them in front of her when she wasn't expecting it. This caused hysteria. Albert and I had a theory about The Mom's fear of snakes. Our theory was based on the science of subliminal advertising. Albert and I studied subliminal advertising in a paperback book called *Subliminal Seduction*, which Albert bought at Caldor because there was a picture of a blonde girl on the cover with big boobs and her shirt half-unbuttoned. Movie theaters used subliminal advertising to sell icy-cold Coca-Colas by interspersing tiny pictures of icy-cold Coca-Colas among the million tiny pictures of a movie. It was a proven fact. It was on *Columbo*. According to our theory, The Mom hated snakes because whenever she looked at a snake she subliminally saw the Snub Nose.

That night was *Kung Fu*. I went into the den and switched on the TV and turned the knob to channel eight and adjusted the rotor so that the antenna on the roof moved to the appropriate direction. The rotor made a grinding noise, and the picture went from fuzzy to clear.

Kung Fu was the story of Kwai Chang Caine. As a boy he was a student of the Shaolin Temple in China, where he learned the ways of the

Shaolin priest. Master Kan told Caine: "When you can take the pebble from my hand, it will be time for you to leave." The boy tried to snatch the pebble from Master Kan's hand but he couldn't do it. He was too slow. He practiced for approximately ten years, while learning to fight kung fu style and duck out of the way of javelins and throw the sharp-sided star-shaped disk, among other things. Then young man Caine snatched the pebble from Master Kan's hand and Master Kan said, "Time for you to leave."

All this happened during the opening credits.

The Dad came into the den. "Did it start yet?"

"Shhh."

"You want me to be quiet during the credits?"

Master Kan said, "Your trip must be light and short, as though your path were upon rice paper. It is said a Shaolin priest can walk through walls. Looked for, he cannot be seen. Listened for, he cannot be heard. Touched, he cannot be felt. This rice paper is a test. Fragile as the wings of a dragonfly. Clinging as the cocoon of the silkworm. When you can walk its length and leave no tread, you will have learned."

The show began.

During the course of any given *Kung Fu* episode, there were one or two fights and one or two flashbacks. These scenes were the best part of the show. During the flashbacks, Master Po, who had eyes like white marbles, said things like "The bird sings in the forest. Does it seek to be admired for its song?"

Whenever Master Po said something like that, The Dad always said one of two things. He said, "Someone ought to be writing this down," or he said, "They're trying to teach us something."

Halfway through the show, The Mom came into the den and sat on the couch. She said, "Are you watching that terrible show?"

The Dad said, "Do you want us to turn the station?"

"It's either this one or the one about the bionic man. That's all you ever watch."

We watched the show. After a while, The Mom asked, "Why are they calling him a Chinaman? He's not Chinese."

I said, "He's a half-breed."

"He's as white as you or me."

"His mother was Chinese and his father was American."

"In real life?"

"On the show."

"Well, I'm sure he's not Chinese. Not even half."

"Shhh."

"Don't shush me."

Eventually the show ended and the credits came on. The music played, and Caine walked alone across the desert.

I left the room.

When I went to bed, they were still in the den. It sounded like they were watching Johnny Carson and laughing at one of Johnny Carson's jokes, but I couldn't be certain. I took my clothes off and emptied the change out of my pockets, checking the pennies for a 1955 double die. Finding none, I went immediately to sleep.

12.
RAINY DAY ACTIVITIES

Every house had a particular smell. Stev's house smelled like lemon polish. Tiger's house smelled like gas from the stove. Our house smelled like Monty. Mik Cosgrove's house smelled like bowling alley shoes, but not exactly. It was a difficult smell to identify. You smelled it as soon as you opened the porch door and walked into the kitchen. It was always there, the Cosgrove smell, which Mik Cosgrove carried with him to a lesser degree wherever he went. His house was the only place in the world where you could get that smell. The smell was strongest in the basement, which we called the Dungeon.

The Dungeon had a tile floor. You could hear your shoes and voice echoing as soon as you opened the cellar door. The Dungeon was an optimal location for watching TV on rainy days. The Dungeon contained the world's longest white vinyl couch, which was shaped like a U and went all the way around the room. The white vinyl couch had space for twenty people to sit on it without touching each other. It was like one of those dining room tables in a castle where the King was eating supper with the Queen but she was fifty feet away and had to ring a little bell to get someone to pass the salt.

Mik Cosgrove opened the cellar door, and Tiger and I went bombing down the stairs. The TV was on. Someone was stretched out on the middle portion of the world's longest white vinyl couch.

Mik Cosgrove said, "Dad?"

Mr. Cosgrove otherwise known as Buddy Cosgrove sat up. He had no shirt on. He was wearing Bermuda shorts and a pair of slippers. He said, "What?"

Mik Cosgrove said, "Can we watch TV?"

"Who's we?"

"Me and the guys."

"Where are they?"

"Right here."

Tiger and I said, "Hi, Mr. Cosgrove."

Mr. Cosgrove got up and stretched his arms, then lifted a glass off the coffee table and drank the rest of whatever was inside it. He shuffled toward us with his slippers scuffing against the tile floor, and halfway across the room he stopped and pointed his index finger at Mik Cosgrove like a pistol and released a fart that made a sound like a tire losing air. "Got ya," he said.

Mik Cosgrove said, "Thanks, Dad. I needed that."

Mr. Cosgrove said, "You bet, buddy." He looked at Tiger and said, "Who are you?"

Tiger said, "Tony Papadakis."

Mr. Cosgrove looked at me and said, "Who are you?"

I told him my name.

He said, "What's on TV that's so important that you three buffaloes had to wake me out of a sound sleep and kick me out of my own basement?"

I said, "Nothing."

He said, "Every time I turn on the TV it's something I've already seen. Repeat after repeat. Don't they make any new shows anymore?"

I said, "It's always repeats in the summertime. The new shows start in September."

He said, "Even the new shows seem like repeats. You get to a certain age and that's all it is, one big repeat."

Mik Cosgrove said, "That's so interesting, Dad. Can you tell us more?"

"Watch it, buddy."

"I'm watching it."

"I'm talking to little Timmy here, you mind?"

"Take your time. We'd rather listen to you than watch TV any day."

Mr. Cosgrove and Mik Cosgrove grinned at each other. They looked very much alike. Both had moon faces that looked like Glen

Campbell. Both were chubby. Both had teeth as white as paper and they grinned ear-to-ear Glen Campbell grins. Mr. Cosgrove did not smell good. He stood next to me giving off the Cosgrove smell interspersed with the lingering aroma of the fart he had just blown.

Mr. Cosgrove said to me, "Your mother is a very pretty woman."

I said, "She used to be an Arthur Murray dance instructor."

"Is that right?"

I nodded. "That was a long time ago."

"I'm not surprised. Nothing surprises me. If you could tell me something that surprised me, I'd give you a dollar."

"Really?"

"Go ahead. Try me."

"But you could just lie and say you're not surprised no matter what I say."

"Trust me."

I said, "I'm not a fig plucker's son but I'll pluck figs till the fig plucker comes."

He said, "I've heard that one before."

"Give me another chance."

"Go ahead," he said. "I got all day."

I said, "Never follow the purser."

"The who?"

"The purser."

"Why not? Because he's got the money?"

"The purser always goes the wrong way. If you follow the purser, he'll lead you down into a sinking ship that's upside down."

"What are you, some kind of smart kid?"

I shrugged, and he reached into his Bermuda shorts, pulled out a roll of bills, peeled off a dollar and handed it to me. "Here's your dollar," he said.

Tiger said, "Can I have one too?"

Mr. Cosgrove said, "Why not? It's only money."

He gave Tiger a dollar and went upstairs.

Mik Cosgrove said, "Finally."

He leaned over the TV and turned the channel past soap operas until finding *The Guns of Navarone* starring Gregory Peck, David Niven and Anthony Quinn as the ruthless Greek, Stavros. *The Guns of Navarone* was just starting. We sat on the world's longest white vinyl couch, sank down into the cushions, put our feet up on the coffee table and watched the movie.

The rain was still falling when the movie ended. We went upstairs. Mik Cosgrove called, "Hey Dad."

There was no answer.

Mik Cosgrove looked into the garage but his father's car was gone. The house was empty except for us.

He said, "Want to play a game?"

Tiger said, "What game?"

"Hide-and-seek."

"Hide-and-seek is stupid. Hide-and-seek is for little kids."

"This is different," said Mik Cosgrove. "I guarantee it. Count to a hundred and come find me."

Mik Cosgrove walked out of the kitchen. We heard him going up the stairs. Tiger and I did not count to one hundred. We opened the refrigerator and looked for icy-cold Coca-Colas. There were none. The refrigerator was empty except for milk, eggs and mayonnaise, Schaeffer beer cans and two bottles of cognac. The best thing about the Cosgroves' refrigerator was there was a lever on the door that popped out ice cubes when you pushed it. I pushed the lever and the machine made a grinding noise and after a while ice cubes started popping out.

Tiger said, "He went upstairs."

I said, "I know."

"He's going to try to scare us. He's going to jump out of the closet and scream and put us in a full nelson."

"I know."

Mik Cosgrove was fifteen, three years older than Tiger and me. He was strong and he liked to put you in full nelsons until you said uncle. His full nelsons were impossible to escape from. Sooner or later you had to say uncle. Mik Cosgrove was strong but he was not fast. We liked telling him, "Gaf a si Evorgsoc Kim," then making a run for it. He couldn't catch you because he was chubby and got winded easily and ran like he was wearing ski boots. You could run through three backyards while he chased, yelling at the top of your lungs, "Hi, I'm Mik Cosgrove and I'm the number-one spaz of all time, of all time, of all time." After a while he got tired and stopped chasing.

Tiger and I tossed the ice cubes into the sink and went upstairs. The rug was very white and very thick. You sank into it as you walked. We walked soundlessly down the hallway sinking into the rug and went into Mik Cosgrove's bedroom and began looking for him. He was not in his closet or under his bed. He was not in the bathroom. He was not standing behind the shower curtain waiting to scream when we pulled the curtain aside like *Psycho*. He was not in his sister's closet or under her bed. I opened his sister's dresser drawers and looked inside and found a pair of white underwear and stretched them out toward Tiger, and he made a gross-out face because Mik Cosgrove's sister was chubby and she looked like Glen Campbell and her white underwear was very big. We put the big white underwear back in the dresser and continued our search for Mik Cosgrove. He was not in the linen closet. He was not in the hallway closet with the half-door that had nothing inside except for a fire extinguisher. There was only one room left to check. We went to the end of the hall and turned into his parents' bedroom and found him.

Tiger said, "You jerk."

I said, "Very funny. Ha ha."

Mik Cosgrove was lying on his back on his parents' king-sized bed with his hands folded across his chest like a corpse and he was not wearing any clothes. His eyes were closed. He was pretending to be dead. He was not moving at all except for his boner, which was sticking straight up in the air.

Tiger said, "Oh look, he's dead."

I said, "What a loss."

Mik Cosgrove did not open his eyes. He did not smile. He did not break out laughing. He stayed dead. The only sign of life came from his boner, which started moving from side to side like the pendulum in a grandfather's clock.

I said, "Maybe if I nailed him with this tennis ball he might wake up."

Tiger said, "Yeah. That might work."

I did not have a tennis ball in my hand. Nevertheless, at the sound of the words "tennis ball," Mik Cosgrove jumped off his parents' bed and began laughing hysterically. He laughed until his face turned red. He punched Tiger in the shoulder and said, "Wasn't that great?"

Tiger said, "It was stupid."

Mik Cosgrove said, "Try it. It's great."

"No way."

"Come on. You're it. We'll count to a hundred and find you."

"I'm not doing it."

"Come on. Take off your clothes and get a woody."

"I don't like that game."

"All right. I know another game."

I said, "Another homo game, I bet."

Mik Cosgrove said, "No. This one's great. You'll like it. Go outside and close the door and ring the doorbell. I'll surprise you."

I said, "Let me guess. You're going to jump out and put one of us in a full nelson."

Mik Cosgrove said, "No, this is different."

Tiger and I went downstairs, out the front door and closed the door behind us. The sun was starting to come out again. The rain was only a sprinkle. It would have been possible to play whiffle ball under these weather conditions.

Tiger said, "What do you want to do?"

I said, "Play whiffle ball."

"Should I ring the doorbell?"

"Go ahead."

Tiger rang the doorbell. Instantly the door opened. Mik Cosgrove was standing in the foyer buck naked with a boner, which he was shaking furiously with his right hand. The shaking motion was the same motion you would use to shake dice before rolling them but ten times as fast as any normal person would ever shake dice. His eyes were closed and his tongue was sticking out of the corner of his mouth.

I said, "Oh look. It's Mik Cosgrove doing something stupid."

Tiger said, "What a surprise."

We waited for him to stop shaking his boner. He did not. He said, "This is good for you. Doctors tell you to do it. It helps your circulation."

I said, "Are you going to do that all day?"

Mik Cosgrove said, "Just until the jism comes out."

"The what?"

"The jism. You know, the cream."

"You mean the white stuff? That's normal?"

"Duh. Of course it's normal. Getting the white stuff out is the whole point. Didn't you know that?"

I did not respond.

Mik Cosgrove said, "Want to see me do it?"

Tiger said, "Do what? What are you guys talking about?"

Mik Cosgrove said, "Watch this," and leaned back and bubbled white stuff out of his boner like a fountain, which landed on the front step.

Tiger said, "Hey. Cut it out."

Mik Cosgrove said, "Oh. Oh."

Tiger and I turned and walked down the steps.

Mik Cosgrove called out, "Hey. Where are you going? I was just kidding."

13.
HOOGA CHAKA

Stev was Jewish. His family ate different types of food. They ate Danish, gefilte fish, noshes, chicken salad, knishes and matzo balls, which tasted like Styrofoam. Stev wasn't supposed to eat shrimp or lobster or anything else that crawled around the bottom of the sea and ate other fishes' crap. Some nights he came over to our house and said, "Greetings, earthlings," and sat in the chair in the corner of the room and watched us eat. He liked watching us eat. He came over to watch us eat all the time. He watched and listened and joined in the conversation when he felt like saying something. He watched us eat so often that sometimes it felt funny when Stev wasn't sitting in the corner, watching and listening and cracking up when The Dad cracked a joke or Albert cut the cheese, which he did every night at dinnertime.

The Mom said, "I heard that, Albert."

Albert said, "It wasn't me. It was low-flying geese."

"That's not funny, young man. If you must expel your foul vapors, then excuse yourself and go to the bathroom like a gentleman. Don't do it at the dinner table. How many times have I told you that?"

"But it's meat loaf, Mom."

"I'd like to have one meal at this table, just one, without flatulence. Do you think that's possible?"

"Probably not," said Albert, and Stev cracked up.

The Mom said, "Don't encourage him, Steven. He's bad enough already."

Stev said, "Sorry."

"You have nothing to be sorry about. You have perfect manners. You're like a little angel in the corner."

I said, "Yeah, right."

The Dad said, "What's for dessert?"

Dessert was brownies. Stev licked his lips but did not accept one when The Mom offered. Stev was not allowed to eat brownies or other chocolate treats because they made him break out.

The Mom said, "Are you sure you don't want a brownie, Steven?"

Stev said, "I'm not allowed. It makes me break out."

The Mom said, "Oh."

After dinner, Stev and I went up to my room and turned on WDRC. Sunday night was "Casey Kasem's Top 40 Countdown," which we listened to every week. The song "Radar Love" by Golden Earring came on.

Stev said, "I like this part."

I said, "Me too."

"I like the bass."

"It's excellent."

We listened to the bass, which was loud.

Stev said, "It's not as good as Dee Murray but it's good."

I said, "No one's as good as Dee Murray."

"But it's close."

"It's close."

The song ended. Casey Kasem played "Annie's Song."

Stev said, "Rule number one. Never listen to John Denver."

I turned down the radio. It was very quiet in the room. I was lying on my bed. Stev was lying on Albert's bed. He was tossing a Nerf football toward the ceiling so that it nearly touched the ceiling but did not and came back down into his hand. He never dropped the Nerf football and he never hit the ceiling. He came within inches of hitting the ceiling with every throw but never hit it.

"Hooked on a Feeling" by Blue Swede came on.

Stev said, "Turn it up. Quick."

I turned it up.

Stev said, "Louder."

I cranked the radio. The radio was a Fisher. It was brand-new from

Caldor. It still had the sales sticker hanging from the volume button, which read: "Model 190-65 AM/FM stereo receiver with automatic turntable and three-way bookshelf speaker system high sensitivity & selectivity wide band AM tuner auto FM mono-stereo switching bass & treble tone control each speaker, 10 woofer 5 mid and 3 tweeter, weight 84 pounds. Reference price $550.00. Your cost $349. Sale price $315." I turned the volume knob halfway, and the Bic pen on the desk started to move around. Still, the knob was only at number 5. I could crank it to number 6 and beyond. If Stev asked, I was prepared to go higher.

Stev said something that could not be heard.

I said, "What?"

He said, "I like this part."

"Me too."

"It's excellent."

"It's the best."

"Hooga chaka hooga chaka," said Stev.

I joined in.

We said, "Hooga chaka hooga hooga hooga chaka hooga hooga."

We got up and stamped around the room, yelling, "Hooga chaka hooga hooga hooga chaka hooga hooga."

The door opened and The Dad appeared in the doorway. He said, "I knew it was a mistake buying that thing for you."

I said, "I'll turn it down."

"Now."

I turned it down.

"Casey Kasem's Top 40 Countdown" continued. We listened for approximately two hours, like we did every Sunday night. When it was over we picked our personal favorite top-twenty songs of the week, and the songs were from number twenty to number one: "Car Wash Blues," "Sure as I'm Sitting Here," "You Make Me Feel Brand New," "Be Thankful for What You've Got," "I Hate Hate," "Air Disaster," "Rock Me Gently," "Rock Your Baby," "Sideshow," "Please Come to

Boston," "Waterloo," "The Air That I Breathe," "Radar Love," "Rikki Don't Lose That Number," "What Made America Famous," "Rebel Rebel," "Don't Let the Sun Go Down on Me," "Billy Don't Be a Hero," "Hooked on a Feeling," and drumroll please, "The Night Chicago Died."

We wrote down the results in "The Music Testament" and made a note of the time and date.

14.
THE GUEST ROOM

The Dad liked having a project. He liked working with bricks and flagstones, making a patio or a pathway that led around the house to the backyard and garden. He liked building bookcases or tables. The Mom didn't have to nag him to do those types of projects. She didn't even have to ask. You'd hear him in the garage early on a weekend morning sawing and hammering, whistling away. After a couple of hours, he'd come into the house and get a glass of water and say, "Boys, come outside for a minute. I want to show you something." This meant he needed help moving a board or holding the measuring tape. If he started work on a project, he wouldn't stop until he finished or until dinnertime. Sometimes he'd go back to the garage after dark, not to work, but to admire what he'd done so far. Later he'd sit at the kitchen table and sketch plans for the next day's work with a pencil and paper. He liked showing Albert and me his plans, although we had no interest whatsoever in his projects and told him so.

One night he put a sketch in front of us and pointed with his pencil and said, "Guess what we're going to do tomorrow?"

We said, "What?"

"We're going to knock down the wall between the guest room and the hall closet. What do you think about that?"

We said, "Sure, Dad, that's great," then faked passing out on the table from boredom.

But early the next morning, The Dad roused Albert and me out of bed and instructed us to move all the junk out of the hall closet. After doing that, we cleared the furniture from the guest room, including the lamp, night table and fold-up cot. Then began the fun part: the sledgehammering. Albert went first. He yelled, "Banzai," and began smacking holes in the Sheetrock wall. When he got tired, I took over. The Dad said things like "Don't hit the stud," and "Watch what you're doing," and "You boys are helluva good workers when you put your mind to it," and "Okay, that's enough, let's sweep up." The Mom stood nearby, watching with her arms crossed over her chest. She said, "I hope you know what you're doing."

After knocking down the wall and dragging away the remains, we got bored. We said, "We quit," and The Dad said what he always said when we quit. He said, "You're quitting on me already, when we just got started?" But he must have planned on us quitting because a couple of minutes later Linwood the carpenter wheeled into the driveway in a beat-up red van and got his tools out of the back and came inside the house. Later the painter arrived. After him came the rug man. They didn't stop working, not even for a soda. You heard deep voices and laughter coming out the windows. You heard Linwood muttering and The Dad saying, "Not like that, that's too rough," and the rug man responding, "You sound like my wife," and the painter answering back, "That's because you got hands like meat hooks." By late afternoon the room was done, and the workmen drove away.

Albert and I stood on the new carpet, looking around. The room smelled like cut wood and paint vapors. "Well," said The Dad. "What do you think?"

Albert said, "Whose room is this?"

The Dad said, "Mine."

He decorated the walls with his framed photographs, hanging them all around the room. Before he got married, The Dad used to buy a new Buick convertible every year, as soon as the new model came out. He'd drive the old model down to the dealership, trade it in, and have the salesman take a picture of him with the new model. There were at least six pictures of The Dad smiling the same smile, standing next to brand-new Buick convertibles with rear fins. The other thing The Dad liked doing before he got married was deep-sea fishing in Florida. He had many framed pictures of himself in fishing action. In one, he and Uncle Sal and Calio are sitting on deck chairs in the rear of a fishing boat with their arms around each other. In another, The Dad is standing on a dock, holding a giant sailfish from a hook with its sword pointing down, as tall as him, the same fish he later had painted and filled with plaster of Paris and mounted to a wallboard, which he hung in the den. Whenever guests came to our house, The Dad would show them the sailfish and tell how he'd reeled it in off the coast of Boca Raton and won a prize for the second-biggest sailfish caught that season. The sailfish hung on the wall until the day Albert and I were playing football in the den and accidentally knocked into it, causing it to smash sword-first onto the floor and break into five pieces, for which Albert and I both got a strapping because The Dad was proud of that fish.

We moved the lamp and night table back into The Dad's room, but not the cot. The Dad told us to take the cot out to the garage and throw it in the trash. "I never want to see that rack again," he said.

"What'll you sleep on?" said Albert.

"You'll see," said The Dad.

Halfway through dinner a delivery truck wheeled into the driveway and two men took an enormous bed out of the back. They carried it up to The Dad's new room and set it on top of a sturdy wooden frame. When they were gone, Albert tore the tag off the end of the mattress that read, "Do Not Remove Under Penalty of Law," and stuck it in his mouth and snarled, "Come and get me, coppers." Meanwhile The Dad tried out the bed. He sank into the mattress, which was high and thick, and stretched his arms and legs. "This is more like it," he said. "Now I'll be able to get a decent night's rest."

From the kitchen came the sound of The Mom banging pots.

15.
TEN CHERRY BUSTERS

The tree house was located between two tall pine trees in the backyard. You climbed a ladder fifteen feet into the air and entered through a portal. There was a window and a hatch in the floor where you could lower a rope and bucket. One time we carried Monty up the ladder and put him inside the tree house. This experiment was not repeated. Monty got very frightened and ran around and peed on the floor and whimpered and barked until we brought him back down the ladder and tied him to his run, which made him happy again.

Every once in a while an intruder came at night and slept in the tree house. This had been happening for approximately three summers. No one ever saw the intruder but we found evidence of his presence afterward, such as cigarette butts, empty potato chip bags, beer cans and, one time, a foot-long turd, curled like a half-moon on the ground next to the ladder. Monty sniffed the turd with unusual interest. Albert pinched his nostrils together and said, "It's human." Albert's theory was that a bum roamed the neighborhood after dark, eating crab apples and picking leftover food out of garbage cans. One night he and I camped out in the tree house, armed with a baseball bat. Albert said the intruder would arrive at the stroke of midnight, like Barnabas Collins in *Dark Shadows*, but midnight passed and nothing happened except we got bit all over by mosquitoes, so we went back to the house, itching.

One morning I found a magazine in the tree house entitled *Ten Cherry Busters. Ten Cherry Busters* was not a normal dirty magazine like *Playboy. Ten Cherry Busters* had no writing or advertisements, cartoons or centerfold, only pictures. Each picture was in color and took up a full page. The three girls on the cover were wearing Catholic school uniforms, but in all the other pictures they were naked. These girls were not pretty with big boobs like the girls in *Playboy.* They looked more like the girls in my class at school, who were flat and skinny and wore pigtails. In addition, the girls in *Ten Cherry Busters* were not alone. They were lying under guys who had boners and were sticking them.

I lifted my shirt and hid *Ten Cherry Busters* underneath. Then I went into the house, intending to show the magazine to Albert. But as soon as I opened the porch door, The Mom appeared and said, "What are you hiding beneath your shirt?"

I said, "Nothing."

The Mom folded her arms cross her chest. "Are you hiding drugs? Is that what I see bulging beneath your shirt? Answer me."

"Of course not."

"What is it?"

"It's a magazine."

"What kind of magazine?"

It was nearly impossible to fool The Mom. She was like Mr. Spock doing a Vulcan mind-meld. She knew what you were thinking all the time. You could be acting normally twenty-three hours and fifty-five minutes out of the day. She would ignore you. In the five-minute period when you decided to sneak into your sister's room and read her diary, she would appear out of nowhere and knock on the door and say, "Timmy, what are you doing in there?"

I reached under my shirt and handed over *Ten Cherry Busters.*

The Mom opened the magazine and looked inside. Then she closed the magazine and said, "Where did you get this? Did someone give it to you? Or did you buy it? Is that why I give you an allowance, to buy filth?"

"I found it."

"Where?"

"Tree house."

The Mom held up *Ten Cherry Busters.* She said, "This is filth. Filth. No son of mine would ever look at this filth."

"I didn't look at it."

"Filth," said The Mom. "You should be ashamed of yourself."

The Dad took a drink of his coffee. He said, "It's natural. He's a growing boy. They like looking at dirty pictures."

"There's nothing natural about filth," said The Mom. She ripped the magazine into pieces and pushed it into the trash among the coffee grounds.

16.
FOOTBALL

Football was the only reason to look forward to going back to school at the end of summer. Football had the cheerleaders. Football had the helmet and uniform and pads, which rattled when you ran. Football had the mouth guard that you heated up in boiling water and stuck in your mouth and chomped down to make the mold. Football had the stinky smell of the locker room and the cleats that crunched on the concrete stairs and asphalt path while you were jogging out to the field. Football had scrimmages and drills and coaches who got red in the face and yelled at you and said things like "Is that what you call hitting? My mother hits harder than that. Go to the back of the line and do it right this time, you little pansy ass."

There were feelings you got from football that didn't happen anywhere else. You took the handoff from the quarterback and followed a blocker upfield. There were eleven guys trying to get you. Your heart was pounding. The wind whistled through the ear holes in your helmet. When they closed in on you, you put your head down and smashed into somebody. Everybody piled on top of you. You got up and pulled a wad of dirt and grass out of your face mask and went back to the huddle.

We played two-on-two touch football in the backyard. The tree house marked one end zone, the clothesline marked the other. The count was five Mississippi. The teams were Stev and me against Albert and Tiger.

Albert said, "Let the games begin," and punted the football. The football spiraled through the air and into my arms. I lateraled the ball to Stev, who began running. I ran ahead of him to block. I was the wedge. Tiger and Albert came at us from the opposite direction. Albert was running in long strides ahead of Tiger. Tiger was running with dainty little steps on his tiptoes. I put my arms in front of my chest to make a block. Albert dodged the block, and Tiger came directly at me. At the last moment before we collided, he got scared and turned his back. I could have stopped myself from lowering my shoulder and drilling him in the lower spine but I did not. There was something about the sissy way he stopped and turned around that made me want to drill him. He made the perfect target.

I drilled him.

I said, "Tony the Tiger goes down."

Tiger flopped around on the grass like a fish tank fish on the kitchen floor. His mouth was wide open but no sound came out.

Stev said, "Pull his shorts out. That's what they do at school. Give him some air."

Albert bent down and pulled Tiger's shorts away from his stomach. Tiger continued to writhe. He said something that no one understood.

I said, "What?"

Tiger said, "My back."

Stev said, "Stop faking it."

Albert said, "He's not faking. You knocked the wind out of him."

I said, "Get up, Tiger."

Tiger said, "My back. It's broken."

Stev said, "I can't believe you broke your back on the opening kickoff."

Tiger writhed for approximately three minutes. Then he got up and hobbled around the side of the house and did not return.

A long time ago The Dad played football for Hartford High School. He was all-state end two years in a row. He had black-and-white pictures of his younger self in a three-point stance with his head up, wearing a funny old leather helmet that had no face mask. Kondrack was the other end. They ran plays called the Flea Flicker and the Statue of Liberty. The Dad kept a newspaper clipping, which was torn and yellow, in his photo album that said, "Hartford Line Ready for Flashy New Britain Backs. All-state ends starred against the Red and Gold last year. Coach Johnny Newell is counting on them heavily tomorrow."

I asked, "Did you win? Did you beat New Britain?"

The Dad said, "Never. We couldn't beat 'em. We lost seven–zero one year and seven–six the next. Kicker missed the extra point."

"Was Kondrack good?"

"He was all-state. We were both all-state."

"What happened to him?"

"Kondrack? How should I know? I never saw him again. Maybe he got killed in the war."

The Dad liked it when some old guy stopped him in the street and said something like "Hey, Bob, is that you? Jeez, I thought it was you. I was telling my wife about you just the other day. Who's this, your boy? Looks like a smart kid. Must take after the wife. Heh heh heh. Let me tell you something about your old man, kid. He hit me harder than any son of a bitch ever hit me before or since. You remember that game, Bob? The Weaver game? When the hell was that? Thirty-eight? Thirty-nine? Jeez, did I see stars."

As a result of his all-state performance at Hartford High School, The Dad got a football scholarship to Syracuse University. He was a freshman and he played on the freshman team. Freshmen were not allowed to play with the varsity. The star of the varsity team was named Sidat-Singh.

I said, "What kind of name is that?"

The Dad said, "It's a Hindu name. That's what he told everyone, that he was a Hindu from India. But that was a lie. Sidat-Singh had a Hindu name because his stepfather was a Hindu but he was in reality a full-blooded Negro from Washington, D.C."

"Why did he lie?"

"Because back then some of the teams wouldn't play against Negroes. They'd walk off the field rather than play Negroes."

"That's not fair."

"That's how it was back then."

"Did he play in the pros?"

"He wanted to be a doctor but he never had the chance. He got killed flying a P-40 on a training flight. Best football player I ever saw."

"Better than you?"

"Are you kidding? Sidat-Singh was all-American. You've never seen anyone throw the ball like he could."

The Dad played football at Syracuse University for one year and smashed his knee during a scrimmage and quit school and moved back to the City of Hartford, where he cleaned out boilers for a living and played semipro football on Sundays for the Hartford Ponies in Dillon Stadium for a dollar a game, though they only got paid if they won.

I said, "Did you win?"

He said, "We won some and lost some."

I said, "What happened then?"

The Dad said, "I got drafted."

The doorbell rang and Tiger's Mother said through the screen door, "I'd like to have a word with you, Robert, if that's possible."

The Dad said, "Stella. Anything's possible. Come in. Sit down."

Tiger's Mother came in and sat down. She said, "Your son Timothy hit my son Anthony in the back when he wasn't looking. My son was injured. I spent two hours at the doctor's office this afternoon. I have the bill in my pocketbook."

The Dad glared at me. "You hit a man in the back when he wasn't looking?"

I said, "It wasn't on purpose."

Tiger's Mother said, "It most certainly was. Anthony swears you hit him on purpose."

"I was trying to make a block."

"Anthony has a severely bruised back. He's wearing a truss. The doctor prescribed bed rest."

The Dad said, "I hope he's all right."

"This has happened before. It's always Anthony who gets hurt. That's because they pick on him."

"Now, Stella. An accident is an accident."

"This was no accident. This was a malicious act."

"We've lived next to each other for a long time and the boys have always gotten along."

"Your son did it on purpose. He's lying to cover up. All boys lie when they get into trouble."

"That's not the way we raised our sons."

"I have a doctor's bill for fifty-five dollars."

"Put it on the table."

"I don't want your money. That's not why I came. I came to talk about your son's behavior."

The Dad said, "I don't want to be obligated."

"Obligated how?"

"I don't want to be obligated. Period."

"I don't understand what you're saying."

"I don't want to be obligated. Which word don't you understand?"

"If you think I'm asking for money, I'm not."

"Put the paper on the table."

"I most certainly will not."

"I pay my bills. You should know that."

"I'm not talking about paying bills. I'm talking about proper discipline."

"Don't tell me how to discipline my boys. I'm their father. That's my job."

"I'll tell you when they misbehave. I'll tell you when they assault my son."

"Football's not a game for sissies, Stella. Someone's bound to get hurt now and then."

"It's not that simple."

"I'll be the judge of that."

Tiger's Mother got up and said, "Fine. You be the judge. I won't say another word." She turned and walked out the door. The Dad and I watched her go down the front steps.

The Mom came to the top of the stairs. She said, "What in God's name was that about?"

The Dad said, "Don't ask."

Later that night I helped The Dad bring the garbage pails to the end of the driveway. The Dad nodded toward Tiger's house, which was dark. Not a single light was on. Somewhere inside that house Tiger was lying in bed in a dark room wearing something called a truss.

The Dad said, "I can't figure it. There's seven of them living in that little house. Right? There's the grandmother, the parents, the four kids. That makes seven. But look at their garbage. One lousy can. They take out one lousy can of garbage every week."

I said, "So?"

He said, "Look at us. Look how many cans we just dragged out."

I counted them. "Six," I said.

"That's right. Six big ones."

"Maybe they burn their trash."

"You can't burn glass," said The Dad. "You can't burn plastic. You can't burn aluminum."

"What do they do with their garbage?"

"They don't do anything with it. They don't have any garbage."

"Why not?"

"Because they don't buy anything. They're cheapos."

I thought about Tiger's record collection. I said, "Tiger only has six 45's."

The Dad said, "How many do you have?"

"Over a hundred. And almost that many albums."

"See what I mean? We got a lot of stuff here. We live like kings."

"We don't have a pool table. We don't have a swimming pool."

"That's your mother's doing. I'd buy those things in a New York second."

"What's a New York second?"

"Just a figure of speech."

We looked at Tiger's dark house approximately twenty New York seconds longer.

The Dad said, "Hey."

I said, "What?"

"You would never hit a man in the back, would you? You wouldn't do a thing like that, right?"

"Of course not."

"I didn't think so. Because a man who hits another man in the back, that's about the lowest thing you can do."

"I know that. You told me that before."

"Good. You remember that."

The night was silent. The sound of a car passed in the distance, going up Avon Mountain. An owl called out. There were many stars. The Dad and I watched the stars for a while. Then we went back inside our house and closed the door and turned out the lights.

17.
KISS ME LIKE THE MOVIES

Daphne came home from summer camp. A van dropped her off in the driveway with her trunk. I went out to the driveway and picked up one end of the trunk and helped her lug it inside. Daphne's face was red and zit-covered. She was having a serious breakout.

I said, "What happened to your face?"

Daphne said, "Mom, Timmy's making fun of me. Tell him to stop or I'll beat the living shit out of him."

The Mom said, "Where did you learn that kind of language?"

"From the counselors."

"I don't believe that for an instant."

"It's true."

"Would you like me to wash your mouth out with soap?"

"No."

"Then don't let me hear that kind of talk again."

Daphne was fourteen, two years older than me and one year older than Albert. When Daphne was a baby she was the prettiest baby anyone had ever seen. The Mom mailed a Kodak picture of Daphne wearing a white bonnet in her Easter dress to a women's magazine, and the magazine published the picture and titled it "Pretty Baby of the Month." When Daphne grew up she was still sort of pretty but she had a tremendous number of zits. All you had to do was mention the word "zits" and she would lose her mind and start blathering and trying to kill you. It was impossible to win a fight with Daphne because she never quit. She was like Joe Frazier. She put her head down and came at you screaming and kicking and scratching and pulling hair and throwing nonstop punches from all directions. She did not fight according to the Marquis of Queensbury Rules. She observed no rules of fighting etiquette whatsoever. Daphne was not wispy-thin like some girls. She was a star soccer player and softball player. Her punches hurt. The best you could hope for was to block her punches and keep calling her Zit Face until she exhausted herself. If you punched back, you were doomed. She would immediately hyperventilate and run and tell The Mom. There was one rule in our house: Never hit a girl. The Mom would tell us, "You can injure her for life. You can give her breast cancer. Is that what you want? To maim your sister?" If Albert or I broke that rule, we would be "severely disciplined," which meant a strapping when The Dad got home from work.

Daphne had three girlfriends in the ninth grade who were extremely pretty. These girls were named Lisa Loomis, Maribeth Donovan and Cynthia Storm. Sometimes they came to our house to sleep over. On such nights they put on pajamas or long T-shirts and slept on the two single beds in Daphne's room. They smoked cigarettes and blew the smoke out the window. They giggled a lot and talked about guys in the tenth grade who were cool. On select occasions they called me into the room while they were lying on the beds and treated me the same way I treated Monty, which meant they grabbed me, ruffled my hair and hugged me, and said, "Oh my God, you're so cute," and "Look how big you're getting," and "How did you get so adorable with that curly black hair?" and "Do you like girls yet? I bet you do." Little did they know that while they were fussing over me, I was copping cheap feels and popping ferocious boners.

I went into the den and turned on the TV. *Gilligan's Island* was on. In this episode, Gilligan won three million dollars from Thurston Howell III in a golfing contest. For that reason, Ginger Grant otherwise known as the Movie Star, played by Tina Louise, wanted to kiss him. She said, "I think you're quite a man, Gilligan. I'd like to play the leading lady in your life story." She came slowly toward him with an open mouth, breathing lipstick breath and swishing in her shiny white-sequined gown. A saxophone went *wa wa wa waaaaaaa wa*. Gilligan fell backward into a water trough. Ginger Grant said, "Oh Gilligan. Let me help you. Where does it hurt?" She leaned over, and her boobs bulged against the shiny white-sequined gown.

I took out my boner and began shaking it furiously.

Shortly thereafter the door opened and Daphne screamed, "Oh my God. Gross."

She ran into the kitchen, yelling, "Mommy, Timmy's playing with himself."

I said, "No, I'm not."

The Mom said, "What's all this yelling about?"

"Timmy was playing with his peter. I saw him, I saw him, I saw him."

"He was doing what?"

"Shaking his peter."

"I won't hear another word of this kind of talk."

"But he was playing with it."

"I was not. I was scratching."

"Leave your brother alone, Daphne."

"But it was gross. He was shaking it really fast."

"I had an itch. I was scratching."

"No, he wasn't."

"Go to your room, young lady."

"But it's not fair. Timmy was playing with his peter."

"You're in big trouble unless you go to your room this instant."

Daphne went to her room.

The Mom said, "I don't understand why you and your sister can't watch television in peace."

I went back to the den and stared at the TV.

The Skipper said to Gilligan, "You've done it again, Little Buddy."

Someone knocked on the front door. I got up and opened the door. Sissi Mandelbaum said, "Is Daphne home?"

I said, “She’s not allowed to come out of her room until dinner.”

Sissi said, “Why not?”

I said, “Because.”

Sissi said, “Let’s go to the tree house and play.”

We went out the back porch door and walked across the backyard. Sissi was Stev’s sister. She was thirteen. She and Daphne went to camp in a place called Casco, Maine, where they had to worry about leeches when they went swimming in the pond. Sissi had straight brown hair and freckles. Her face was red, but not as red as Daphne’s, and she had no zits.

We climbed the ladder into the tree house and sat down on the wooden floor.

I said, “How was camp?”

Sissi said, “There were a lot of older guys.”

“What did you do?”

“A lot.”

“Like what?”

“I’ll take off my shirt if you give me a dollar.”

“Okay.”

Sissi took off her shirt and folded it and placed it on the floorboards. She was wearing a white bra and she had lots of freckles. I looked at her and didn’t say anything.

Sissi said, “You don’t have to pay if you’ll be my boyfriend.”

I said, “Mik Cosgrove is your boyfriend.”

“No, he’s not.”

“Mik Cosgrove tells everyone that you’ve got bee stings and that you don’t know how to French kiss.”

“I hate Mike Cosgrove. I hate his guts.”

“He tells other stuff.”

“Like what?”

“I don’t remember.”

Sissi took off her bra. She had bee stings. The only difference between her chest and mine was that her nips were pointy. A squirrel walked across the top of the tree house and looked in the window and twitched his nose and twirled an acorn with his little fingers and ran away. I looked at Sissi's nips for approximately ten seconds. Then she put on her bra and shirt.

I said, "What should we do now?"

Sissi closed her eyes and put her face next to mine and said, "Kiss me like the movies."

I put my lips against her mouth and held them there for a long time.

She said, "I'll show you mine if you show me yours."

I said, "Okay."

"You go first."

"No, you."

Sissi pulled down her shorts and underwear and waited approximately five seconds, then pulled them back up. I looked but didn't see anything except that she had no hair. She said, "Your turn."

I took out my boner.

She said, "Why is it so big?"

I said, "I don't know. I think I have to go to the bathroom."

We got up and climbed down the ladder and walked across the backyard and went into the basement. Monty came over and sniffed Sissi's legs and butt. I patted him and ruffled his fur.

Sissi said, "We're boyfriend and girlfriend now."

Sissi always had two or three boyfriends at the same time. One was a kid named Matt. No one at school liked Matt. He was in the grade above mine and he had the shortest haircut in school, which he called a whiffle and everyone else called a crew cut. Most kids refused to get their hair cut, but not Matt. He went to the barber once per week, cutting it shorter and shorter. He was stocky, with shoulders as straight as a board, and he never slouched. He had a pasty white face and lots of zits. When he came to visit Sissi, he knocked on the front door and said like Eddie Haskell, "Hello, Mrs. Mandelbaum, I've come to see Sissi." One time

Stev and I were listening to records in his room when Matt came upstairs. Sissi called out, "Don't look, Matt. I'm getting dressed, so whatever you do, don't look." I stuck my head into the hallway and looked at Sissi, who was standing in the doorway of her bedroom wearing only her underwear. She was not trying to cover up or get dressed. Matt stood on the top step with his hands over his eyes and said, "Are you dressed yet, Sissi?" and Sissi said, "Not yet, I'm still naked, so don't look, please don't look," and she stood waiting for him to look. Sissi liked when boys looked. She liked undressing with her door open. She liked losing at strip poker. She liked having séances and talking to dead people and saying things like, "Yes, I hear you, yes, I do, yes, I will take off my shirt if it will help you in the other world, Mr. Green." She liked crawling into the tent, which Stev put up in his backyard, and taking off her clothes and saying, "You can come in now. You can look but don't touch." We crawled into the tent, one at a time, and looked at Sissi in her underwear, but we didn't touch. Sissi never allowed anyone to touch.

Sissi and I went into the kitchen. Mik Cosgrove and Albert were sitting in the swivel chairs.

Albert said, "Watch this." He got behind Mik Cosgrove and started turning Mik Cosgrove's swivel chair around and around, and Mik Cosgrove said, "Faster faster faster faster."

We watched him spinning but could not see his face because he was turning so fast. After a minute, Albert got tired of spinning, and Mik Cosgrove got out of the chair and took one wobbly step and fell onto the linoleum floor. He tried to get up and fell down again and started laughing.

Albert said, "Want to try it?"

Sissi said, "I'll throw up."

Mik Cosgrove said, "I never throw up. You can spin me all day and I won't get sick."

The Mom said, "You're making me dizzy with all that spinning. Go upstairs and play with Daphne if you want something to do."

We went up to Daphne's room. She was lying on her stomach on her bed, reading a book. She closed the book and said, "I caught Timmy playing with his peter. He was shaking it like he was trying to yank it off. He was doing it on the couch in front of the TV. It was really really really gross."

Mik Cosgrove said, "What was he watching? *Petticoat Junction*, I bet."

Daphne said, "I don't know."

I said, "I was watching baseball and I wasn't doing anything."

Mik Cosgrove said, "If you play with your dick enough times it'll get huge. It will get humongous."

Albert said, "That's not true. You'll go blind and grow hair on your palms is what happens."

Mik Cosgrove said, "The dick is a muscle, just like Jack La Lanne. It gets bigger when you exercise. Some guys play with it so much they can't get their hands around it. They can't even fit it into their pants. I've seen pictures in *National Geographic*. There's a guy with a dick as big as a watermelon. He carries it between his legs in a wheelbarrow."

I said, "There's no such picture."

Mik Cosgrove said, "Trust me. I've seen it."

Sissi looked at me and said, "So that's why."

I said, "Why what?"

"You're *National Geographic*."

"I am not."

Daphne said, "Stop denying it. We all know the truth. You play with your peter."

"I don't."

Sissi said, "Then why is it so big? Tell me that."

I said, "It's not big."

"It is too. It's really big."

Daphne said, "How do you know? Did you catch him playing with it?"

Sissi said, "Yes. In the tree house. He said he had to go to the bathroom but he didn't."

I said, "I showed her mine because she showed me hers."

"That's a lie," said Sissi.

"She said we were boyfriend and girlfriend."

"Stop lying."

Mik Cosgrove picked up the flashlight and pointed the beam in my eyes. He said, "This is a test by the Emergency Broadcast System. For the next sixty seconds you will be experiencing a test. Do not get alarmed. Relax. Take a deep breath. Fart if you must. No one who lies can pass the test. Liars always laugh. If you are telling the truth, do not laugh. Repeat after me: 'I am telling the truth.' "

I looked into the flashlight and said, "I am telling the truth."

Mik Cosgrove said, " 'I am not lying.' "

I said, "I am not lying."

Mik Cosgrove kept the flashlight beam in my eyes. After approximately fifteen seconds I started cracking up.

Mik Cosgrove said, "That proves it. He's lying. He pulls back skin. He's a jerk-off artist. He pounds his pud like there's no tomorrow."

The Mom called from the kitchen, "Dinner's ready. Everyone come down."

We went down to dinner. Dinner was meat loaf. Sissi and Mik Cosgrove went to their separate houses.

The Dad said, "Did anything exciting happen around here today?"

Daphne said, "I caught Timmy playing with his peter."

The Mom said, "Do you want to go to bed without dinner, young lady?"

I said, "It's not true. I was scratching."

Daphne said, "He's lying. Everyone knows it. Ask Albert."

Albert had gobs of Rice-a-Roni in his mouth. He said something that was impossible to understand.

The Mom said, "Don't talk with your mouth full."

Albert swallowed half the portion of yellow mush and said, "*National Geographic.*"

Daphne said, "See? It's a fact. Timmy plays with his peter."

The Mom said, "Go to your room."

Daphne got up and went to her room.

18.
LOOSE

Monty was a brown boxer with a black patch over one eye and a white tuft of fur on his stomach. He liked patrolling the backyard while attached to his line, sniffing things with his nose high in the air, but what he really liked was getting out without a leash. He got out whenever possible. His ears sprang up whenever he heard the squeak of the mail truck stopping at the end of the driveway. He waited. When you opened the door to get the mail from the mailbox, he sprang past you and bolted up the street toward the mountain. For this reason, we kept Monty tied to the run in the backyard for most of the day, spring, summer, fall and winter. He had a doghouse but he never ventured inside it. In thunderstorms he sat by the back door scratching and barking until we let him in. The Dad built the doghouse with nice new wooden planks, and he nailed a sign above the doorway that said, "Monty." We put dog bones and biscuits, a dog pillow and blanket and old tennis balls inside the doghouse. Albert and I tried to lure Monty into the doghouse by going inside ourselves and pretending to eat his dog biscuits, but Monty wanted no part of it. It was beneath his dog dignity to crawl inside the doghouse and sit with his snout out the opening like some mutt who didn't have a real home.

One morning I woke to discover that Monty wasn't lying in the front doorway where he usually slept. I said, "Where's Monty?"

The Mom looked up from her coffee cup and said, "Oh dear. He must have gotten out when I went to the end of the driveway to pick up the newspaper."

"Where's Dad?"

"He left already for Locust Street."

"On a Saturday?"

"That's what I said."

Whenever Monty got out we would go with The Dad in his car to look for him on some dirt roads off the mountain. Instead, Albert and I walked up the street calling, "Monty Monty Monty. Where are you, Monty?" We went into the woods at the top of the street, calling, "Monty Monty Monty," but there was no response other than birds and woodpeckers and the sound of leaves and sticks crunching beneath our feet. You could walk all the way to the top of the mountain and never leave these woods. The woods went on and on, up and up. There were no houses up there. Once upon a time during the Revolutionary War, George Washington and his soldiers set up campsites in these woods. We learned this fact in school and went on a field trip to see the place. The campsites still existed, partially covered by leaves and dirt and branches, just like the day George Washington slept there. No one knew about the campsites other than our teachers and the people who lived nearby. There were no signs that read "George Washington Campsites This Way." There was no path. You walked through the woods and came to a little clearing and there they were. The campsites were made out of stones arranged in the shape of giant horseshoes. The teacher told us, "One thousand men warmed their hands over these fires. They gave this country freedom. This happened in your own backyard."

Albert and I walked around the campsites and kicked over some of the stones. Then we felt bad and put the stones back in place.

I said, "One thousand men warmed their hands over these fires."

Albert said, "I bet they farted a lot."

"Everyone farts at campfires."

A deer approached from behind us. The deer stood still and looked at us with big eyes. Then he ran away.

We called, "Monty Monty Monty. Where are you, Monty?"

He was somewhere in these woods, running and crouching low to the ground, sniffing and stalking animals, peeing on tree stumps and fallen logs. He always went into the woods when he ran away. This was his territory. The danger was that he would wander onto Albany Avenue otherwise known as Route 44, located nearby. Everyone drove fast on Albany Avenue. There were always dead animals lying by the side of the road, such as squirrels and raccoons, cats and dogs, and once in a while a deer lying on his side with his neck broken and tongue out and eyes open and legs crossed.

Albert looked up and said, "Aaaagh."

I said, "What?"

"Snake."

I looked up and saw a snake hanging on a tree limb above our heads. The snake was coiled up, silently flicking its tongue. We bolted.

The Mom said, "Did you find him?"

She was sitting at the kitchen table with The Myra. The Myra was pouring herself a J&B.

I said, "No."

The Myra said, "Who are you looking for? Steven? He's playing tennis with his sister at the club."

"We're looking for Monty. Have you seen him?"

"Should I have seen Monty?"

"He's loose."

"I wish I was loose."

"What do you mean?"

"You don't want to know."

I went upstairs and stood in the hallway, peeking around the corner.

The Mom said, "What's wrong, Myra? You're not yourself today."

The Myra said, "I've got a rash on my ass that's driving me bananas."

"Have you seen a dermatologist?"

"Do you know who my dermatologist is?"

"No."

"It's Dr. Silberstein."

"So. He's a doctor. He's seen everything."

"He's a member of Tumblebrook and he's gorgeous and he's not going to see my ass in this condition. How could I look him in the face if he saw me like this?"

"You're being silly."

"You want me to show my ass to Dr. Silberstein looking like this? Here. See for yourself."

The Myra leaned against the kitchen table, bent over, raised her skirt and pulled down her big white underwear. There were red blotches covering her haunches and butt cheeks. It looked like someone had tied her down and spanked her with a paddle fifty times and then scratched her butt with sharp fingernails.

The Mom stood back and looked. She said, "Well. I don't know."

The Myra said, "How does it look?"

"It looks inflamed."

"Inflamed? My ass is as red as a fire pole."

She pulled up her underwear and walked toward the sink, out of my viewing area.

I went into my room to listen to the radio. When I looked out the window I saw Albert. He was standing on top of the garage, holding a handsaw. His feet made crunching sounds against the little white pebbles on the garage rooftop.

I opened the window and said, "What are you doing?"

He said, "Watch and learn."

He grabbed the branches of a pine tree and pushed them out of his way and began cutting the tree with the handsaw. After approximately one minute of sawing, the top of the pine tree fell off and landed on the front lawn like a miniature Christmas tree. There were four pine trees planted in a row alongside the garage. One by one Albert cut off all four treetops.

Albert said, "That should do it."

I said, "Do what?"

"You'll see," he said, and then he disappeared down the ladder.

The Myra was having a fit. It was a bona fide nervous breakdown. She was crying black tears and smearing them over her face with her hands. This was not an unusual event. The Myra had nervous breakdowns fairly often. She cried and drank and complained. Meanwhile The Mom tried to console her by saying such things as "I know exactly how you feel," or "You have every right to be upset," or "This is the thing, this is the very thing I've always told you."

The Myra said, "I'm married to a man who calls me shicker. You'd think that was my name. You're shicker, he says. Shicker shicker shicker. Ten times a day I hear that word."

The Mom said, "You need a vacation."

"I need another drink."

"You really should go away. Go to the beach. It'll do wonders for you."

"Ask me where I want to go."

"Where?"

"I want to go back to my roots."

"You want to go back to Newark? Why?"

"Did I say I wanted to go back to Newark? I never want to see Newark again."

"What are you talking about? What roots?"

"Niles Street."

"Niles Street in Hartford? Niles Street near Scoler's Restaurant? You lived on Niles Street for two years. How can that be your roots?"

"It was my first apartment away from home. The children were babies then. We were so happy."

"Still, I wouldn't call that your roots."

"Don't you remember that feeling, having a newborn baby in your hands? When everything feels fresh and clean?"

"Of course."

"Let's get in the car and drive to Niles Street and go up to the third floor and knock on the door. Maybe they'll let me see my roots, whoever's living there."

"Don't be silly. We can't go there. It's not a nice neighborhood anymore."

"Do you think I'm shicker?"

"Right now I would say yes. After four drinks, yes."

"You think I'm shicker?"

"I think you're shicker."

The Myra laughed. "You're right. I am shicker. I'm shicker as hell."

The Myra laughed some more and then she stopped laughing and put her head down on the kitchen table and started crying. She cried for a long time. The Mom said, "Now, Myra. What are you crying for?"

The Myra said, "I don't know. I just am."

I went down the stairs and told The Myra, "I know something that will make you feel better."

The Myra raised her head. "What?"

I said, "Wait here."

I went into the living room and got the brass duck off the mantel. No one knew why The Myra liked the brass duck so much, but she did. It always made her happy to hold the brass duck in her hands and rub it against her cheeks and forehead. The brass duck was ice cold. It was better than putting a steak on your eye if you had a black eye. I handed the brass duck to The Myra and said, "The duck will make you feel better."

The Myra took the brass duck from my hand, pressed it against her forehead and closed her eyes. She said, "You're right. It makes me feel better."

I said, "It never fails."

The Myra said, "Come here."

She grabbed me around the shoulders and pulled me toward her. She hugged me tightly and kissed me on the cheek. Her face was wet and sticky and she smelled like smoke, J&B and perfume.

The Mom said, "Go wash your face, Timmy."

I said, "Why?"

The Myra said, "I got my mascara all over you. You look like a French whore."

Dinner came and went and The Dad didn't come home.

The Mom said, "Your father is a liar."

I said, "Do you think he's playing golf?"

"Where else?"

"What are you going to do?"

"Nothing. I couldn't care less what that man does."

The Mom was strangely calm. She was the calm before the storm. She was like the SS *Poseidon* floating happily along on New Year's Eve before the tidal wave struck and capsized the ship and all hell broke loose and the enormous fake Christmas tree fell over, crushing numerous passengers, and the purser screamed, "Stay where you are, for God's sake," and some panic-stricken weasel screamed back, "We're going to die. We're all going to die."

I said, "Aren't you going to call the club?"

She said, "What makes you think I care where he is?"

"You always track him down."

"I'm not going to lift my little finger."

Daphne walked into the room. She was wearing a mud mask to cover her zits and dry them up. She said, "Did Monty come back?"

I shook my head.

She said, "He's going to get run over. That's what happened to Lisa Loomis's dog. He got run over by a flower delivery truck and squashed flat. The same thing's going to happen to Monty. I know it."

The Mom said, "Monty is as wild as a moose. Boxers are like that. They're high-strung."

Daphne said, "Why does he run away?"

The Mom said, "He's young and he wants to play. He smells the scent of a deer or a rabbit or some other animal and he can't resist. It's in his blood. He'll come back when he's done carousing."

"He will not," said Daphne. "He's going to get squashed."

Daphne went up the stairs. She weighed approximately the same as me but when she went up the stairs, you'd think an elephant was loose in the house.

Saturday night was the best television of the week. We tuned to CBS and did not change the channel. It began at 8 P.M. with *All in the Family* starring Carroll O'Connor, Jean Stapleton, Sally Struthers and Rob Reiner as Mike Stivic, the Meathead. *All in the Family* was recorded before a live studio audience. At least once per episode Carroll O'Connor otherwise known as Archie Bunker got red in the face and turned to his wife and said, "Stifle yourself, Edith." This was the moment everyone waited for. When it happened, the live studio audience broke out in hysterical laughter.

After *All in the Family* came *M*A*S*H*, *The Mary Tyler Moore Show*, *The Bob Newhart Show* and *The Carol Burnett Show* with Harvey Korman and Vicki Lawrence. We usually watched these shows together, in the den, all of us lined up on the couch except Albert, who liked to lie on the floor with his head propped on two couch pillows and his feet sticking up in front of the picture tube. Sometimes he would lie so close to the TV that The Mom said, "Move back, Albert. You'll get radiation that way."

Everyone had their favorite show. The Dad liked *All in the Family*. Albert and I liked *M*A*S*H*. Our favorite character was Frank Burns, who was the world's biggest weasel. Daphne liked *Mary Tyler Moore*, especially when Mary spun around and tossed her winter cap high in the air and the singer said, "You're gonna make it after all." The Mom liked *Carol Burnett*. Every week when Carol Burnett pinched her earlobe during the ending credits The Mom said, "That means she's saying good night to her children and telling them to get to bed."

Laughter was contagious. Whenever one of us broke out laughing, the rest joined in. You couldn't help laughing, even if you hadn't thought the particular joke was funny at first. That was why someone invented canned laughter. The Mom laughed politely, with her hand covering her mouth. Daphne snorted when she laughed. Albert and I laughed as loud as we could, but not as loud as The Dad. The Dad belly-laughed. Sometimes he laughed so hard that he pulled out his handkerchief and wiped the tears out of the corners of his eyes.

Without him, the den was quiet. The Mom knitted, clicking her needles. Daphne and Albert were in their rooms. I sat on the couch, eating slices of white bread. I ate eight slices in all, piling the crusts to the side. Usually The Mom complained when I left the crusts or tossed them to Monty. Usually she would say something like "There are children starving in Africa and in this country too, in the Appalachians, so only take what you can finish."

But she didn't mention starving Africans, nor did she laugh, not once during *All in the Family*, not even when Carroll O'Connor said, "The reason you don't understand me, Edith, is because I'm talking to you in English and you're listening in dingbat."

I said, "Why aren't you laughing?"

"That man reminds me of your father."

"He doesn't look anything like him."

"I'm not talking about looks," she said. "He's low-class. He's crude like your father."

At 10 P.M. the announcer said, "From television city in Hollywood, it's the *Carol Burnett Show* with Harvey Korman and Vicki Lawrence."

I said, "Can we turn it?"

The Mom said, "No. This is the only show I like."

The Dad came home while Harvey Korman was imitating a Nazi. He walked into the den and said, "Watching TV?" His face was red and he was smiling largely.

The Mom said, "What does it look?"

I said, "Dad, Monty got out. We waited for you to look for him in the car."

The Dad said, "Did he come back?"

"No. He's still out."

"Let me change my clothes and we'll go find him."

"It's too dark. We'll never see."

The Mom said, "If that dog gets run over, it's on your head."

The Dad said, "My head? I'm not the one who let him out."

"No. You're the one who hung around the golf club until ten o'clock at night while we had an emergency."

"For your information, I haven't been golfing in a month."

"That's a bunch of bull."

"Listen. I don't like walking through that door after working ten hours on a Saturday and hearing this kind of crap. That's not the kind of welcome I expect."

"You expect a welcome? What are you, royalty? You want us to get on our knees and bow? Is that what you want?"

"I want a little consideration. It's me who pays the bills around here. Not you. You don't do a goddamn thing."

"I don't come home with my face as red as a beet, that's for certain."

"Who the hell are you kidding? I haven't touched a drop. I spent the day boarding up a building. Me alone. That's where I been. Slaving on a Saturday. And I have to come home and listen to this crap."

"Save it for your lawyer."

"What's that supposed to mean?"

"You figure it out."

"You threaten me with a lawyer? That's a laugh."

"Go ahead and laugh. See if I care."

"I'd like to talk to a lawyer myself. I'd like to talk about loss of consortium. Ever hear of that?"

The Mom said nothing.

I said, "What does that mean?"

The Dad said, "What does it mean? You want to know what it means? I'll tell you what it means. You're old enough to know."

The Mom said, "You shut your mouth."

The Dad said, "It means not being allowed to sleep in the same room with your wife. That's what it means. It means sleeping in the guest room like some sort of goddamn flunky. What's that worth? How do you put a price on that?"

"How dare you talk that way in front of the children? What kind of a father are you?"

"There's nothing wrong with your back. You're a faker."

"I'll never let you back in my bedroom. Never. You hear that, mister? Not until hell freezes over."

"I wouldn't go back in your bedroom if you paid me. Not for all the tea in China."

"Good. 'Cause that's as close as you'll get. China."

Daphne came into the room. She said, "You're always fighting. I can't stand it when you fight."

The Mom and The Dad continued yelling at each other. The yelling was simultaneous. It was no longer possible to understand what each person was saying, except for the words "loss of consortium," which The Dad repeated many times, like a sorcerer's spell.

Suddenly Daphne screamed, "I hate you. I hate you both."

I said, "Shut up, Daphne."

Daphne said, "I hate you too."

The Mom said, "There. I hope you're happy. Look how upset she is."

The Dad said, "She's hysterical. Just like her mother."

Daphne said, "I am not hysterical." Then she let out an ear-piercing scream that lasted approximately ten seconds. No one could scream as loud as Daphne. It was so loud I had to put my hands over my ears and wait for her to stop.

After that, the room was silent. Daphne turned and stomped off.

The Mom said, "Do me a favor. Empty your pockets."

The Dad said, "My pockets?"

"You're the big breadwinner. Show us what you got."

"You checking up on me, is that it?"

"I'm curious. Humor me."

"You want to see what's in my pockets? There. That's what's in my pockets." The Dad pulled out a big wad of cash, which he called a Michigan bankroll, and threw it on the couch next to The Mom. He said, "Take a good look, lady. Count it. That's what keeps this family going. Me. Big Bob. My money. You'd be like lost sheep without me."

The Mom said, "Keep going."

"You want more? There. There's some change."

"Turn the pockets out."

"Here. Have it all. Every goddamn cent."

With a quick motion, The Dad pulled out the inside of his pockets. Some pennies dropped to the Oriental rug and then a red golf tee popped out and bounced once and landed next to the coins. He stood looking down at the golf tee. The white lining hung out of his pocket like a miniature flag of surrender, dangling a long thread.

The Mom said, "I've got a pile of them in the laundry room. Always the right pocket. For ten years I've been taking golf tees out of that right pocket."

The Dad said, "So I got in a quick nine holes. What's the crime in that?"

He picked up the wad of cash. Then he went to the kitchen and opened the cabinet and uncorked the J&B.

The Dad stored cases of J&B in the Restricted Area, which was located in the basement. The J&B was piled in cases to the ceiling, along with other assorted alcoholic beverages, such as Schlitz, Johnnie Walker, Seagrams V.O. and Martell's. Whenever The Dad finished a bottle of J&B, he tossed it into the trash and said, "Another dead soldier." When we were little no one was allowed to go into the Restricted Area except for The Dad. He locked the door with a key he kept on the ledge above the cabinets. No one could reach the key except for him. But then Albert got tall and one day he stood on his tiptoes and grabbed the key and we unlocked the door to the Restricted Area and went inside and opened a bottle. The

J&B tasted lousy. It was like trying to swallow mouthwash. Albert spit it out and said, "Not so good." We opened a can of Schlitz and spit that out too, so Albert put the key back on the ledge and we never again snuck into the Restricted Area. Sometimes The Dad asked us to go downstairs and get a bottle for him, but most of the time he went himself.

The Mom came out of the den and stood at the top of the stairs, waiting for him. When he reached the top step she said, "Having a drink?"

The Dad said, "Why?"

"I'd like one too."

"You would?"

"Yes, I would. If you're going to get drunk every night, I might as well too."

"Might do you some good," said The Dad. "Might loosen you up a bit."

"Give me that," said The Mom. She took the bottle and went over to the sink and got two glasses out of the cabinet. She set the glasses on the counter and snapped open the J&B and looked at The Dad and said, "On second thought, I'm not very thirsty." Then she turned the bottle over and began pouring the J&B into the sink. The J&B glugged and splashed.

The Dad said, "Sure. Pour it out. Why not?"

The Mom said, "I certainly will."

"Pour out the milk and orange juice while you're at it. You don't pay for it. It's no skin off your ass."

The Dad watched her pour out the J&B. Then he went downstairs and came back approximately one minute later with a new bottle.

The Mom said, "Give me that bottle."

The Dad said, "The hell I will."

She raised the empty bottle and threw it toward him with a spastic girl's throw. The Dad stepped out of the way, and the bottle bounced once off the linoleum and hit with a thud against the wall but did not break.

The Dad said, "Break the window while you're at it."

The Mom said, "I won't have you drinking in this house any longer."

"This is my house," said The Dad. "I'll drink from noon to night if I want. You got that?"

She pointed at me and said, "Not when it affects my children, you won't."

The Dad said, "Him? What the hell is wrong with him?"

"Watching his father come home at ten o'clock and stumble around the kitchen? You think that's good for a boy?"

The Dad said, "You're out of your goddamn mind."

"Out of my mind?" said The Mom. "I want a divorce. You heard me, a divorce. How's that for out of my mind? What do you say to that?"

"Don't make me laugh."

"Go ahead and laugh. That's what drunks do. They laugh all the time."

"Who you calling drunk?"

"You are, mister. Drunk as a hoot owl."

"I'm as sober as a judge. You've never seen me drunk in your life. In your life."

"You're drunk tonight and you were drunk last night and every night before that as long as I can remember. I'm so sick of looking at your drunk red face that I could scream. I can't bear the sight of you."

"Why do you think I drink? Any man would drink, living with a woman like you."

"Get out," said The Mom.

The Dad said, "You want me out? Maybe I'll go someplace I can drink in peace."

"That's fine with me," said The Mom, and she turned and walked upstairs.

The Dad called after her, "You're not getting rid of me, lady. I'm not going anywhere. This is my house. Mine."

From upstairs came the sound of The Mom slamming her bedroom door, so The Dad raised his voice. "You think it's easy? You think it's some kind of free ride? Think about it. Think long and hard. You might get what you want."

Then he bent down and picked up the empty bottle of J&B and set it on the table. "Sin to waste good scotch," he said to me. He took a glass out of the cupboard and went into the den, carrying the fresh bottle of J&B.

I went upstairs and opened the door to our bedroom. The room was dark, so I turned on the overhead light.

"You're exposing me," said Albert.

He was kneeling in front of the window with his eyeball pressed against the surveyor's equipment, looking toward Stev's house. The surveyor's equipment belonged to The Dad. He told us never to fool around with it because it was expensive and something we could break easily. The surveyor's equipment was like a telescope, only heavier. The Dad used it to measure distances and draw straight lines when he built square-shaped industrial warehouses on Locust Street in the City of Hartford. You looked into the lens and saw miles away, much farther than binoculars.

I turned off the light and said, "You missed a good fight."

He said, "I heard."

"Pretty good, huh?"

"Adequate." Albert adjusted the knob with his hand.

I said, "What are you doing? Spying on Stev?"

"Negative. I've got The Myra."

"Can you see something?"

"Affirmative. The tree is no longer an obstacle. We now have direct access."

He watched for a long time. I sat on the bed watching him watch. I said, "What's she doing?"

He said, "You won't believe it."

"Is it good?"

"It's unbelievable."

"Let me see."

"Not yet."

I waited. I said, "Come on. You've been watching all night. Lemme have a turn."

Albert said, "Behold," and moved aside.

The window was foggy from all his heavy breathing. I wiped off the window with the bedsheet and pressed my eyeball against the lens. I adjusted the knob, and the Mandelbaums' master bedroom came into perfect focus. It was like watching a movie in Technicolor.

The Myra was standing bare naked swinging a set of dumbbells. She raised the dumbbells over her head, pushed the dumbbells forward, dropped the dumbbells to her side. She continued this procedure over and over. Meanwhile her boobs moved from side to side. Approximately ten feet away, Mr. Mandelbaum was sitting at the table in front of the window, looking out at the darkness. He was cracking open peanuts with his fingers, carefully putting the shells into a dish and popping the peanuts into his mouth. He appeared to be looking directly at me although he could not see me and had no clue that I was watching him through the surveyor's equipment. Not once did he turn and look at The Myra. He just kept staring out the window, eating the peanuts.

Albert said, "Well?"

I said, "The surveyor's equipment is the greatest invention ever created by mankind."

We watched Mr. Mandelbaum eat the entire bag of peanuts. After he finished he picked up the plate and dropped the empty shells into the wastepaper basket. Then he went into the bathroom for a few minutes. When he came out, he put on his pajamas, took off his glasses, got under the covers and reached up and turned out the lamp on the night table next to his side of the bed and went to sleep. Meanwhile The Myra put down the dumbbells and put on a nightgown and got into bed. She took a book off the night table and started reading.

Albert said, "I wonder if it's a dirty book."

I said, "Maybe it's *The Instrument.*"

The Instrument by John O'Hara was a book that The Mom and The Dad kept on the top shelf of the closet, which we were not allowed to read. Albert and I tried reading *The Instrument* once but it was boring and we could not find any good parts and we wondered why the book was forbidden.

The Myra read for a long time, wearing half glasses that made her look like an old lady. She licked her finger and turned the pages, page after page. After a while she got out of bed and went to the bathroom and came back and got under the covers and propped up the pillows and continued reading the book.

"Is she still reading?" said Albert.

"Affirmative."

The Dad yelled from downstairs. He said, "Hey, lumberjacks. Come down here. Quick."

Albert and I looked at each other for a New York second. Then we jumped up, hid the surveyor's equipment under the bed and ran downstairs.

The Dad said, "Look who's here. Look who decided to come home after a day on the mountain."

Monty was sitting politely on the floor with his mouth open and his tongue hanging out. He was covered with burrs and had leaves stuck in his collar. When he saw us, he barked three times.

The Dad said, "He came back. He runs away. He comes back. That's what he likes doing."

We stood looking at Monty. Daphne trudged down the stairs and joined us. "Hey," she said. "What's going on? What's all the noise about?"

We said, "Monty came back."

I said, "He must be hungry, Dad."

The Dad tossed a piece of bread, and Monty snatched it out of the air.

19.
FIVE MISSISSIPPI

The next day, The Myra telephoned. She said, "Did your dog come back?"

I said, "He came back last night. He ate ten pieces of bread and barfed on the living room rug."

She said, "That's nice."

"I had to clean it up because he's my dog."

"Is your mother home?"

"She's at church."

"What about your father?"

"Hold on," I said. Then I yelled downstairs, "Dad. Telephone."

We had two phones. One was located upstairs on The Mom's night table. The other was located in the kitchen. I often eavesdropped on telephone calls with my hand placed over the receiver, sometimes hearing confidential information. Once I overheard The Myra tell The Mom, "Leonard was a wolf last night. He wouldn't stop. I don't know what got into him. I can barely sit down today."

The Dad picked up the phone in the kitchen. He said, "I got it."

I said, "Okay, I'll hang up," and I pushed down the button and counted five Mississippi, then softly released the button and placed my hand over the receiver.

The Myra said, "When did she leave?"

"Ten minutes ago. I'll tell her you called."

"What's your rush? Can't you talk to me for one minute?"

"It's Sunday morning."

"So?"

"So I'm reading the paper."

"What's so important about that? You can read the paper anytime."

"The hell I can. Ten minutes a day. That's all I get to myself."

"Why don't you come over?"

"I just told you. I'm reading the paper."

"I ask you to come over and you tell me you're reading the paper?"

"Yeah. I'm reading the paper. What the hell's wrong with that?"

The Myra said, "Leonard took Steven and Sissi to the club."

"You should go too. Get yourself some sun."

"Who needs sun? That's the last thing I need, sitting by the pool listening to that shrieking."

"Well. Stay home then."

The Myra exhaled. "You act like I'm asking you to jump off a cliff."

The Dad said nothing.

The Myra said, "You're worse than Leonard. Next you'll be telling me I'm shicker. Go ahead. Tell me I'm shicker."

"Shitter? What the hell are you talking about? What's shitter?"

"You are. You're a first-rate shitter."

"What the hell's gotten into you?"

"Nothing. Nothing at all. Good-bye."

Then came the sound of the dial tone and The Dad muttering, "For Christsake."

20.
MIDNIGHT SNACK

The Mom announced that she was going to Cranston, Rhode Island, to visit Aunt Ethel. She took her luggage and her handbag and got into the Station Wagon.

She said, "You children take care of yourselves. Do what your father tells you."

Daphne said, "When are you coming back?"

"In a few days."

"Why are you leaving?"

"I have to see Aunt Ethel. We have to talk about important things."

"What about?"

"Don't be nosy. Adults have problems too, you know."

"Duh, Mom."

"Don't use that expression. It's not attractive. Now, I'll call you collect every night. When the operator asks you the question you say, 'I accept the charges.' Got that?"

Daphne said, "Okay."

"Do you understand, Timmy?"

I said, "I accept the charges."

The Mom said, "Good."

She put the gearshift into *R* for Reverse and backed out of the driveway.

With The Mom gone, I stayed up late watching TV. I flipped from one station to the next, but all the stations showed Richard Milhaus Nixon, who kept saying the same thing: "Let me say this about that. This president is not going to leave the White House until the end of his term." Then he shot his hands above his head like a referee signaling a touchdown.

After the news and the late movie, the announcer said, "This concludes our programming for this evening. We would like to thank you for viewing. From all of us here at Channel Forty, this is Dean Sias, wishing you a good night."

High Flight came on. This was the last program of the night. Channel Forty played *High Flight* every night before the screen went blank. *High Flight* was the best part of watching late-night TV. *High Flight* was only one minute long. It consisted of aerial photography of an air force jet. As the pilot did spins and somersaults, a narrator with a deep voice read poetry. The poetry began with the following words: "O I have slipped the surly bonds of earth."

Daphne came into the den. She had pink zit cream all over her face and her eyes were puffy from sleeping. She said, "What are you watching?"

I said, "Shhh."

"Is this a movie?"

"Just shut up for a second. It's almost over."

High Flight was Albert's favorite TV program. He knew the words by heart. He made the same comment every time the camera showed the air force jet from the side angle. He said, "You see that sucker? That's all engine. Every inch of it." Albert wanted to be an air force pilot when he got older. He liked to say, "I got twenty-twenty vision. They wouldn't take you. You got glasses. They only take you in the air force if you got twenty-twenty, like me."

I told Daphne, "You see that sucker? It's all engine."

"What is?"

"The plane."

"I can't see without my glasses on," she said, squinting.

We watched the air force jet fly into the clouds and the narrator said, "And touched the face of God."

The screen went blank and the high-pitched noise sounded.

Daphne said, "I can't sleep. Dad's keeping me up snoring. He sounds like he's choking."

"Just bang on the wall and he'll shut up. That usually works."

"I tried that. They should sleep in the same room. That's what parents are supposed to do."

"Mom and Dad are different. They fight a lot."

"Everyone's parents fight. Mr. and Mrs. Mandelbaum fight but they sleep in the same room."

"They have a bed as big as a trampoline. Did you ever see it? It's the size of three beds."

Daphne said, "Mom and Dad should get one like that. There'd be more room and maybe they wouldn't fight."

"Dad has his own room now," I said. "He likes it in there."

We turned off the TV and went into the kitchen and made bologna and cheese sandwiches. While we were eating, The Dad came down the stairs wearing his leopard pajama bottoms and said, "What's going on here? It's two o'clock in the morning."

Daphne said, "I couldn't sleep because you were snoring."

"I'll stop."

"You always say that but you don't."

"I'll turn on my side. That's all I have to do."

"Why don't you move back in the room with Mom?"

"Are you crazy? When I can have my own room all to myself?"

"I'm serious, Dad."

The Dad turned on the tap and poured a glass of water, drank half of it and pitched the rest down the sink. He said, "You kids have to understand something about your mother. She's a high-strung woman. She's like one of those French poodles. Yap yap yap. She has no sense of humor. You say something funny and she looks at you like a deer in the headlights."

Daphne said, "Don't you like Mom anymore?"

The Dad said, "I'm not saying that."

"Then why don't you move back?"

"Your mother cares the world for you kids. That's her whole life, ever since the day you were born, starting with you, Daphne."

"But that's good."

"Of course it's good. You're what matters to her. You kids. You should be proud of her. She's the best mother any kid could hope for. Don't forget that."

Daphne said, "We won't."

"Good. Now get to bed."

We went back to our rooms, listening to The Dad cleaning up the mess we'd made. He wrapped up the food and put it back into the refrigerator. He washed off the plates, put them in the dishwasher and checked the doors to make sure they were locked. There was a big bolt on the back porch door. The last thing The Dad did every night was slam that bolt into place, which meant the house was safe and sound. I listened to the bolt snap into place and turned on my side and went immediately to sleep.

21.
GOOD HUMOR MAN

Mik Cosgrove did not grow up on Apple Hill Road like the rest of us. He was a newcomer. His family came from Arizona. There were four Cosgroves, all of whom looked like Glen Campbell except the mother, whose name was Vanya. At first, all Mik Cosgrove talked about was Arizona. He told us how great school was back in Arizona and how pretty his girlfriend was back in Arizona. We didn't believe him. We didn't believe that he French-kissed his girlfriend back in Arizona. We didn't believe that he went to third base with her. The only proof Mik Cosgrove had to support his stories was a Kodak picture of a girl wearing a bikini. The girl in the bikini was pretty. On the back of the picture, the following word was written: "Wendy." Mik Cosgrove was not in the picture. We said, "This picture doesn't prove squat." Mik Cosgrove said, "That's her. That's Wendy. She French-kisses like you wouldn't believe. You don't even know what that means, do you?" Stev said, "Tongue. You use the tongue." Mik Cosgrove said, "Correct. That's her specialty." After he lived on our street for approximately one year, Mik Cosgrove stopped talking so much about Arizona.

Every afternoon the Good Humor ice cream truck turned up our street. The guy driving the truck rang a bell, causing an immediate effect. Front doors opened. Little kids stormed from their houses, ran to the end of their driveways and waited. The ice cream truck moved from one driveway to the next. The ice cream man dressed all in white except for a blue bow tie and a silver change belt. When he reached the end of Mik Cosgrove's driveway, he stopped the truck, jumped out of the front seat and came around to the back of the truck and said, "What'll you have, Glen Campbell?"

Mik Cosgrove said, "Fudgesicle."

The ice cream man said, "Fudgesicle. Who's next?"

Stev said, "Toasted Almond."

The ice cream man said, "Toasted Almond. How about you?"

I said, "Drumstick."

"Drumstick it is. Okay. Here goes," he said, and he grabbed the big handle and opened the freezer, releasing a puff of cold air, and reached deep into the back without looking where his hand was going and pulled out the correct items.

He said, "That's seventy-five cents each. Except the Drumstick. That's ten cents extra."

The ice cream man dispensed our change from his silver change belt, using one hand to pop out dimes and nickels. He said, "Nice doing business with you, gentlemen."

A voice from behind us said, "Not so fast, buddy. I haven't decided yet."

We turned around. Mik Cosgrove's father was standing behind us. He was wearing Bermuda shorts and slippers. He had no shirt on. His belly was hanging over the front of his Bermuda shorts and his chest had absolutely no hair on it.

Mr. Cosgrove said, "You got soft ice cream?"

The ice cream man said, "No. Just frozen."

"You got chocolate chip?"

"We got chocolate ice cream bars and vanilla ice cream bars."

"How about peach?"

"No peach."

"What else you got?"

"We got Chocolate Eclairs. We got ice cream sandwiches. We got Coconut Bars. We got everything on the menu except Candy Center Crunch."

Mr. Cosgrove studied the menu, which was pasted to the rear corner of the truck. He said, "You say you're out of Candy Center Crunch?"

The ice cream man said, "Yeah. Ran out about two streets ago. There was a big push on Candy Center Crunch over on Lostbrook Drive."

"Don't you load up after you run out of something?"

"Oh no. We just keep going until the end of the day."

Mr. Cosgrove said, "Huh," and studied the menu some more.

The ice cream man said, "So what'll it be?"

Mr. Cosgrove said, "You got a strawberry cone?"

"We got Strawberry Shortcakes. Does it say strawberry cone on the menu?"

"No. I'm asking."

Mik Cosgrove said, "It's an ice cream truck, Dad, not Friendly's."

Mr. Cosgrove said, "It doesn't hurt to ask, does it?"

"Not unless you enjoy sounding like a retard and taking ten minutes to order a Fudgesicle."

"I'm sick of that lip, buddy."

"It's the only lip I got."

"You keep it zipped when I'm talking to the man here."

"I'm zipping it," said Mik Cosgrove.

Mr. Cosgrove said, "Fudgesicle."

The ice cream man said, "Fudgesicle. Like father like son."

In the *Star Trek* episode entitled "I, Mudd," Mr. Spock short-circuits a computer by telling it the following statement: "Everything I say is a lie. I am telling the truth."

Listening to Mik Cosgrove was like that. You never knew whether he was lying or telling the truth. Once Mik Cosgrove told us that he jumped out of an airplane and his parachute didn't open until the last moment but he didn't get killed because he landed in a lake. Another time he told us that he whipped out his dick on top of a bridge and pissed on some well-dressed ladies who were walking on a sidewalk below. The happiest I ever saw Mik Cosgrove was one day after he got a crew cut at the barbershop. His ears, which usually stuck out, stuck out twice as far because of the crew cut. His grin, which was usually pretty big, was twice as big because he was so happy. He was standing at the top of the stairwell outside the barbershop tossing nickels and dimes and pennies down the stairs. A gang of little kids was running around at the bottom of the stairs, picking up the coins and screaming for more. Mik Cosgrove threw the coins and said, "Go get 'em. Here's some more. Ha ha ha. Go get 'em." After he threw all his coins, he went back inside the barbershop and got one hundred pennies for a dollar and came back out and threw them all down the stairs to the waiting children. He stood watching and grinning while the children scrambled for his pennies.

The ice cream truck drove up the street and turned the corner. The bell faded. All was quiet again. You could hear birds chirping and grasshoppers buzzing and Tiger's Brother tapping a screwdriver underneath the hood of some hot rod. These sounds were always there. You didn't hear them until they stopped.

Mr. Cosgrove peeled the white paper wrapper and stuck the Fudgesicle in his mouth. He said, "What was that thing you told me, kid?"

I said, "Me?"

"Yeah, you. When I gave you the dollar."

"I told you, 'Never follow the purser.' "

"There was more to it. Something about a sinking ship."

"I told you, 'Never follow the purser because he will lead you down into a sinking ship which is upside down.' "

"Yeah. That's it. A sinking ship that's upside down."

Stev said, "*The Poseidon Adventure.*"

"Correct," said I.

Mr. Cosgrove smacked his belly and said, "Upside down. The world is upside down. Everything's topsy-turvy. Up is down and down is up. You know what I mean, buddy?" I shrugged, and he licked the Fudgesicle, looking off into the distance. We watched him watching the distance. After approximately fifteen seconds, he said, "You know something. I could eat ten of these. You ever do that? Eat ten Fudgesicles in a row? Jesus. That would be something. One fucking Fudgesicle after the other."

Mr. Cosgrove turned around and shuffled back to his house and went inside and closed the door.

Stev said to Mik Cosgrove, "Your father is weird."

"What's weird about him?"

"He doesn't go to work. He just stays in the house all day."

"He's on vacation. Doesn't your father take vacations?"

"That's not what I heard."

"What did you hear?"

"I heard he got fired."

"Who told you that?"

"Somebody."

"Did somebody also tell you that I fingered your sister? Well, I did. I fingered Sissi and she moaned and begged for more."

"Just like you fell out of the airplane and landed in a lake."

"I got skydiving pictures and a skydiving helmet to prove it. Skydiving is big back in Arizona, if you must know."

"Sure it is."

"I mean it."

"I believe you."

"Do you want me to kick your ass? Is that what you want?"

"I'm scared."

"I'll do it, you little faggot."

"I'm shaking in my shoes," said Stev.

There were two white-painted rocks at the end of Stev's driveway. One rock was called Stev's Rock and the other rock was called Sissi's Rock. I sat on Sissi's Rock and unwrapped the foil and started biting the nuts, chocolate and caramel that coated the top of the Drumstick. Stev sat on his rock and bit into his Toasted Almond. Mik Cosgrove stood in the middle of the street sucking on his Fudgesicle without biting it.

Stev said to Mik Cosgrove, "Where's your mom? Is she on vacation too?"

Mik Cosgrove said, "What did you say about my mom?"

Stev said, "I said, Where is she?"

"She's in Arizona with my sister."

"That's not what I heard."

"What did you hear?"

"I heard she took off. I heard she left 'cause you're fat and stupid and your father has no job."

"What else did you hear?"

"I heard she's got a mattress in back of the firehouse and she's taking customers."

Mik Cosgrove pretended to laugh. Then he rushed Stev, who jumped off the rock and bolted. Mik Cosgrove didn't chase. It was pointless to chase Stev, who was as fast as a dog. Instead, Mik Cosgrove reared back and threw his Fudgesicle like a tomahawk, which zipped past Stev's ear and landed in the grass.

After a minute, Mik Cosgrove walked gingerly onto the grass and peered around the side of the house, where Stev had gone. Seeing nothing, he picked up his Fudgesicle, wiped it on his shirt and sat down on Stev's white-painted rock. He stuck the Fudgesicle in his mouth.

"They're on vacation," he told me.

22.
CAT'S AWAY

With The Mom away, The Dad went on a golfing extravaganza. Each morning at 8 A.M. he put on his brightly colored slacks and short-sleeved shirt and zoomed out of the driveway in the Mark IV. He was playing in a members-only tournament at the country club. Each night when he came back he showed us his scorecard. The Dad was a nine handicap, but he said he was hitting the ball like a scratch. He and Pinky were playing their hearts out, he said. He described in great detail what shots he made on what holes, even though we didn't care and told him so. On the third day of the tournament, The Dad didn't come home until nine o'clock. We were waiting for him in the kitchen when he came through the door. He had a gold trophy in his hand, approximately three feet tall.

He said, "You should have seen it. Picture this. I'm on the eighteenth green looking at a thirty-foot putt, uphill with a break to the right. The entire clubhouse is watching. You can hear a pin drop. I get out my Ping Putter and line it up. If I make it, Pinky and I win. If I two-putt, we go to sudden death."

"Did you make it?" I asked.

He put the trophy on the kitchen table. "Does that answer your question?"

Daphne said, "Big deal. We're hungry."

Albert said, "Are we going to a restaurant?"

Daphne said, "Yeah. What's for dinner?"

The Dad scratched the stubble on his cheek and said, "Waffles."

Daphne said, "Waffles are for breakfast."

"Things are going to be a little different around here from now on," said The Dad. "While the cat's away, the mice will play. That's what they say, right?"

"Who's the cat?"

"Your mother's the cat."

"Different how?"

"Waffles for dinner. Ice cream for breakfast."

"What else?"

"No bedtimes."

"Really?"

"Get your plates ready. I'll get the waffle iron. This'll be fun, right, kids?"

We said, "Sure, Dad. Real fun."

The Dad said, "Pinky said it was the finest putt he's seen in ten years. You should have heard the crowd."

After dinner, The Myra came over while The Dad was washing the dishes. She walked into the kitchen, took a puff on her cigarette and said, "How is she?"

The Dad said, "She's in Cranston. What else do you want to know?"

"Poor woman. She has limits like anyone else."

"What about my limits? Kicking me out of my own bedroom? Pouring my scotch down the drain?"

The Myra stubbed her cigarette in the ashtray and pushed up the sleeves of her tight beige sweater. The Dad rinsed the plates and handed them to her, one at a time, and she loaded them into the dishwasher. She said, "She calls every day wanting to know what's going on over here."

The Dad said, "What does she think? I'd throw a cocktail party?"

The Myra glanced at me and said, "Go watch TV. Your father and I are talking."

I said, "I haven't finished my pecan roll."

She said, "You're done. You're listening to us is what you're doing."

"So?"

"So it's rude."

I got up and went into the den and turned on the TV. The screen was black but the sound came on, playing the theme song to *Nanny and the Professor.*

Nanny and the Professor was about a special maid who comes to stay with a family. She may have magic powers, like Samantha Stephens in *Bewitched* and Jeannie in *I Dream of Jeannie,* but you never knew for sure. The nanny's name was Phoebe Figalilly.

The Professor is played by Richard Long, who also played Jarrod Barkley on *The Big Valley.* Richard Long looks and acts exactly the same on both shows. He talks the same way and he makes the same facial expressions. In one show, he is a lawyer in cowboy times. In the other show, he is a professor in modern times. But you could not tell the two characters apart. Richard Long even wore the same type of clothes for both roles.

At the first commercial I went quietly into the living room and looked through the slats in the door with my head twisted to one side.

The Dad said, "She's an excitable woman. You'd think it was a crime, going to the club."

"Excitable, my ass," said The Myra. She was bending to put the plates into the dishwasher. "She's a saint to put up with you."

"That what she tell you? Some kind of sob story?"

"I know what I see with my own two eyes."

"What the hell do you see?"

"A lot. I see a lot."

"You don't know the half of it."

"No," said The Myra. "You don't know. You come home and dinner's on the table and the floor's scrubbed and the clothes are folded, nice and clean. Who do you think does all that work, with three kids running wild?"

"I offered plenty of times. She always says the same thing. No maids."

"Who can afford maids?"

"You think I can't?"

"There're bills enough to pay without a maid. Lots of them. And they're piling up, from what I hear."

"You let me worry about the bills," said The Dad. "You keep your nose out of it."

The Myra said, "I'm only trying to help."

The Dad turned off the faucet and pointed his finger at The Myra. "You come over here every day, drinking my liquor and whining to my wife. I've got enough to worry about without you getting her all riled up, making me out to be the bad guy. You should spend more time at your own goddamn house worrying about your own goddamn business."

The Myra said, "I'll never step foot in this house again if that's what you want."

"Did I say that?"

"Ever." The Myra turned away from him, and tears started pouring out of her eyes.

The Dad lowered his finger. "Hey," he said. "Don't do that."

She said, "I don't know why I even try."

The Dad said, "Look, Myra. It's been a long day." He dried his hands on the dish towel, got the J&B out of the cabinet and poured two glasses. He placed them on the kitchen table, and they sat down. He said, "Here. Have this."

The Myra wiped her eyes and said, "I've got nothing to do all day. Do you know what that's like?"

"I thought you cook and clean."

"I said your wife cooks and cleans. Not me. Sissi and Steven take care of themselves."

"What about Leonard?"

"Leonard's away on business."

"What about when he's not away?"

"He takes his clients to restaurants. Or else he plays tennis at the club. That's all he does."

"So," said The Dad. "Play tennis. Get yourself a hobby."

The Myra took a sip of J&B. "Like swimming?" she said. "You think I should take up swimming? That's what Leonard says."

"Do you good," said The Dad. "Get some fresh air. Exercise."

"Don't tell me that. I'm not some child, for God's sake. I need swimming lessons like I need another hole in my ass."

"Who knows. You might like it."

"No, I would not like it. Not one bit. Not swimming lessons. Not tennis lessons. Oh, what's the use? You don't care."

The Dad took out his handkerchief. She raised her chin, and he leaned forward and wiped the tears from her face.

She said, "You're a ruffian, yelling at me like that. You're a brute."

"I told you I was sorry."

"No, you didn't."

"Well, I am."

He poured some more J&B into her glass. She raised the glass and said, "This is my hobby. The only hobby I need."

The Dad clinked his glass against hers.

"Cheers," he said.

23.
STORM

Thunder woke me. I checked the clock on my desk, as I always did when I woke. It was exactly 2 A.M. The room was pitch black but lightning flashed periodically, showing momentary views of the green shag carpet, yellow bean bag and Elton John posters on the walls. Albert was lying on his back in bed with his hands crossed over his chest. The thunder was louder than the loudest bass notes during "Radar Love" played on the Fisher stereo at high volume, yet Albert slept peacefully. I wondered if he had died. Only a dead person could sleep through a storm louder than "Radar Love."

I got out of bed and went to the window. Despite the thunder and lightning there was no rain, not even a drizzle. Clouds rolled by in fast motion. A lightning bolt exposed the green grass of the front lawn, like an instant of daylight, and I saw The Dad standing in the driveway. He was wearing the bottoms to his leopard pajamas, smoking a cigarette. He raised and lowered the cigarette, looking at the sky over Stev's house. The storm roared above him. Some of the lightning flashes were very bright, making jagged fluorescent lines in the black sky. Other flashes were dim and flickering.

I thought my eyes were playing tricks on me. Standing outside in the middle of the night was not normal behavior for The Dad. When he woke, he usually went to the bathroom, where he would sit on the toilet and smoke and read the newspaper. The bathroom door had no lock. Often Albert or Daphne or I would walk in unexpectedly. You'd open the door with eyes narrowed from sleep and find The Dad, his hair standing up, turning his head toward you and lowering the newspaper, the bathroom hazy with Marlboro smoke. You'd say, "I have to go the bathroom, Dad." And he would always say the same thing: "Go downstairs. I'm reading the paper." The bathroom was The Dad's preferred smoking chamber. He was not required to smoke outdoors, like

Mr. DiLorenzo, who smoked on his front stoop wearing his high-water pants, looking impatient, like he was in a hurry to be done with his cigarette. The Mom did not object to The Dad's smoking in the bathroom, so long as he turned on the fan. But he often forgot to do so. When this happened, Albert would raise his nose and sniff and yell, "Dad. Turn on the fan. It stinks." Albert was like a coal mine canary. He could detect smoke from any room in the house, whether it were the laundry room, the den or the rec room, where he fiddled with pieces of electronic equipment that he learned about in *Popular Mechanics*. He complained about the slightest whiff of smoke, but I liked the smell, which was thick and warm. I would open the bathroom door and take a deep breath, filling my lungs with the Marlboro cloud. The Dad smoked at various times in the day. He smoked after every meal and whenever he crapped and whenever he woke in the middle of the night, but he rarely smoked outside, especially not during thunderstorms with no shirt on and dark clouds racing above.

The storm grew louder. A lightning bolt cracked, followed by a sonic boom of thunder, and rain started falling all at once. An instant later Monty scurried into the room and crawled underneath my bed. Only his hind legs were visible. The hind legs were shivering. I knew he was quietly whimpering even though I couldn't hear him above the noise of the storm. Thunderstorms terrified Monty. He always hid beneath my bed during thunderstorms. He lay with his nose two inches from the wall, drooling and shivering. He probably wouldn't come out until daylight, and when he did he would act embarrassed, as if he had done something wrong.

I sat on the bed, stroking his hind legs, saying, "It's okay, Monty. It's only a storm."

After a while the lightning dimmed and the thunder became a low rumble. When I looked out the window, a normal darkness had returned to the night. The streetlight glowed faintly. I could see no one out there. It seemed impossible that The Dad had been standing in the driveway during the midst of the storm, but when I went into his room his bed was empty, and downstairs, I found the front door open. I stood in front of the screen door, looking out. A breeze touched my face.

"Dad," I called.

Then in a louder voice I said, "Are you out there, Dad?"

A light went on and off across the street. I heard the sound of a door closing, or maybe it was a shutter banging against someone's house.

After a while I went into the den and turned on the TV. All the channels were off the air. I sat on the couch and watched the test pattern and listened to the high-pitched tone. The raindrops pelted against the window. The wind blew low chords.

"Hey," said The Dad.

I opened my eyes and blinked a couple of times. He was standing in the doorway, wearing his leopard pajama bottoms and slippers. His hair was wet and slicked back. I looked at the clock above the TV. Approximately thirty minutes had passed, although I did not remember falling asleep. I had been hypnotized by the red light of the test pattern, just like the lady scientist in *The Andromeda Strain*.

The Dad hit the off switch, and the test pattern slowly dissolved to one small light in the middle of the tube, then nothing. He said, "Storm wake you?"

I nodded.

"Passed right over us," said The Dad. "Nothing like a summer storm to shake the rafters."

"What were you doing outside?"

"Couldn't sleep."

"Is it because you had too many cups of coffee?"

"Nah. Coffee never keeps me up. In the army we drank it like water. Gallons of it, every day. The men would yell and scream if they didn't get their coffee. Only thing that got them mad. They'd do anything you'd ask, so long as you gave 'em hot coffee."

"It tastes lousy," I said.

"You'll like it someday."

"I like Coke."

"Coke'll rot your teeth."

"It tastes pretty good, though."

"Hear that?" said The Dad.

We listened to the rain. It fell quietly against the window and on the rooftop.

"Nice, huh?" he said. "That sound. That's one of the best sounds there is."

I yawned.

"Go back to bed," said The Dad. "The rain'll put you to sleep."

24.
THREE FINGERS

The next afternoon I knocked on the Mandelbaums' front door and went inside. The Myra was sitting on the couch in the den watching figure skating, puffing on a cigarette, blowing a cloud of Pall Mall vapors. She had an empty glass in her hand. She was wearing a tight beige sweater and her boobs bulged against the fuzzy material.

I looked at the TV and said, "Spanning the globe to bring you the constant variety of sport. The thrill of victory and the agony of defeat. The human drama of athletic competition. This is ABC's *Wide World of Sports*. Hi, I'm Jim McKay and I have bad breath. Hi, I'm Jim McKay and I like watching the guy fall off the ski jump and smash his head open. Hi, I'm Jim McKay and I'm looking for Stev."

The Myra said, "He's playing tennis at Tumblebrook with his sister. It's a tournament. It takes all day."

"What's it called?"

"How do I know what it's called? It's the brother-sister tournament."

"You mean mixed doubles?"

"For heaven's sake, I'm trying to watch figure skating."

"It's a repeat."

"Here," she said, handing me her glass. "The bottle's on the counter in the kitchen. Pour the rye until you reach three fingers. Measure it with your hand. Three fingers, no more. Add a splash of water. No ice."

"What kind of drink is it?"

"I just told you. It's rye."

"I mean, what's the name for it? Is it a Manhattan or a martini or a sidecar or what?"

"There is no name. Some things don't have names. They just are."

"If they didn't have names, they wouldn't exist."

"I want a rye. That's the name. Plain old rye."

I took the glass and went into the kitchen. There were red lipstick smudges around the sides of the glass and one perfect red set of lips, like someone had drawn them. I looked around. No one was home. I took out my boner and stuck it inside the glass and rubbed it around the sides. I did the same thing to the outside of the glass and gave special attention to the rim, where her mouth would go. I rubbed my boner all over the place.

The Myra called from the den, “Three fingers. Measure it.”

“I'm measuring,” I said.

When I was done the glass was cloudy with dick smudges. It looked like a hundred or more people had passed the glass from hand to hand. I poured the Seagrams V.O. and went into the den and handed the glass to The Myra. I watched closely as she raised the glass to her lips and drank the rye while she watched Janet Lynn glide across the ice and jump double axles and double salchows and smile a beautiful fake smile.

“You forgot the splash of water,” said The Myra.

25.
DIVORCE

The Mom came back from Cranston, Rhode Island, and her new favorite word was Divorce. She said the word ten times a day. She didn't think we heard but we did. We listened while she talked on the phone, making an appointment with a lawyer. "In regard to what?" said the lady on the other end of the line. "In regard to a divorce," said The Mom. We heard her talking to Aunt Ethel and Aunt Mabel, saying things like "I've tried for a long time. He hasn't changed. It's the only answer." We heard her say, "He's in for a surprise, I can promise you that. I'm going to take him for every cent he's got."

One afternoon while The Dad was at work, she called a family meeting. We, the children, sat on the couch, lined up, staring at her. She said, "I have something very important to tell you. I want you to hear this together. This isn't easy to say but it has to be done."

Albert said, "Let me guess. You want a divorce. What else is new."

The Mom said, "Why, yes. That's why I called you together."

Daphne immediately started crying. "It's not true, Mom. You don't mean it."

The Mom said, "Your father and I can't get along."

"Why not?"

"We've tried but it's just not possible anymore. I can't go on like this. I can't live with that man a day longer. I've thought this out very clearly. I've decided."

Daphne said, "But Mom. We need Dad."

"We most certainly do not."

Daphne glanced at Albert, who nodded. Then she said what we agreed she should say.

"Without Dad, the house would fall apart. He does important things for us. He checks the oil tank to see if it's empty or full. He restarts the furnace when it turns off. He goes onto the roof and cleans out the gutters."

The Mom said, "I can hire people to do those things."

Daphne said, "He does other stuff too. He helps with our homework. He's good at math and geography. When we can't sleep he tells us stories about Italy and Africa and other places he's been. He tells us what a good mother you are, that you're the best mother anyone could have."

She said, "He told you that?"

Daphne nodded.

The Mom said, "Well. He's perfectly right about that. That's why I have to do this. For the good of you children. In the long run, you'll see. In the long run, you'll agree with me. Someday you will."

Daphne said, "What about Dad? What does he say about it?"

"This isn't your father's decision. He has no choice in the matter whatsoever. I'm sorry but that's the way it is. He's going to have to move out of the house. From now on, it'll be just the four of us. We'll get along fine without him. It'll be like an adventure. You'll see."

Daphne began hyperventilating. She tried to talk but sounded like a retard. The only words that made sense were "Daddy would never leave us."

Albert said, "Real smart, Mom. Look what you did to Daphne."

The Mom straightened her skirt. "Daphne will be fine. We're all going to be just fine. We'll be better off, I promise."

"Don't be stupid, Mom. It'll never work. You'll never convince Dad to go."

The Mom said, "I've spoken to a lawyer. Your father will do what the judge orders. He will continue to support this family. The court will make sure of that. And I'll get a job. I've already looked into it. There's an opening at town hall that pays seven dollars per hour. That's more than two hundred dollars per week."

I said, "That's nothing. Dad makes that in a day."

"And he spends it just as fast. Like a drunken sailor he spends. He's been bankrupting this family for years, Timmy. The best cars, the best golf clubs. He acts like a big shot at the club, buying drinks for those hooligan Italians. Meanwhile he neglects his work. Meanwhile the electric company calls and threatens to turn off the power. You kids don't know the half of it. I never wanted you to worry."

Albert said, "We're not worried."

"Well, I am," said The Mom. "And it's past time I did something about it."

Albert said, "If Dad goes, we go too."

Daphne said, "Yeah."

The Mom got up from the chair. "You children will not tell me what to do. Not when your future is at stake. Until you're of age, you have to go along with my decision. That's final."

Daphne said, "We'll run away."

"Don't be melodramatic." The Mom got up and left the room.

Albert looked at Daphne and me. "Don't worry. She won't do it. She'll cave in."

Daphne said, "Are you sure?"

Albert said, "Trust me."

26.
FRANKS AND BEANS

Lunch usually consisted of bologna and cheese sandwiches, but once in a while The Mom made franks and beans, which was a treat. Franks and beans was our favorite. When The Mom put the plates in front of us, we would say, "Beans, beans, the musical fruit, the more you eat the more you toot," and The Mom would respond, "That's a myth. Eat slowly and you'll have no problem." But the power of franks and beans was no myth. It was an indisputable fact. Albert and I would gobble the franks and beans as quickly as possible to intensify the effect. In addition, Albert ingested the third element, a glass of V8. Franks and beans were bad enough. But when Albert brought V8 into the mix, the results were cataclysmic.

One afternoon, after bolting our lunch, Albert and I went looking for Stev. We found him in his den. He and Tiger were sitting on the rug, trading baseball cards, which were laid out on the rug in neat rows. Stev held up his Thurman Munson card and smiled his liar's smile and said to Tiger, "This baby is worth a mint. What'll you give me for it?"

Tiger said, "I'll give you Hank Aaron."

Stev said, "No way."

"Hank Aaron and Frank Howard."

"Not even close."

"Hank Aaron, Frank Howard and Harmon Killebrew. The three home run kings. Take it or leave it."

"Nope."

"You don't even like Thurman Munson. How come you won't trade?"

"Because you want it so bad."

He moved the Thurman Munson card back and forth in front of Tiger's eyes, like a hypnotist. Everything about the Thurman Munson card was special. His picture on the front of the card was horizontal, not vertical. The picture was an action shot, not the usual smile-for-the-camera pose. There was some guy sliding face-first into home base with his feet in the air and dirt flying and Thurman Munson squatting and tagging him out. In addition, there was a miniature gold trophy superimposed on the lower left corner of the card that said: "Topps 1970 All-Star Rookie."

Albert got off the couch and stood next to Tiger. He said, "What's so great about that card? Lemme see it."

Albert took the Thurman Munson card from Stev, turned it over and studied the statistics on the back of the card. He said, "Huh, look at that," and he bent over so that his butt was sticking in Tiger's face and blasted him. The fart made a sound like a lawnmower sputtering to a stop.

Tiger said, "Hey. Cut it out. We're trying to trade."

Albert said, "Take a whiff, sucker."

"It stinks."

"I had franks and beans. Plenty more where that came from."

Albert was the tallest kid in his class. He was six feet. He had growing pains. At night while I tried to sleep he grunted and groaned and got up and stretched and went back to bed. He grew three inches in four months. Clothes did not fit him. The coaches refused to let him play football because the equipment wouldn't fit and he weighed more than 160 pounds, which was the limit for his grade. Instead, he played soccer. He was the goalie. The soccer team went from lousy to good just because Albert was standing in front of the goal, blocking shots. One time after a game some kids from the other team surrounded Albert in the parking lot and pushed him and said, "You think you're so big and tough, don't you?" Albert did not fight back. He never picked on anybody. He was not mean like other kids who were twice your size. Albert was a joker. He was voted class clown two years in a row in the school yearbook. He liked crank-calling people. His favorite thing to do was call a house and ask for Moe Gladstone. Then after the person told him he had the wrong number, Albert would wait a minute and call back and say, "Hi, this is Moe Gladstone, did anyone call for me?" The other class clown was a kid named Mac. Albert and Mac were best friends. Mac was a year older because he stayed back a grade for being stupid. Mac was almost as tall as Albert but he was overweight. His pockets were always filled with Yodels, Ring Dings and Twinkies. Albert and Mac walked around school together wearing funny ties that were four inches wide but only two inches long. They called themselves the Mad Engineers because they carried Swiss army knives in their pockets and unscrewed the hinges off doors and lockers when no one was looking. Kids would walk down the hall and push the door, and the door would crash to the floor. This went on for approximately one month. A janitor named Orlando worked full-time screwing things back together, muttering in Spanish. Mac had the ability to burp at will. He burped until his voice went hoarse. Teachers would yell at him to stop burping, and Mac would say, "I can't help it. I ate too much for lunch." Like any fat kid, Mac farted a lot, and his farts smelled awful. Mac was the person who originated the bicycle pump method. He demonstrated one afternoon in the locker room with an air pump he stole out of the football coach's office. He stuck the end of the hose in his butt and pumped himself up for approximately thirty seconds, then pulled out the hose and immediately let loose a fart that never ended. As the fart went on and on, Mac made a perplexed expression and he cupped his hand around his ear like someone straining to hear distant voices even though the fart was as loud as a jackhammer. Then he would pretend that he was playing the accordion, fluctuating the tone and rhythm of the fart. Mac and Albert loved to fart on people when they weren't expecting it. They farted into their cupped hands and released the fart in your face, which they called a hand fart. They farted into empty milk bottles, which made a musical sound, and covered the opening and stuck the bottle under some unsuspecting kid's nose and said, "Do me a favor. Smell this. Tell me what it smells like." In math class they sat on opposite sides of a girl named Dodie who liked to pick her bottom lip and they farted silent-but-deadlies until she raised her hand and asked the teacher to be excused because she wasn't feeling well. They farted in the back of the school bus in wintertime, when the windows were shut tight and couldn't be opened. They farted silently next to some kid in the hallway talking to his girlfriend and walked away and watched the girl blush and hold her nose, and the kid would say something like "Hey, that wasn't me, I didn't do it."

There was nothing good on TV, only soap operas and games shows. Albert got off the couch and stood next to the TV and began turning the channels.

Tiger said, "Why are you bending over?"

Albert said, "I'm changing the station."

"No, you're not. You're trying to fart. I know that look."

Tiger backed out of range, and Albert said, "Get him. Hold him down."

Stev and I tackled Tiger and pushed him onto the rug. He flailed and threw girly punches and screamed girly screams but we held him down easily because he was not strong.

Albert said, "You got him?"

Stev said, "Go."

Albert dropped his pants and squatted like a baseball catcher an inch above Tiger's face and blasted a high-pitched fart that sounded like a question through his Fruit of the Looms. The smell was immediate.

Stev said, "Oh my God. Dog fart."

I said, "It always smells like that when he has V8."

Stev said, "It's unbelievable."

Albert remained in the squatting position. He said, "Ah, the sweet, sickly aroma. How's the air down there? Is it balmy?"

Tiger said, "Lemme go."

Albert said, "I'm afraid that's not possible."

Tiger said, "You guys are being dicks."

Stev said, "Give him another."

Albert said, "I'm not ready yet."

We sat on top of Tiger huffing and puffing and waiting.

Albert said, "Okay, I'm ready," and he ripped three farts in a row like firecrackers, the third being the longest and deadliest.

Tiger squirmed away. He jumped to his feet and stood back against the wall. He said, "I didn't smell a thing. I held my breath the whole time."

Stev said, "You did not."

Tiger said, "I did too. I can hold my breath for longer than that."

"You're lying. Admit it, Tiger. You got smoked."

Tiger walked out of the den and out the front door.

Albert pulled up his pants and said, "Time for a V8."

We watched *Mike Douglas*, *The Big Valley* and *Gomer Pyle*. Albert got the runs during *I Dream of Jeannie*. He raised his leg to fart and realized that it was diarrhea and went running home.

Stev said, "Jeannie is the number-one fox of all time."

"She's top ten," I said. "But not one."

"Who then?"

"Audra Barkley."

"Audra's prissy."

"Still."

Stev said, "If I was Major Nelson, I'd jump Jeannie constantly."

"He can't jump her. She's only five inches tall."

"That's when she's in the bottle. Otherwise she's full-grown."

"No. The bottle is her true size. She's a midget. She's the tiniest midget there ever was."

"She's always got her pajamas on. She can sleep anywhere."

"Those are genie pants, not pajamas."

"What about the girls in *Land of the Giants*? They're tiny."

"No. They only look small because the giants are so big. They're actually normal size. In theory."

Stev said, "If I was Major Nelson, I'd make a wish for Audra Barkley."

"Jeannie would never grant that wish. She's jealous. She wouldn't let Major Nelson go off with Audra."

"She has to. He's the master. She has to do anything he says."

"She might grant the wish but she wouldn't do it right. She'd turn Audra into a salamander or something like that."

My dinner bell rang. I heard it faintly through the screen door. I went outside. It was a sunny day. I squinted into the sunlight with my television eyes and saw something in the cherry tree. I walked across the street and stood under the tree and shaded my eyes.

I said, "Hey, Tiger. What are you doing? You're not allowed to go up there. That's a violation."

Tiger was sitting on the highest branch, the one that hung out over the driveway. No one climbed on that branch, not even Stev. Only raccoons went out that far. If the branch broke, he'd fall onto the driveway, which was black asphalt.

I waited for Tiger to say something but he did not, so I said, "I'm coming up."

I went onto the lawn and placed my foot on the bottom branch and started to pull myself up, and Tiger screamed, "No." The scream struck my ears and stopped me like a photograph and traveled all the way to Avon Mountain and rebounded back to where I was standing. The scream was not normal. The scream was something out of a mental institution.

I said, "Okay. Don't spaz out."

I could not see Tiger without shading my eyes. The sun was directly behind him, glaring the view. He might have been an enormous crow perched up there, black against the sun, silent and motionless.

I said, "Are you going to stay up there forever?"

My dinner bell rang again.

I said, "That's my bell. I gotta go."

Tiger's Mother disliked telephone calls. She said we tied up the phone. She said telephones were for emergencies. Nevertheless, I dialed the number.

Tiger's Mother said, "Hello. Hello. Who's calling?"

I said, "Is Tiger home?"

There was no answer.

I said, "Hello?"

The line went dead.

27.
HUMBUG ON THE ROAD

Going on a car trip made The Dad happy. No matter where you were going, no matter how far the trip might be, you had to leave first thing in the morning. The Dad refused to leave any other time. On the day of a trip, he would wake everyone at exactly 6 A.M., with sausages and bacon already frying, and say, "Everybody up. Get out of bed. Up up up." He would whistle and clap his hands and serve the breakfast. While packing the luggage into the rear of the car, he would say the same thing over and over: "Humbug on the road. Humbug on the road. We gotta get going 'cause there's humbug on the road."

The Dad and Albert loaded the trunk into the back of the Station Wagon. The trunk contained everything that Albert needed for summer camp in Cape Cod, including sporting equipment, beach towels, baseball caps, peanut butter, socks, underwear, bathing suits, shorts, shirts and other clothes stitched with tiny red and white labels on the waistbands or collars that read "Albert."

The Dad said, "All set?"

Albert said, "Affirmative."

"All right. Let's go."

The Dad started the ignition and wrote down the mileage on a scrap of paper, which was what he always did before a trip. Albert rolled down the window and said, "Don't play my records."

I said, "I would never play your records."

"I'll kill you if you do."

"You'll never know, will you?"

"I'll know. I have my methods."

The Dad said, "That's enough of that kind of talk. You boys gotta stick together. You're a team. No one can beat you if you stick together. Together you can lick the world. Remember that."

We said, "Sure, Dad."

The Dad said, "Say good-bye to your brother."

Albert said, "See you in hell, sucker."

Approximately one hour later Stev opened the front door and came into the kitchen. He said, "It's going to be a hundred degrees."

"I heard."

"That'll be hot for driving."

"Yeah."

"I'm leaving now. My dad got a cop to drive me."

"A real cop? In a cop car?"

"In my mom's car. He's not wearing a uniform or anything. He just drives people around when he's not working as cop."

We looked out the window toward Stev's driveway. Mr. Mandelbaum was talking to some fat guy with a crew cut. Stev said, "That's the guy."

I said, "Tiant got the loss last night."

Stev said, "I know. He got bombed."

"Did you watch the whole game?"

"Yeah. I stayed up late."

"Me too. The National League always wins."

"I know."

Across the street, Mr. Mandelbaum honked the horn.

Stev said, "I gotta go."

I said, "Okay."

"I got stamps and envelopes and all that stuff."

"Me too. I'll send the Big D surveys."

"Definitely send the surveys. And any articles you see about Elton. Cut them out and send them to me. Ask my mom for my *Rolling Stone* if you want."

"Okay."

Stev went out the front door and walked across the street. He shook hands with his father, hugged The Myra and pulled Sissi's pigtails. Then he turned and waved to me and got in the car and drove away toward a place called Casco, Maine, which was where he went every summer at the end of July.

28.
SLEEPOVER

Shopping was Daphne's favorite activity. Her closet was stuffed with clothes. She had more clothes than everyone else in the family combined, but she always needed more. She went shopping with her girlfriends almost every day. They would walk around the center of town and look at boys and go into shops to try on tops, skirts, corduroys and bathing suits, saying to each other, "How do I look, does it make me look fat?" At the end of the day her girlfriends would drop off Daphne in our driveway, and she would come into the house carrying shopping bags from Sam's Army Navy and Youth Center.

I said, "Was that Lisa Loomis in the car?"

Daphne said, "Your girlfriend Lisa, you mean?"

"She's not my girlfriend."

"No, but you wish she was."

"Don't be queer."

"You wish all my friends were your girlfriend, don't you? You probably think about them when you shake your peter like the time I caught you."

"I was scratching."

"They're coming for a sleepover tonight. I'm going to tell them what I saw. They think it's neat that I have brothers. They don't have brothers. Only Maribeth has a brother but he's just a baby."

"Who's coming?"

"Lisa Loomis and Cynthia Storm and Maribeth Donovan."

"Don't tell them."

"I'm telling them everything."

"Come on, Daphne. Stop kidding around."

"What makes you think I'm kidding?"

Daphne bent over and imitated me shaking my boner. Then she grinned and walked upstairs, swinging her shopping bags.

I wanted to say, "Hi, I'm Daphne and I'm a certified zit face," but I changed my mind, thinking better of it under the circumstances.

There was no air conditioner upstairs. The only air conditioner was in the kitchen, and was built into the wall above the refrigerator. The air conditioner was industrial strength. The Dad had removed it from one of his square-shaped warehouses on Locust Street. Standing in the airstream was like putting your head out the car window traveling fifty miles per hour. The cold air blew your hair back. The air conditioner cooled off the entire house except for Daphne's room because she kept her door closed when Lisa Loomis and Cynthia Storm and Maribeth Donovan slept over.

I knocked on the door and Daphne screamed, "Who is it?" and I opened the door.

Daphne said, "Oh my God, it's you. I thought you were Mom."

She passed the cigarette she was smoking to Cynthia Storm, who giggled and puffed. I came in and closed the door. It was hot in the bedroom. The temperature felt like one hundred degrees even though it was late at night and the moon was out. The room smelled like cigarette smoke and something stronger, something musty, like stinky feet.

Daphne's friends were lounging on the twin beds listening to Carole King. They were hot and sweaty and pink-faced. Strands of their hair were sticking to their cheeks. Lisa Loomis and Maribeth Donovan were wearing extra-long T-shirts. Their legs were bare. Cynthia Storm was wearing pink pajamas. All of them were pretty. Lisa Loomis had straight black hair parted in the middle and a mole on her cheek. She was the prettiest. She was short and had a butt shaped like a little pumpkin, which stuck out behind, the bump visible under her extra-long T-shirt. Cynthia Storm had curly blonde hair, freckles and bright teeth. She laughed a lot and made a snort noise when something was really funny. Maribeth Donovan had an overbite and big boobs. She was the tallest. Every time Maribeth Donovan saw me, she said in a high voice, "Oh my God, look at you, you're so cute." Maribeth Donovan wore no bra underneath her extra-long T-shirt and her nips pointed at me like tiny fingers.

She said, "Whatcha doing, cutie?"

"Nothing," I said.

"Want a sip?" She offered a little brown airplane bottle that said "Jack Daniels." I put my nose over the opening and sniffed. The bottle smelled the same as the J&B.

I said, "Not now."

She said, "It smells bad but you get used to it. Try it."

Daphne said, "He better not. He'll tell my mom or get sick or something."

Lisa Loomis said, "You wouldn't tell on us, would you?"

"No."

"We can trust a nice boy like you, right?"

I nodded.

"Look, he's blushing. That's so cute. Come here."

Before I could move, Lisa Loomis grabbed my arm and pulled me toward her. She said, "You're my boyfriend, right?"

"He's mine," said Maribeth Donovan, and she hugged me with her boobs pressed against my arm, and Lisa Loomis tried to pull me back toward her. They smelled like girl sweat, smoke and J&B.

Daphne said, "Want to do something for us?"

"Like what?" I said.

"Go downstairs when no one's looking and pour some of Dad's booze into a paper cup and bring it back up. Don't let them see you."

I said, "He might find out."

"He'll never know if you pour a little water back into the bottle. Not much. Just a little."

"I don't know," I said.

"Please," said all the girls at the same time, like they had rehearsed it.

I said, "Okay," and they all clapped.

Getting the J&B was easy. The Mom and The Dad were watching

Sonny and Cher in the den. They didn't hear a thing. Sonny and Cher were singing, "I got you, babe, I got you, babe," over and over. It took me approximately two minutes to complete the operation and return to Daphne's room with the paper cup. But when I came back and handed the cup to Daphne, the girls were quiet and sad.

Daphne said, "Ask Timmy. He played on the football team last year."

Lisa Loomis said, "Do you know Al Nance?"

I said, "What grade is he in?"

"Next year he'll be in the tenth."

"Is he a football player?"

"He's the quarterback."

"Yeah. I heard of him."

"Do you know what he's like?"

"He doesn't say much. He talks real low, like the Fonz."

"Does he have a girlfriend, do you know?"

"I could find out, if you want."

"Oh, don't bother."

Lisa Loomis made a face like she was about to cry.

Daphne said to me, "Come back later, okay, Timmy?"

"Do you want me to bring another paper cup?"

She said, "I'll tell you if we need it."

I turned and went out the door, and as the door closed I heard Maribeth Donovan say, "Your brother is so cool," and Daphne said, "I know."

I went into my room and put my ear against the wall. I could hear voices and faint music and individual words like "sleazebag" and "shit-faced," and once in a while there came an explosion of laughter, but I could not follow the conversation. It was unfortunate that Albert was not present. He was missing it. He never spoke a word to Daphne's friends when they slept over because he was too shy, but he spied on them through the crack in the door when they went to the bathroom and once placed a tape recorder under Daphne's bed, which we listened to the next day though all the voices were muffled.

I turned the radio on. WDRC was playing "Don't Let the Sun Go

Down on Me" by Elton John. I took out "The Music Testament" and reviewed recent entries. By my calculations, "Don't Let the Sun Go Down on Me" had the best rating and therefore qualified as the number-one song of the week, knocking out "The Night Chicago Died." This was a serious decision. Stev had to be consulted.

I got out a piece of paper and wrote:

> Dear Stev.
>
> Right now I'm listening to, you guessed it, Elton. The song is "Don't Let the Sun Go Down on Me." By my calculations, this should be the new number one. Do you confirm? Well, that's it. Timmy. PS. You left for camp today. PPS. It's hot. PPPS. Materials used to write this letter: orange juice, a stale Danish and a snot-colored felt pen.

I folded the letter into an envelope and wrote "Steven Mandelbaum, Camp White Oak, Casco, Maine" on the outside of the envelope and licked it closed.

Stev liked when I made jokes about orange juice and stale Danish because that was what he ate for breakfast every morning of his life. He liked when I wrote a lot of PS'es. Sometimes I wrote entire letters to Stev comprised of PS'es. Stev liked getting letters because there was nothing to do in the woods in Casco, Maine, except wait for the mail and listen to the radio and go swimming in leech-infested lakes and play sports like Bombardment, which was his favorite.

A new song began. The new song was "Wildwood Weed" by an unknown artist. I could not hear the DJ identify the name of the artist because there came an explosion of laughter from Daphne's bedroom.

Someone knocked at my door.

I said, "Enter."

Daphne opened the door and said, "Come into my room for a minute."

"Why?"

"Just come on."

"Your face is bright red."

"We're laughing. Come on."

I got up and followed Daphne into her room. I said, "What do you want?"

Daphne said, "Go sit next to Lisa. She wants to tell you a secret."

Lisa Loomis was lying on her stomach on one of the twin beds. Her pumpkin butt was sticking up. Maribeth Donovan and Cynthia Storm were sitting on the other bed. I went over and sat on the edge of the bed next to Lisa Loomis and said, "What?"

Lisa Loomis said, "I have something very important to tell you."

"What?"

"It's a secret so you have to promise not to tell anyone else. Do you promise?"

"Yes."

"Are you ready to hear the secret?"

"Yes."

"Are you sure you're ready?"

"Yes. Tell me."

"Okay, then, here goes," she said, and she squinted and sucked in her breath and wrinkled her nose and farted deep like a man. All the girls immediately began laughing so hard that nothing came out of their mouths. Lisa Loomis rolled onto her back and kicked her feet in the air. Maribeth Donovan and Daphne collapsed against each other. Cynthia Storm slid off the bed and landed on the rug with her legs spread like she was doing a split. She laughed speechlessly except for an occasional snort.

They laughed on and on.

The only thing worse than a dog fart was a girl fart. I held my nose with two fingers because Lisa Loomis's fart smelled bad, and they pointed at me and started laughing all over again.

Cynthia Storm tried to say something but couldn't get the words out.

I said, "What?"

She said, "I'm . . ."

"You're what?"

"I'm wetting my pants."

I looked at her pajamas, which were pink. A stain appeared between her legs and got bigger and bigger while she sat on the floor with her legs out to each side, snorting.

Daphne said, "Oh my God, she is."

The girls screeched and howled like lunatics in a movie. They yelled so loud that The Mom banged on the door and said, "Girls, please. The neighbors will complain."

At the sound of The Mom's voice there was immediate silence.

Daphne jumped up and grabbed me and said, "Quick. Get out of here," and she pushed me out the door and slammed it.

The Mom was standing in the hallway. She said, "What's going on in there?"

"Girl stuff," said I.

29.

THE NIGHT CHICAGO DIED

The Mom never cooked on Saturday night. She called it her "night off." Sometimes we got Chinese takeout but afterward The Dad always said the same thing. He said, "You pay all that money and you're hungry an hour later. It's not worth it." Also, Chinese food made a mess of the kitchen with all the little white boxes and packets of sauce and paper bags and cookies we smashed open just to read the fortune, which usually said something stupid, like "He who wait come to good thing." Albert and I preferred pizza, particularly Dino's pizza. Dino's Pizza Parlor was the best pizza in town. Pizza West was greasy. Pizza Palace made a good grinder but the large pepperoni with double cheese always caused stomach cramps and subsequent diarrhea, or at least it did to Albert and me. The Dad disliked Dino's because they charged extra for the cheese, but Albert and I insisted because Dino's had the secret sauce, which Jimmy the Pizza Man cooked in a big pot he continuously stirred, like a witch concocting her brew. The sauce tasted sweet. It tasted like no other pizza sauce. Just thinking about the sauce made my stomach growl.

One night The Dad went to pick up a large pepperoni at Dino's but didn't come back. The Mom and I sat at the kitchen table in front of our place mats, waiting.

"What's taking him so long?" I said, sipping on an icy-cold Coca-Cola.

The Mom said, "God knows. He's like some teenage boy, always looking to get away with something."

"Maybe he crashed his car."

"I doubt it. More likely he stopped for a drink at the nearest bar. At six o'clock on a Saturday."

The Mom tapped her fingernails against the shiny wooden tabletop. After waiting for an hour and twenty minutes, she started banging pots on the stove. She said, "We'll have spaghetti. You like spaghetti, don't you?"

"Not really."

"Then we'll have sandwiches. That's quick. Bologna and cheese sandwiches."

"Where's Dad, do you think?"

"I couldn't care less. Whatever that man does is fine with me. Perfectly fine."

"Why didn't he bring home the pizza?"

"You ask your father that question when he comes back. See what he says."

The Mom went to the refrigerator and took out the bologna, cheese and mayonnaise. She began putting together the sandwich. She said, "Do you want a pickle?"

"No thanks."

"This'll be better than pizza."

She finished making the sandwich and set the plate in front of me. I lifted the top piece of bread, which was soggy with mayonnaise like a wet sponge. The sandwich consisted of four slices of American cheese and a thin strip of bologna. The mayonnaise spilled out the sides, enough for ten bologna and cheese sandwiches. Only a dummy would make a sandwich like this one.

She said, "Do you want anything else? Do you want some potato chips?"

I shook my head. "I guess I'm not really that hungry."

The Mom did not answer. She stared out at the driveway.

I went upstairs to my room and turned up the radio. WDRC was playing "The Night Chicago Died."

"The Night Chicago Died" was the best song of all time. It was like the sound track to a movie that never got made. In the song, cops and gangsters on the west side of Chicago have an all-night shoot-out. Sirens blare and people run through the streets yelling things like " 'Bout a hundred cops are dead." Meanwhile, a kid waits at home with his mother for his father, who's a cop, to come back. They worry. The house is silent except for a ticking clock. All you hear is the tick-tock, tick-tock. Then the door bursts open and the father barges into the room and kisses the mother. That's the end of the song, except for the fade-out, during which the singer goes, "Na-na na, na-na na, na-na na na na na na."

I listened to the song, tapping my feet.

The Dad came home during *M*A*S*H*. The Mom heard his car wheel into the driveway, and she jumped off the couch, went into the hallway and locked the screen door. She stood in the doorway, glaring.

The Dad said, "I got the pizza here."

She said, "Get out."

"What are you talking about?"

"I said get out and I mean it."

The Dad jiggled the handle of the screen door. He said, "This is my house. You can't lock me out."

"Get out or I'll call the police."

"Just what the hell is going on?"

"You tell me."

"There was smoke coming out of the engine. I blew a gasket, all right? I was waiting on the mechanic the past three hours."

"I don't want to hear your excuses," said the Mom. Then she lowered her voice. I couldn't hear what she said except for the last words, which were, "For God's sake."

The Dad said, "I don't know how you got it into your head but . . . Look. Just open up."

"Get out and don't come back." She slammed the front door and locked it.

After a while The Dad called out, "I've got the key right here. Don't make me take the screen door off the hinges."

The Mom threw open the front door and said, "If you so much as set foot in this house I'll call the police. Do you hear me? The police."

"Ah, to hell with it," said The Dad, and he dropped the pizza box onto the stoop, turned, went down the steps and got into the Mark IV.

The Mom slammed the door and locked it. She went to the kitchen window and stood with her arms crossed, looking out. She and I watched The Dad sitting in the Mark IV. He did not start the car. He just sat in the front seat, going nowhere. After approximately two minutes, The Mom went to the sink and began washing dishes. She said, "What's he doing?"

"Just sitting in the car."

"What's on TV next?"

"*Mary Tyler Moore.*"

"What's on after that?"

"*Bob Newhart.*"

"That's a good show, isn't it?"

"Not really."

From the driveway came the sound of the car door slamming. The Dad charged up the front steps taking two steps at a time and banged on the screen door. "Open this goddamn door. You can't lock me out of my own house."

The Mom said, "Go hang yourself."

"I'll break it down. You watch me."

"Try it. I'll have the police here so fast it'll make your head spin."

The Dad's face appeared in the kitchen window. He said, "Where do you get off threatening me with the police? Huh? This is my house."

The Mom picked up the kitchen phone and said, "Operator. Operator. Get me the police."

The Dad grabbed the screen door and wrenched it, which made a sound like a tree falling. Then he pulled out his key and unlocked the front door and barged in. He stood in the kitchen with his hands on his hips and said, "Lock me out of my own house and for what? Look at what you made me do. Who's gonna fix that door? Me, that's who."

The Mom said into the phone, "Apple Hill Road. Number thirty-five."

The Dad said, "Who are you kidding? There's no one on that line."

The Mom dropped the phone, and the receiver fell to the floor with a thud and gave off the sound of the dial tone.

The Mom collected Christmas plates. Each Christmas, The Dad gave her a new one. He special-ordered the plates from G. Fox Department Store in the City of Hartford. Each plate featured a different wintry country scene, such as a barn with snow covering the roof, a rabbit in a snow-covered field, a horse, a wreath, a sleigh. On the bottom of each plate was the date, such as 1960. There were fourteen plates in all. They hung on the kitchen wall like paintings.

The Mom took Country Christmas 1971 off its hook and said, "So help me."

The Dad said, "You wouldn't dare."

"Wouldn't I?" She hurled it. Country Christmas 1971 flew past The Dad and smashed on the marble floor in the front hallway.

The Dad said, "Hey."

The Mom grabbed another plate and heaved. It hit the wall and smashed, spraying broken pieces of plate onto the linoleum.

He said, "Stop that. Those are worth a fortune."

The Mom yelled, "Get out," and she threw another plate. The Dad tried to catch the plate but it thudded off his chest and fell to the floor without breaking.

He said, "You're gonna hurt someone like that."

The Mom reached out with both hands, grabbed two plates off their hooks and hurled them simultaneously, sending them spinning end over end. The Dad stood perfectly still. He did not move his head to see the plates smash against the wall. He said, "Fine. Break 'em all, for all I care," and he turned and stepped over the broken pieces in the front hallway, pushed aside the screen door, which hung crookedly from one hinge, and walked out to his car. The car started and he drove away.

I examined the wreckage. Country Christmas 1963 had incurred no damage whatsoever. Of the others, Country Christmas 1970 had broken cleanly down the middle. I fitted the two pieces back together.

You couldn't tell the difference. I held up Country Christmas 1970 with the pieces fitted together and said, "I can glue this."

The Mom said, "Oh Timmy. I broke them all."

"No, you didn't. You only broke four. And I can fix this one."

"Can you?"

"It'll be as good as new."

The Mom looked out the window. "I can't bear lying," she said. "Lying and cheating. I just can't bear it."

Daphne came home during *Carol Burnett*. She walked into the den and stood in front of the TV. "What happened to the screen door?"

I said, "She locked him out so he busted it."

"Why'd she do that?"

"I don't know. Get out of the way, will you? I'm trying to watch TV."

"Where's Dad?"

"Took off."

"But it's late. Where did he go?"

I shrugged.

"Maybe he went to a hotel," said Daphne. "You think so?"

"Will you please move your fat ass out of the way? I'm missing *Carol Burnett*."

"That's mean. Why can't you ask nicely?"

"Because you're a big, fat pig and I can't see around the TV."

Daphne immediately started crying. "Why do you have to be so mean?" she said between sobs.

A moment later The Mom appeared in the doorway. "What in God's name is going on?"

Daphne said, "He called me names for no reason. He said I was big and fat."

The Mom shook her finger at me. "Why do you torment your sister? She's never anything but nice to you. You won't be happy until you give her a complex."

"I'm trying to watch *Carol Burnett*."

"Not any more, you aren't. Go to your room."

"It's okay for you and Dad to fight and wreck things. But I can't even watch TV."

"Your father has nothing to do with this."

"You fight all the time. You're like a broken record. Now he took off and it's your fault."

"How dare you talk to me that way? Go. Right now."

I got off the couch and walked past them. As I went up the stairs I heard The Mom say to Daphne, "Now shush. Your brother didn't mean it. I'm sure he didn't."

I sat in bed, reading *TV Guide* and making check marks next to the shows that I had seen that week. After finishing *TV Guide* I picked up the new issue of *Popular Mechanics* and read an article about radio antennas, which caused immediate boredom.

At precisely eleven o'clock The Mom and Daphne came upstairs. I listened to them getting ready for bed, opening and closing cabinets and closet doors, turning the faucet on and off, flushing the toilet and saying, "Good night." Then they went into their rooms.

After a while I got out of bed and opened Daphne's door. I stuck my head inside the room. All the lights were out but I could see the lump of her, underneath the covers.

"Are you asleep?"

"I don't want to talk to you. Just get out."

"I'm sorry I said that stuff."

"You really hurt my feelings. Why'd you call me those names?"

"I didn't mean it."

"I know I'm fat. But you don't have to tell me so."

I said, "You're not fat."

"No. I am. I know I am."

"Don't be stupid, Daphne. All the guys like you. They talk about you all the time."

"Yeah, right."

"It's true."

"What guys?"

"The guys in your class. John Lowe and Geebee. Those guys."

"Really?"

"Yes, really. They're nice to me because you're my sister. Otherwise they'd give me wedgies and titty twisters, like everyone else."

"They're just guys. I don't care about them."

"Still. They like you. They say you're a fox."

"If they're not nice to you, you let me know. I'll take care of them. You bet I would."

"Thanks, Daphne."

"Go to sleep now."

I said, "Do you think Dad will come back?"

"Of course he will."

"They had a pretty bad fight."

Daphne said, "Don't worry."

I closed the door and went into my room. I lay on the bed for a long time, staring at the ceiling and listening for the rumble of The Dad's car. I did not fall asleep, not even after replaying the movie *Killdozer* in my head. *Killdozer* was the story of a bulldozer operated by an invisible alien entity that chased Clint Walker around a Pacific island, trying to kill him and other construction workers. Meanwhile I watched the clock spin off minutes. It seemed impossible that two hours could pass while I stared at the clock replaying *Killdozer* in my head, but that is precisely what happened. Then suddenly I was asleep, dreaming that *Killdozer* was chasing me, raising and lowering its shovel, making a tremendous banging noise.

I opened my eyes and it was daylight.

I got out of bed and went downstairs. The Mom was sitting at the kitchen table, wearing her housecoat and sipping a cup of tea. The curtains were closed, which was unusual. The first thing The Mom did each morning was throw open the kitchen curtains, look out at the sunshine and say something like "What a glorious day."

I said, "Where's Dad? Did he come home?"

She said, "Your father doesn't live here anymore."

30.
SINKING SHIP

I hadn't seen Mik Cosgrove for approximately ten to twelve days, so I went over to his house one afternoon to see what he was doing. When I knocked on his back door, there was no answer for a long time. Then he called, "Come in," and I entered the Dungeon.

Mik Cosgrove was sitting on the world's longest white vinyl couch next to his dog, a French poodle named Gidget. The TV was off. The only light was dim sunlight coming through the curtains in front of the well windows near the ceiling. It took my eyes some time to focus.

"What are you doing?" I asked.

"Nothing," said Mik Cosgrove. He reached into a bag of potato chips and dipped some of the chips into a bowl filled with a huge gob of mayonnaise.

I said, "Do you like potato chips like that? With mayonnaise on them?"

"Yeah. Don't you?"

"I like them with mustard."

"They're better like this." Mik Cosgrove petted Gidget while he talked. Gidget barked and tried to get up but Mik Cosgrove held her tight. He said, "She's not supposed to go outside. She's high-strung."

"I see her outside all the time."

"Want to see her do a trick?"

"Like what? Shake hands with her paw? Every dog does that."

"No. This is different. Watch," he said. He turned Gidget onto her back, held her down, put his hand between her legs and started rubbing back and forth. Gidget pointed all four legs in the air and whimpered, cocked her head and stuck out her tongue. She went perfectly still, like he'd shot her with a dart from a blowgun, and Mik Cosgrove continued to rub, faster and faster, and said, "Watch this, watch this, here it comes, here it comes," and suddenly Gidget stuck her snout in the air and howled like a wolf.

Mik Cosgrove released her, and Gidget flopped over and moved down the couch approximately five feet and lay down on the cushion with her head between her paws.

Mik Cosgrove began laughing. He said, "Ha ha ha. Look at her. She always makes that sad face. Isn't that great? When she howls like that, that means she's getting off. Wooooooo. Wooooooo. Isn't that great? Did you ever try that on your dog?"

I said, "Monty's a boy."

"So. You could do it to him. The vets do it all the time. It's good for dogs. It keeps them healthy."

"I don't think so."

"It is."

"He'd bite me if I grabbed him down there. He doesn't even like his stomach rubbed."

"Nah. He'd like it."

"There's no way I'm doing it," I said.

Mik Cosgrove reached over and took some potato chips out of the bag and put the chips inside his mouth and crunched them up.

I said, "Is your mom still on vacation?"

"Who told you she was on vacation?"

"You did. You said she went to Arizona with your sister."

"So what?"

"So nothing."

He looked at me and blinked a few times, like he had something stuck in his eye. Then he said, "There's lots to do in Arizona, you know. There's swimming and rock climbing and skydiving."

"So when's she coming back?"

Mik Cosgrove scratched the dog's ears. He said, "Gidget does all kinds of tricks. Want to see another?"

"You're going to stick your finger in her butt, right?"

"Why would I do that?"

"I heard some kids do that to dogs to make them crap."

"No. That's stupid."

"What is it then?"

"Watch," he said, and he got up and whipped down his shorts and pulled out his boner and sat back on the couch.

"What are you doing?"

He said, "This is great. You'll like this. Watch what she does."

Mik Cosgrove reached over to the bowl on the coffee table, scooped a gob of mayonnaise and spread the mayonnaise onto his boner. He said, "Here, Gidget, here, Gidget," and Gidget's ears went up and she jumped up and immediately began licking the mayonnaise off Mik Cosgrove's boner with short, fast dog licks. She kept going until the mayonnaise was gone. Then she barked three times, "Ruff ruff ruff," and Mik Cosgrove reached over and gobbed some more mayonnaise onto his boner and she licked her chops and resumed licking it off.

"Quit it," I said.

"Why?"

"She's gonna bite your dick if you keep doing that."

"She never does that. Here. You try it."

He pushed the mayonnaise bowl toward me.

I said, "No way."

"You'll like it. It's good."

"You're a homo," I said, and I started up the stairs.

Mik Cosgrove said, "Hey. Don't go up there. Go out the back door."

"Forget it." I always did the opposite of what Mik Cosgrove asked. Everyone did. It was standard operating procedure not to do what Mik Cosgrove told you.

I went up the stairs, opened the door to the kitchen, took one step and stopped. Mr. Cosgrove was sitting at the kitchen table, wearing white underwear and black socks and nothing else. He was slumped over the table with his stomach sticking out like a big baby in a diaper. There was a dumpy-shaped bottle on the table that said "Hennessy." After waiting a moment I said, "Hi, Mr. Cosgrove."

He raised his head and looked over his shoulder, squinting his moon face at me. "Where did you come from?"

"Downstairs."

"I've been sitting at this table for three hours. You been down there that long?"

"I just got here five minutes ago."

"That's impossible."

"No, really."

"You're the sinking ship kid. Right?"

"I guess."

"You don't know how right you are."

"What do you mean?"

"The sinking ship that's upside down. That's what you said."

"I got that from a movie. *The Poseidon Adventure*. It's not real."

"Oh, it's real, all right. You can take that to the bank."

"I mean, the movie isn't real. It's make-believe."

Mr. Cosgrove picked up the bottle, refilled the glass and drank a small sip. Then he lowered the glass and looked into the liquid for a long time. "It's all crap, kid," he said. "Take it from me."

From the basement came the sound of Gidget barking. She barked in perfect rhythm, like a bass drum in a marching band. She went, "Ruff. Ruff. Ruff. Ruff. Ruff."

He said, "You hear that? I've been listening to that all day."

I said, "It's Gidget."

Mr. Cosgrove pushed his chair back and got up from the table and took three wobbly steps toward me. I moved out of the way, and he opened the basement door and yelled, "You shut that goddamn dog up. I'm sick of that noise. You hear me? Are you listening to me? Don't make me come down there, buddy, or so help me."

The barking continued. "Ruff. Ruff. Ruff."

I said, "I should get going, Mr. Cosgrove."

He ignored me. He said, "I'm talking to you, goddamnit. Answer me."

The barking did not stop.

Mr. Cosgrove closed the basement door and staggered back to the table and sat down. “Bunch of crap,” he said. “That’s all it is. Crap.”

I said, “I gotta go.”

“Go already. Who’s stopping you.”

I opened the front door and went outside.

31.
A LOVELY DAY

The Mom came into the den while I was watching *Gomer Pyle*. She said, "It's a lovely day. Why don't you go outside and get some fresh air?"

I said, "I'm busy right now."

"Spending so much time inside's not good for you. Ever since Albert and Steven left for camp, that's all you do. Why don't you play with the guys?"

"There's no one around."

"What about the Cosgrove boy? He's part of the gang, isn't he?"

"He's a weirdo."

"What's weird about him?"

"He's weird, that's all."

"Everyone your age uses that word, weird. I don't know if it's supposed to mean good or bad."

"It means weird."

The Mom said, "I should have sent you to summer camp with your brother. I knew it was a mistake separating you."

"I don't like camp. It's stupid."

"You've never been to overnight camp. It's different from day camp. It's a lot more fun."

The Mom looked into her handbag and ruffled around. She said to herself, "Where did I put the green stamps?" Then she found the S&H Green Stamps booklets and said, "I'm going food shopping. I'll be back in an hour."

I said, "When's Dad coming home?"

She said, "Your father is not coming back. He's not welcome here anymore. He left and that's that."

"He didn't leave. You locked him out and threw plates at him just because he was late bringing home the pizza."

"This has nothing to do with pizza. It's much more serious than that."

"He'll come back. You'll see."

"What gives you that idea?"

"I just know."

"What do you know? Have you spoken to your father? Have you been in contact with him?"

"That's for me to know and you to find out."

"Don't be coy with me, young man. Answer me when I ask you a question."

"Why should I?"

"I'm your mother and you will do as I say."

On TV, Sergeant Carter was screaming at Gomer Pyle, who had a stupid expression on his face. This was the best part of the show, when Sergeant Carter nearly popped a blood vessel. "I'm trying to watch the show," I said.

The Mom said, "When I ask you a question, I demand an answer."

I said, "Dad took off because of you. You're always spazzing out."

She said, "He's your big hero, isn't he? He can do no wrong in your eyes. Maybe you should go live with him. Go ahead. See if you like it, living in a filthy house with no food on the table and him out God knows where and the electric company calling to disconnect the power. Doesn't that sound nice?"

"It sounds peachy."

"I've got enough to worry about without listening to this sort of back talk. If your father calls this house I want to know immediately. I have Myra keeping a lookout. She tells me the instant anything happens. If he shows up, I'll call the police, do you hear? You tell him that if you want to tell him something."

She exhaled and went out the front door.

After she left, I watched the end of *Gomer Pyle* and half of *The Edge of Night*. Then I got bored watching TV and went into the kitchen and waited for the mailman.

There was no one home except for Monty. We sat in the kitchen, looking at each other. The clock clicked off the seconds. After a while Monty made a funny face and put his head down and barfed on the floor. A blue marble popped out and rolled across the linoleum. He flopped onto his side, yawned and smacked his chops, which had yellow barf on them. I went to the sink and poured some water onto a dish towel. Then I wiped his snout, picked up the blue marble and cleaned it, and put it in my pocket.

I said, "Where did you get the shiny blue marble?"

Monty placed his paw on top of my wrist and licked the back of my hand.

"Good boy. That's a good boy."

I cleaned up the dog barf with the dish towel.

Getting the mail was a high point of the day. Mail could bring many interesting and important items, such as letters from Stev or Albert, records from the Record Club of America or magazines like *TV Guide, Sports Illustrated* and *Popular Mechanics*. The mailman usually arrived sometime after two o'clock. When he did, I ducked behind the curtain, so as to avoid detection. This was standard operating procedure in our house. The mailman loved the New York Yankees and if he saw you, he would immediately begin telling you about yesterday's game and which players made mistakes or did well. It was all he wanted to talk about. You'd think it impossible for anyone to have so much to say about the New York Yankees, but the mailman proved you wrong. He usually made the same general observations over and over, such as "The only thing Bobby Mercer's got in common with Mickey Mantle is they're both from Oklahoma," or "Joe DiMaggio is the greatest ballplayer who ever lived. Period."

After the mailman delivered and walked back to his mail truck, I went out to the front porch and collected the mail. The only item addressed to me was a letter from Albert, which I opened. The letter read:

Dear Timmy,
I made a lamp in arts and crafts out of a Schweppes Ginger Ale can. It's pretty cool. We can put it in our room. I'm going to make one for you too. Do you want Coke or Dr Pepper or Shasta? Albert

There were no letters from Stev, not one since he left. Stev usually sent three or four letters per week from Casco, Maine. I had a pile of old letters in my desk, saved from past summers. In the letters he told me the names of songs he heard on the radio and the games they played at camp, like Bombardment, and the names of the girls he danced with at the camp dances. If he made out with a girl at a camp dance, he would place the initials M.O. next to the girl's name. He wrote about the outings that they went on with the counselors, such as concerts at a place called Tanglewood, where he once saw Seals and Crofts. He wrote:

The concert was great except our seats weren't so great but we could hear. Livingston Taylor was good but I didn't know the songs he sang. Seals and Crofts sang "Hummingbird," "Funny Man," "Summer Breeze," "Diamond Girl" and "East of Ginger Trees." They played others but I didn't know them. We got back to camp around two A.M. and I turned on the radio and "Taxi" was playing and it was great. Stev.

I picked up the telephone and dialed The Myra. When she answered I asked, "Do you have any letters for me?"

She said, "Should I have letters for you?"

"Sometimes Stev puts my letters inside envelopes addressed to you to save stamps."

"The only thing I have for you is a magazine. It's called *Rolling Stones*."

"I thought there might be some letters."

"I wish there were letters. He hasn't sent one. I had to call the camp director to see if my son's alive."

"Is he sick?"

"Did I say he was sick? He's fine. He's busy. That's what they told me. Do you want the magazine or not?"

"You already brought that over."

"Then why are you asking?"

"I'm not asking."

"Fine," said The Myra, and the line went dead.

I hadn't seen Tiger since the day Albert blasted him, so I went over to his house and knocked. A minute later Tiger's Mother opened the front door a few inches and peered out, with half her face visible through the crack. I said, "Is Tiger home?"

"There's no one here named Tiger."

"Tony, I mean."

"You're always making fun of him, calling him names. You and the others. Does that make you feel good?"

"I'm not making fun."

"You're not? Is it a compliment calling him Tiger, like he was some great, big bully? He's a sensitive boy."

"He likes being called Tiger."

"He most certainly does not. Would you like being called Killer or Big Foot or something like that? Of course you wouldn't."

"It's because his name is Tony," I explained. "Tony the Tiger. You know, Frosted Flakes."

She said, "Don't try to lie your way out of it."

"I'm not lying."

"You're always making fun of him and picking on him and bullying him every chance you get. I can't tell you how many times that boy has come home crying. I tried to talk to your father but he said he knew better. Well. This is the end. Do you hear? There'll be no more of this abuse."

"But we're friends," I said.

"That's not how friends behave."

I peered through the crack. I knew Tiger was standing behind his mother somewhere in the room, listening. It wasn't true what she said about calling him Tony the Tiger. He liked being called Tony the Tiger. He went around the neighborhood saying, "They're grrrrrrr-eat." He was known for it. It was his favorite thing to say.

I said, "You know when Tony says, 'They're grrrrrrr-eat'? That's because it's what Tony the Tiger says."

She said, "You should be ashamed of yourself. Go home. Don't come knocking anymore. Anthony doesn't want to see you. Do you hear? Now go."

She closed the door.

Tiger's Brother came out of the garage. He said, "Hey you."

I said, "What?"

He said, "How would you like it if I beat the crap out of you? Would you like that? Answer me."

"No."

" 'Cause I thought you were a big shot. Picking on little kids. Isn't that what you do?"

"No."

"You pick on Tony. He's smaller than you."

"He's my friend."

"That's how you treat your friends. You pick on them and fart on them and hit them in the back. You must have lots of friends."

I said, "He likes being called Tony the Tiger. He told everyone to call him that."

"What the hell are you talking about?"

"Why we call him Tiger."

"Go on," said Tiger's Brother. "Get out of here. Before I change my mind and smack you."

I walked back to my house and went upstairs to my room. I sat at my desk, thinking. After a while I picked up the Bic pen and got out a piece of paper. I wrote:

Dear Albert.

Dad took off. He hasn't come back for four days. He and Mom had another fight. Tiger won't talk to anyone since the time you blasted him. I want the lamp made out of the Coke can. Make that one for me. A Schlitz can would be cool if they let you but they probably won't. Timmy. PS. When are you supposed to come home? Can you leave early?

32.
TO THE MOON

I hopped onto the World's Greatest Bicycle otherwise known as the Chopper otherwise known as the Green Machine and took off down the street, smacking my hand against the signpost that said Apple Hill Road. I turned onto the sidewalk, rode past the brook, crossed Albany Avenue, took the shortcut through the field of tall grass and emerged by the old farm on Flagg Road. When I reached the center of town, I chained my bike to a parking meter outside Mechanics Savings Bank and went across the street to The Dad's office.

I tried the door and peered through the window. I checked the rear of the building, where The Dad and Uncle Sal usually parked their Lincolns. The parking slots were empty.

It was late afternoon. The sun glared high in the sky above the First Church of Christ.

I went into The Lodge to look at some records, and the guy who worked behind the counter nodded to me and said, "Hey." His name was Tom Majusiak. Everyone knew him.

I said, "Hey."

I checked the counter for new surveys, but none had arrived. I thumbed through albums by Elton John and The Who and bands no one ever heard of, like Triumvirate. The Triumvirate album was entitled *Illusion on a Double Dimple*. I studied the front and back cover of *Illusion on a Double Dimple* for approximately two to three minutes, reading the names of the songs and band members.

Tom Majusiak said, "That's a pretty good band. If you like art rock, you'll like them."

I said, "I never heard of them before."

"They're like Yes only heavier on the synthesizers."

"Cool," I said.

"They're Danish, I think, or something like that."

Tom Majusiak was six feet seven inches tall and had curly black hair that went halfway down his back. He taught guitar to all the kids who wanted to learn guitar in our neighborhood. He was twenty-eight years old and played in a band called Legerdemain that performed at junior high and high school dances. On certain songs he stepped on a pedal that made his guitar sound like it was talking baby talk. Everyone cheered when he did that trick, or when he sang high-pitched vocals on such songs as "Roundabout" and "Stairway to Heaven," or when he goosenecked across the stage, soloing mightily. Although he sang in a high-pitched voice, his speaking voice was low and thick, like certain late-night DJ's on WCCC and WPLR. At dances, during the sudden silence after the last song of the night ended, he would lean close to the microphone and say something that no one understood, like "Who of you remembers what the dormouse said?" Then the lights would go out and he would be gone.

I handed *Illusion on a Double Dimple* by Triumvirate to Tom Majusiak, and he said, "You'll dig it, man."

I said, "Cool."

"That's four and a quarter with tax."

I doled out my money, and he put the record in a paper bag, handed it back to me and flashed a peace sign.

Outside Dino's the exhaust fan blew pizza vapors into my face, making me hungry even though it was an hour before dinnertime. I opened the door and went inside to order a slice of pizza with extra cheese.

When Jimmy the Pizza Man saw me he stopped stirring his giant pot of spaghetti sauce and wiped his hands on his apron. He said, while gesturing furiously with his fat, stubby fingers, "Your father already picked it up. About an hour ago. Large pepperoni."

I said, "My dad was here?"

Tenino the Salad Man nodded. "Yeah. Large pepperoni to go. About an hour ago."

Jimmy the Pizza Man said, "I just told him that. What do you gotta repeat everything I say for?"

Tenino the Salad Man had a deep scar across his forehead. He always looked like he was frowning. He frowned his scar-frown and said, "Might not a been that long. Might a been less."

I said, "You sure it was him?"

Tenino the Salad Man said, "I know your father. He give good tip. He always give good tip."

I ran back to Mechanics Savings Bank and unchained my bike from the parking meter. I rechecked The Dad's office, but it was locked, the parking lot empty. I wheeled up and down Main Street, looking for the Mark IV. I saw a man outside Baskin Robbins, and another leaving Herb's Sports Shop, but those were other tall, dark-haired men with their hair Brylcreemed back from their foreheads, wearing Clark Kent glasses. Not The Dad.

I went into Harvey's Package Store. Harvey's Package Store was where The Dad bought all his alcoholic beverages, including the cases of J&B. When I came through the door, Harvey looked up from behind the counter. He said, "One. You're too young to come in here. Two. You just missed him."

I said, "Who?"

"Who else. He was here about twenty minutes ago."

"You sure?"

"Sure, I'm sure. A bottle of cognac and a bottle of champagne. Martell's and Dom Perignon. He said it was a special occasion."

"Which way did he go?"

Harvey shrugged.

"Because I'm looking for him," I said.

"Everyone's looking for somebody. Haven't you heard the song, kid?"

"What song?"

Harvey laughed. "He's a card, your old man. Listen to this. Listen to what he told me. Three guys go into a bar. A Jew. A guinea. And a Polack."

I waited for Harvey to finish the joke, and when he did I said, "So which way did he go?"

"To the moon," said Harvey. "That's where he went. Same place you're going."

"What do you mean?"

"I mean, shoo. I mean, get the hell outa here. That's what I mean."

33.
SCREEN STARS

The next day I sat in my room with an apple on my desk, reading *Screen Stars* magazine and listening to WDRC. It was midafternoon. The Mom and Daphne were out. I was alone in the house, which for some reason gave me a boner.

Elizabeth Taylor was on the cover of *Screen Stars* magazine. She was chubby but her face was pretty and her boobs were big. The Mom often said, "Elizabeth Taylor is the most beautiful creature who ever lived." I did not agree. In my opinion, Sandra Wilder was prettier than Elizabeth Taylor. I flipped the pages to the Mark Eden Developer and Bustline Contouring Course advertisement and studied the pictures of Sandra Wilder, bust 36 and bust 41. Sandra Wilder was not chubby and puffy-faced like Elizabeth Taylor. Sandra Wilder had shapelier bosoms. Sandra Wilder's bosoms were taut and they turned up like a ski jump. Elizabeth Taylor's bosoms were big, freckled and wobbly. Sandra Wilder had a nice, bright smile, whereas Elizabeth Taylor looked like she wanted to kill the photographer. I flipped the pages back and forth between Sandra Wilder and Elizabeth Taylor. Meanwhile I held the Swedish Massager against my boner. After the requisite period of vibration, I made the Ernest Borgnine face and shot white bullets into the shag carpet.

I closed the magazine and turned up the radio.

WDRC was playing "Americans" by Byron MacGregor. "Americans" was a difficult song to rank. To call "Americans" a song was probably a mistake. "Americans" was an oration put to patriotic music. There was a marching band in the background, playing flutes and snare drums. During the music, Byron MacGregor talked about everything in America that was great. He had a deep voice. He told you: We won the war. We saved the world for democracy. We put a man on the moon. Even when we make mistakes, like Watergate, we put the problem in the store window for everyone to see. And so on. Listening to "Americans" was like being in school when you stand up and say the Pledge of Allegiance. For some reason, "Americans" made me feel good, even though I knew the song was queer and Stev would not like it. At one point, when Byron MacGregor was talking about flying to the moon, molecules from all over my body rushed to my head and detonated like an atom bomb, which we Americans dropped on Hiroshima and killed the dirty Japs to win the war and save democracy. I closed my eyes and waited for my brain to unlock, like when I drank a milk shake too fast.

"Americans" ended.

A new song came on. The new song was "The Bitch Is Back" by Elton John. I got out a piece of paper and wrote:

> Dear Stev.
>
> I'm listening to "The Bitch Is Back" on WDRC. I am including an article from *Rolling Stone* about all the great singing stars on an English soccer team. There is a good picture of Elton holding the ball. That's it. Timmy. PS. Did you get my letters and surveys?

A commercial came on WDRC. I turned down the volume and waited for the next song. Meanwhile I turned *Screen Stars* magazine to the Mark Eden Developer and Bustline Contouring Course advertisement. Said Sandra Wilder: "I always wanted fuller and shapelier bosoms, but I didn't think it was possible."

Reading the word "bosoms" gave me another boner.

I examined Sandra Wilder's full and shapely bosoms and wondered what they looked like without the bikini top covering them. For some reason, I wondered whether Sandra Wilder ever farted like Lisa Loomis. Lisa Loomis had a butt shaped like a little pumpkin, which stuck out behind. Before farting, she had squinted her eyes and held her breath and concentrated and scrunched her nose and pushed and pushed and used all her muscles. Sandra Wilder was much bigger than Lisa Loomis.

If she farted, the sound would probably be much deeper and louder, although Lisa Loomis's fart was pretty deep. I could not remember whether the force of Lisa Loomis's fart had puffed up the fabric of the T-shirt covering her pumpkin butt. The T-shirt must have flounced, if only a little. I tried to remember whether there had been a flounce. I thought about kissing Lisa Loomis just before she farted, when her face was tense with concentration and effort. I thought about kissing Lisa Loomis just after she farted, when relief washed over her features like sunlight. Meanwhile I stuck my Bic pen into the middle of the apple, which was mealy, and hollowed out the core so that the apple looked like a doughnut. Then I stuck my boner inside the apple and moved it back and forth as fast as humanly possible. After the requisite time period, I made the Ernest Borgnine face and shot white bullets into the shag carpet.

I tossed the remnants of the apple into the wastepaper basket. There were apple shavings and apple pits and apple juice all over the place.

I decided to take a bath.

I went into the bathroom and closed the door, turned on the water and sat in the tub. The water began to rise around me. A noise came from outside the door. It was Monty, scratching with his nails.

"Wait a minute," I said.

I got out of the tub and walked across the tile floor, dripping water, and opened the door. Monty walked across the wet tiles and carefully stepped into the bathtub and sat down in the water.

"Move over," I said.

I got in next to him.

Monty loved baths. Whenever he heard bathwater, he came running, and he would scratch the bathroom door and whine until you let him in. He liked to sit in the tub and lap the lukewarm bathwater out of your cupped hands. Sometimes he tested the temperature of the water by putting one paw in first, barely breaking the surface of the water. He liked drinking bathwater, so long as the water was not soapy. He would drink lukewarm bathwater forever, if he had his way.

I scooped some lukewarm water into my cupped hands like a dog bowl, and Monty drank, shooting out his tongue.

"Good boy," I said. "Want some more?"

After he drank approximately ten handfuls of lukewarm water, I said, "All right, that's enough."

I gave him a push. Monty stepped carefully out of the tub and vigorously shook himself off, spraying water everywhere. Then he padded out of the bathroom on his wet paws and thumped down the stairs until I could no longer hear him.

I got out and started to towel off.

Then I had an idea.

I closed the bathroom door. I got back into the tub, kneeled in front of the faucet, turned the water on full blast at medium temperature and stuck my boner beneath the stream. My boner did not bend at all. It was like a piece of wood under a waterfall. The splashing water sounded liked peeing, like when Cynthia Storm peed her pajamas. I wondered whether Cynthia Storm ever peed in the bathtub. I wondered what she looked like naked while she peed. Cynthia Storm had smiled brightly and snorted while she pissed her pajamas. The stain between her legs had gotten bigger and bigger, darkening her pink pajama bottoms. I thought about Cynthia Storm's face while she pissed her nice pink pajama bottoms. Meanwhile I held my boner beneath the stream of water for the requisite time period and made the Ernest Borgnine face and shot white bullets, which went down the drain.

Afterward I toweled off and put on a fresh pair of Fruit of the Looms.

The Mom came home. I heard her placing various shopping bags on the table. She said, "Timmy?"

I said, "I'm upstairs."

"Go out to the car and get the rest of the shopping bags. I bought you some pecan rolls. Your favorite."

"Okay." I put on the rest of my clothes and went downstairs.

The Mom said, "You look clean."

I said, "I took a bath."

"You didn't let the dog in the tub, did you?"

"Just for a little while."

"You know he drinks too much water in the tub. You better put him outside before he starts whining and has an accident."

"Okay."

The Mom ruffled my wet hair. She said, "You take more baths than anyone I've ever known. Mrs. Mandelbaum has to bribe Steven to get him into the tub. She has to give him money for records or he won't do it. I'm glad you're not like that. What a nice, clean boy you are."

I went out to the car and got the shopping bags and carried them inside. I helped The Mom unpack the groceries. There was a package of six pecan rolls. I tore off the cellophane and one by one ate all six pecans rolls, unrolling the strips into my mouth like a conveyor belt until reaching the soft and tasty cores.

In the last shopping bag, I found the new issue of *Screen Stars* magazine.

Raquel Welch was on the cover.

34.
HERE'S TO YOU, JELLYBEAN

After *Kojak* ended, I snuck out of the house and hopped on my bike. The night was hot and muggy. Mosquitoes and other insects swarmed around my head, trying to inject me with bug venom. I pedaled furiously, sweating into my Bermuda shorts and Lobster Pot T-shirt, which had a smiling red lobster on the front.

All the stores and restaurants in the center of town were closed. The stoplight made a buzzing noise when it changed from green to yellow to red, but hardly any cars went by. There was a pink Cadillac parked outside Mayron's Bakery, but otherwise Main Street was empty. I passed a man walking a dog along the sidewalk. The dog barked at me as I wheeled by, and his owner said, "Stop that, Truman. Be a good dog, Truman."

The clock above Mechanics Savings Bank flashed the time and temperature in bright yellow numbers. The temperature was eighty-two degrees. The time was 9:45 P.M.

There was a light on in The Dad's office.

I wheeled around to the back of the building. The Mark IV was parked in the lot, by itself. I put a hand on the hood, because I had seen Columbo do that to check if a car had been recently driven. The hood was cold.

The rear window of the office was open, and faint transistor radio music was coming from inside. The music was easy listening, which was The Dad's favorite. I rolled my bike soundlessly into the darkness near the bushes beneath the window. A moment later a shadow crossed in front of the window shade. Then I heard The Dad's voice, which was startlingly loud and close to me, say, "Where the hell did I put them?"

"Put what?" said a woman's voice, farther away.

"The goddamn glasses."

"We don't need them. We'll drink out of the bottle."

"Like hell. This is Dom Perignon."

"Then we'll drink out of my shoe."

"Your feet are too big for that."

"Hey," screeched the woman.

"I never seen a pair that big."

"They're not big. They're petite. Everyone says so."

"Who says I'm talking about your feet?" said The Dad, and the woman laughed.

I heard the sound of cupboard doors closing, and then The Dad's shadow moved away from the window. He and the woman were in the back room, where we used to go weekend afternoons to nap, before The Mom found out and put an end to it.

"Are you ready?" said The Dad.

"You bet."

"Here we go."

A cork popped out of a champagne bottle. The sound made me flinch.

"Watch out. It's fizzy," said the woman. Her voice was low-pitched and raspy.

"Move over," said The Dad.

"Aren't you going to make a toast?"

"Here's to you, jellybean."

"That's not much of a toast."

I heard The Dad exhale and sink into the saggy old leather couch. "Here's to you, jellybean" was the expression The Dad used whenever he gave you something. He would take the birthday present or Christmas present and drop it into your lap and nine times out of ten he would say, "Here's to you, jellybean."

The Dad said, "How's that champagne?"

"Not bad."

" 'Not bad,' she says. This stuff costs fifty bucks a bottle and she says not bad."

"Now you sound like Pinky."

"He should be happy spending it on you. You got it coming."

"I wish. That son of a bitch watches every dime."

"Pinky does?"

"Damn right he does. He makes me keep accounts in a schoolteacher's ledger he brought home from Maxwell's Drugstore. He graphs out the columns with a ruler. Food and drink. Utilities. Insurance. Miscellaneous. I'm supposed to enter the amounts with receipts, like an accountant."

The Dad yawned. "Pink's a stand-up guy," he said.

"Oh, he's a big spender at the club, all right, buying rounds for the house. But it's a different story at home. At home he's whining night and day. Says I'm putting him into the poorhouse."

"You got expensive tastes. Pinky should have known that when he married you."

"The son of a bitch is as tight as they come."

The Dad exhaled loudly. He said, "It's hot as a bastard."

"I don't mind. I like being all sweaty and naked."

"Drink up," said The Dad. "This stuff doesn't keep."

"Are you trying to get me drunk? Is that your plan? So you can have your way with me?"

"If I have my way with you one more time, Gladys, I'll drop dead."

"Look who's complaining. You were singing a different tune an hour ago."

"What do you expect? Body like yours."

"You're sweet, Bobby. You know how to treat a lady. Pinky could take a page out of your book."

"Pink's okay. You're too hard on the poor bastard. That's a tough racket, selling cars. All that smiling and glad-handing. No one wants to pay list price anymore."

"Oh please. Spare me."

The Dad yawned. "Jesus, it's hot. You want another glass?"

"I can't, Bobby. It's late. I should be getting back."

"Okay."

"Hey. Don't sound so anxious to see me go. You'd think I was holding you hostage."

The couch squeaked and then came a loud, bare-flesh slap, and the woman yelled, "Ouch," and The Dad said, "Look at that. Now that's an ass."

For the next couple of minutes, I heard the sounds of them moving around the back room, hallway and bathroom: the click-clack of her heels, the faucet going on and off, a toilet flushing. Then I heard the front door open and close.

I rolled my bike forward and peeked around the side of the building. The woman came down the steps in the ray of the light above the door, clutching the rail, looking at her feet. She was wearing a tight yellow dress, which gripped the rolls of fat around her hips and butt. Her hair was a gold beehive, piled on top of her head. She clicked onto the sidewalk on her high heels, walking in short stiff steps.

Whenever The Mom saw a woman on TV who looked like this, she always used the word "blowser," which rhymed with "schnauzer." She would say something like "That Jacqueline Susann is starting to look like a blowser. And she used to be so pretty when that book first came out."

I wheeled soundlessly into the street and watched the woman make her way along the sidewalk, her heels clicking loudly. Halfway down the street, outside Mayron's Bakery, she fumbled inside her purse and dug out her keys. Then she unlocked the pink Cadillac, started the motor and roared off down the street.

35.
GETTING OUT

The noise began as The Mom and I were sitting down to dinner. Screams and yells wafted through the screen door like barbecue vapors.

The Mom said, "What on earth is that commotion?"

I said, "I don't know."

"Go take a look."

I went outside. The sun was going down the color of an orange Popsicle. A murder of crows flapped overhead, flying to someplace else. I walked to the end of the driveway and looked down the street.

Franky DiLorenzo was standing on his front lawn, yelling at the top of his lungs. "You fucking bitch. You cocksucking old whore."

Doors opened. People started to come outside. Mr. Mandelbaum came out on his front porch and put on his glasses and looked. The whole Papadakis family lined up on their front lawn like bowling pins, all seven of them, including the grandmother, watching the show.

Franky DiLorenzo said, "You can't kick me out. Dad's not around. I run things around here. I'll kick you out."

Mrs. DiLorenzo came out onto the doorstep and screamed, "Go away. Just go away. I never want to see you again."

"I'm not going anywhere. I'm not listening to you anymore. You got that?"

"You're no son of mine. You never were."

She went inside the house and tried to slam the door but Franky DiLorenzo leaped onto the stoop and put his foot in front of the door, grabbed her by the arm and pulled her outside.

She yelled, "Franky. You're hurting me." She stumbled on the steps and fell, and Franky DiLorenzo grabbed her by the hair and dragged her across the lawn, like Chief Jay Strongbow pulling Lou Albino around the ring. Mrs. DiLorenzo screamed a constant, unwavering scream. She had curly black hair, which Franky DiLorenzo pulled with both hands. In a movie, her hair would come off in one piece and he would go tumbling backward with the wig in his hands and his mother would be bald. But this was not a movie and her hair did not come off.

He said, "How do you like that? Huh? How does it feel?"

Mr. Mandelbaum said in a loud voice, "I'm calling the police."

At that moment there came the sound of a siren wailing in the distance, growing louder.

Franky DiLorenzo let go of his mother's hair and stood over her screaming, "I hate your guts, I'll kill you, you fucking bitch," and he reared back and kicked her in the stomach, and she clutched her stomach and stopped screaming.

Franky DiLorenzo's sister appeared. She stood on the lawn, waving her hands in the air, yelling, "No, Franky. No, Franky. No, Franky."

Franky DiLorenzo looked at her and opened his mouth to say something but before he could speak he heard the siren and froze. He looked both directions, up and down the street. He looked at his mother, lying like a bag of clothes at his feet. Then he bolted, heading for the woods at the top of the street. He ran past the Papadakis family, who turned their heads in unison and watched him go. He ran past me without looking. He ran past all the people standing in their driveways watching him. You could hear him taking big gulps of air, his sneakers smacking the pavement. He looked back once, and kept running, arms pumping high like Bob Hayes, the world's fastest man.

I ran to the front door. The Mom was standing in the doorway, looking out the screen door.

I said, "Mom. He's getting away."

She said, "Who?"

"Franky DiLorenzo. He beat up his mother. He kicked her in the stomach and pulled her hair."

"Lord save us."

"The police are coming."

I opened the screen door, and Monty came out of nowhere. He dashed through the opening before I could close the door. I lunged for him but it was too late. He got past me. He went down the front steps, his nails clicking on the flagstones, and galloped toward the street, pushing with all four legs.

Chasing people was one of Monty's favorite things to do. He thought it was a game, running after someone. It was something we did in the backyard. Albert and I would run around and he would chase after us with his leash tied to the line, which made a noise like fishing twine going out. He could not resist chasing someone who was running.

I said, "Monty. No."

Monty ran the length of the driveway. He was moving fast but everything happened slowly. He ran into the street and immediately got hit by the police car. There was a screech of tires and a squeal, which briefly seemed to be the same sound. The police car skidded to a stop and the squeal continued, like a pig. Squealing, Monty ran in a circle in the middle of the street, around and around like he was chasing his tail except he had no tail, only a little Boxer stub.

The Mom said, "Dear God."

I reached him just as he stopped running in circles and went down. He lay in the middle of the street, on his side, panting.

I said, "Monty. Monty. Are you okay?"

I touched his head. He whimpered and licked my hand. There was a black tire track across his stomach, where he didn't like being touched, as clear as if someone had painted it on. You could see the separate tracks of the tire. But there was no blood, not a drop. The white fur of his stomach was spotless except for the tire track.

The air smelled like burned rubber. The cop got out of the police car and slammed the door, saying, "Goddamnit. Goddamnit."

Monty panted, slower and slower, looking at me.

I rubbed his head softly. I said, "Get up, Monty. Come on. Get up. You can do it."

The Mom said, "Help me lift him."

I looked up. She was standing over me, and the cop was standing behind her.

I said, "He's okay. He's not bleeding."

The Mom said, "We've got to get him to the doctor."

"He's tired. He wants to rest, that's all."

The Mom leaned down and picked up Monty's front legs. I held his back legs, and we carried him to the Station Wagon, with the cop walking beside. We put Monty into the backseat and laid him on his side. I wrapped him in the army blanket that we kept in the backseat. Only his head was sticking out of the blanket, the tongue hanging down.

The cop said, "Where are you taking him? I'll call ahead and tell them you're coming."

The Mom said, "This is a residential street. What were you doing, driving that fast?" She closed the car door.

I said, "Can't I come?"

"No."

She got in the front seat, started the car and took off. I ran to the end of the driveway and watched the car go down the street.

All the people from all the houses were standing outside watching me and the crowd of people on the DiLorenzos' lawn, helping Mrs. DiLorenzo.

The cop said, "I'm sorry, son. I didn't see him coming. He came out of nowhere."

I said, "He's not bleeding. He just needs some rest."

I went inside the house and waited.

Late that night, when everyone else was asleep, I noticed a light in the backyard, a faint glow, like a firefly hovering in the air, flickering on and off. I stood in the darkness of the kitchen, looking out the back window at the light. Monty liked the backyard. The backyard was his home. He spent half his life out there, lying on the grass, sniffing, listening to sounds that other animals made. If you watch a star for long enough, that star seems to move across the sky like a plane at night. I watched the flickering light and decided that the light was not real, just my eyes playing tricks. But as I watched, the light flared bright white and dropped to the ground and went out. The light did not return. Finally I went to bed. Just before I fell asleep I realized that the light had been coming from the tree house.

36.
DOG HEAVEN

We buried Monty in the backyard. I dug the hole near the pine tree where he liked to sit in the shade. I used the shovel to dig and the pinch bar to loosen the dirt, wearing a pair of work gloves. It took me almost the entire morning.

After I was done two guys from the veterinarian's office arrived in a van. They carried Monty, wrapped in a burlap sack, around to the backyard and placed him in the hole.

They left, and I went inside and told Daphne and The Mom to come out. We stood over the grave, holding hands.

The Mom said, "Monty was a good dog for us. He had a good life here for a long time. He was part of the family. He watched over us and looked out for us. Everybody knows how much Timmy loved that dog. Now he's in dog heaven, chasing rabbits and birds."

Daphne said, "There's no such thing."

"Of course there is. There's a heaven for all creatures."

"He got squashed. He ran in a circle squealing."

"Don't think about that. Think about how he was."

I said, "What happened? Did he just stop breathing?"

The Mom said, "The doctor gave him a shot. He didn't feel any pain. He put his head down and went to sleep, like always."

"But he wasn't bleeding. He was okay."

"He had internal bleeding."

"Couldn't they operate?"

"There was nothing they could do. He was all broken up inside."

"He was my dog. He was my birthday present."

"We'll get you another dog. Any kind you like."

"I don't want another."

"I know you don't."

Daphne said, "We have to tell Albert."

I said, "I'll do it."

The Mom said, "Are you sure you want to, Timmy?"

"It was my fault. I'm the one who let him out."

"It was no one's fault. It just happened. Sometimes things happen and there's nothing you can do about it no matter how hard you try."

"I should have checked before opening the screen door. I always check to see if he's there. I forgot this time."

"Don't think that way. You'll make yourself sick thinking that way."

Daphne said, "We'll never see Monty again."

After they went back to the house, I filled in the grave with dirt and hammered a two-by-four into the soft ground as a grave marker. The sign on the doghouse said "Monty." The words were engraved into the wood in script. I pried the sign off the doghouse and nailed it to the grave marker.

37.
TOAD

A croaking woke me. It was past midnight. Everyone else was asleep. I sat up in bed and listened to the croaking, which was like no noise ever before made in my bedroom. I turned on the light and looked around. The room was empty. The door was closed.

I realized that the sound was coming from underneath my bed. I got on my hands and knees and peered under the bed and found a big, fat toad.

I said, "Where did you come from? How did you get in here?"

The toad did not try to get away. He sat there croaking while I picked him up and he peed toad pee all over my hands. I held him with both hands like a sandwich and stepped into my slippers and went downstairs, opened the back porch door and walked into the backyard, wearing my pajamas. The backyard was silent except for crickets and grasshoppers rubbing their legs together, making a quiet racket. I took the toad to the garden and let him go. He sat there for a moment in the dirt. Then he hopped into the darkness.

The sky was covered by stars. I looked up and watched the stars glimmering like sequins on Ginger Grant's gown. There were no clouds, only stars, enough to count forever.

I walked across the yard and stood at the bottom of the treehouse ladder. I looked up toward the dark opening.

I said, "Franky. Hey, Franky."

There was no answer.

I said, "Franky. You in there?"

He said, "Who's there?"

"It's me. Timmy."

"What do you want?"

"Nothing."

Franky DiLorenzo appeared in the treehouse doorway. He said, "You scared me. I was sleeping."

"You got a blanket?"

"Yeah. I got one out of the car."

"What car?"

"Your car. The station wagon."

"That's the blanket we wrapped Monty in. He got run over."

"I saw it. That helped me get away."

"He had internal bleeding."

"Oh yeah?"

"We buried him over there," I said, pointing at Monty's grave.

Franky DiLorenzo said, "You got anything to eat?"

"We got leftover turkey."

"Turkey's good. Go get me a big turkey leg. Bring it back out."

"I saw you last night. You were smoking a cigarette. I saw the light coming from the treehouse doorway. I figured it was you."

"It got cold as a bitch last night. Too cold to stay out here. I broke into your garage and slept in the backseat of your station wagon."

"How come you always come here when you run away?"

"You got the best treehouse."

"We thought it was someone else. A bum maybe."

"There ain't no bums around here."

"I guess not."

"Hey," said Franky DiLorenzo. "Go get me that turkey leg. I'm starving."

"Are they looking for you? The cops, I mean."

"I think so."

"You kicked your mom in the stomach."

"Yeah. Well. What the fuck, right?"

"You should go back and apologize."

"What is this? You wanna get me that turkey leg? I was sleeping nice till you bothered me. Now I'm hungry as shit."

"Okay."

"Get something else too. Cranberry sauce. Potatoes. All that stuff."

"I don't know if we have any."

"Just grab a big plate of something."

"Okay."

"Get me a pack of your dad's cigarettes too. What does he smoke?"

"Marlboro."

"Marlboro's good."

I went inside the house, turned on the fluorescent light and stood squinting in the brightness. There was a half-eaten turkey in the refrigerator, stuffed with an onion and covered by a sheath of Saran Wrap. I carried the plate to the counter and started piling white meat and turkey legs onto a paper plate.

The Mom came down the stairs. She said, "What are you doing awake?"

I said, "There was a toad in my room. A big one. He was under my bed. I put him outside in the garden."

"I thought I heard the door open."

"That was me."

"Goodness. A toad. We'll have to call the exterminator."

"He was a toad, Mom. You can't exterminate a toad. He got in the house, that's all. He hopped through a window or door or something."

"Did you wash your hands? They have warts, you know."

"They don't."

"They most certainly do. Wash them immediately."

I turned on the faucet and washed my hands with cold water and wiped them with the dish towel.

The Mom said, "What are you doing with all that food?"

"I'm hungry."

"You can't eat all that. You'll be sick. Sit down. I'll make you a sandwich."

"I'll do it."

"Please. You're making a mess."

The Mom got out the white bread and mayonnaise and started picking out the good pieces of white meat. She said, "When I heard you walking around the kitchen, I thought it was Monty. I see him in the backyard when I look out the window. I see him lying in the doorway. I see him sitting on the couch but it's just the brown pillow."

"I see him too."

"I guess we'll have to get used to it."

"I guess. It seems funny without him."

"I know it does."

The Mom placed the sandwich in front of me and cut it into four parts. She watched me eat with my Adam's apple going up and down. She said, "Do you want another sandwich before I put everything away?"

"No thanks."

"Albert comes home next week. Steven too."

"I know. He hasn't written any letters."

"Maybe he's too busy."

"That's what Mrs. Mandelbaum said."

"You didn't sleep last night, did you? You're dead tired. Look at you."

I finished the sandwich. Turkey has a special chemical that puts you to sleep. The chemical took effect immediately. I felt the turkey chemical seeping into my veins and moving toward my head. My eyes got droopy and my sight blurred, like James West after drinking a drink poisoned by Dr. Miguelito Loveless.

The Mom put the food away, locked the back porch door and snapped the bolt into place. She said, "Go up to bed. Before you fall asleep in the chair."

I said, "Okay," and went up to my room, got into bed and fell immediately asleep.

38. CAUGHT IN THE RAIN

The next night, after *Kung Fu* ended, I waited until The Mom went into her bedroom to do her nightly knitting. Then I snuck out the back door and rolled my bike silently out of the garage.

After I had been pedaling for approximately two minutes, the rain struck. It came on in one giant gust, like the tidal wave that capsized the SS *Poseidon*. I rode through the downpour, squinting and wiping my eyes, spraying a trail of water with my back tire. Cars splashed past me in the dark, with their windshield wipers flapping at full speed and high beams lighting the sheets of rain coming from the opposite direction.

The rainwater was warm and tasted slightly salty from the sweat coming down my face. As I pedaled I yelled into the oncoming darkness because it was too loud for anyone to hear me and because I liked yelling at the top of my lungs. I yelled, "The process is reversing." Then I laughed hysterically and yelled, "I'm not Artemis, I'm his twin brother, Adolphis."

The center of town was deserted. The rain pelted the asphalt, kicking up droplets of water like pockmarks. The stoplight above Main Street swung back and forth on its cable, moving with the wind. Thunder sounded like giant wooden boards breaking in half, and lightning flashed in the distant sky.

I stopped beneath the Mechanics Savings Bank overhang and squinted through the downpour.

There was a light in The Dad's office.

I crossed the street, laid my bike against the rail and knocked on the door for approximately one minute, but no one answered so I began pounding the door with my fist.

I said, "Hey, Dad. Open up. It's me."

The light above the door came on. Then the door opened and The

Dad stuck his head out. He said, "Jesus, what are you doing here? You're soaked."

I said, "I got caught in the rain."

"Get inside before you catch cold."

He held open the door, and I followed him down the hallway. He said, "Does your mother know you're here?"

"No. I waited until she went to bed."

"Good." He got a hand towel out of the bathroom and handed it to me. "Dry yourself off."

We went into the back room. He was wearing a white undershirt, a pair of black pants and black socks without shoes. There was a pile of rumpled clothes on the couch. I pushed them aside and sat down.

The Dad lifted the bottle of J&B and poured a glass. "Take this," he said. "It'll warm you up."

"I've tried it. I don't like it."

"Try again. It grows on you." He handed me the glass. The J&B looked and smelled like cough syrup. I took a sip, and a moment later felt my cheeks flush and my eyes start to water.

"Didn't I tell you?" he said. "Nothing like a good belt."

He took the glass out of my hand and drank what was left. The room smelled like Old Spice aftershave and cigarettes. There was a pile of Dino's Pizza Parlor boxes stacked in the corner approximately one foot high, stained on top with grease.

I said, "Monty died. He got hit by a car."

"I heard."

The Dad sank into an easy chair, and when he realized he was sitting on a newspaper, he got the paper out from beneath him and set it on the floor alongside the J&B.

"We buried him in the backyard."

"I wanted to come over but your mother, well, she didn't think it was a good idea. She's got a piece of paper from the court saying when I can come and go."

"That's not fair."

"Goddamn right it's not."

I noticed that his bad eye was bright red, and the skin around it was bruised and swollen.

"What happened to your eye?"

"Poked myself on the job with a piece of wood."

"Does it hurt?"

"Nah. I can hardly feel it."

He picked the bottle off the floor and poured himself a drink. He looked around the room, sipping. There was an old fan in the corner, buzzing and blowing muggy air.

"You need a TV," I said.

He nodded. "That would come in handy."

"I could bring you the black-and-white. It's not heavy."

"Better not," he said. "No use aggravating your mother."

"I could do it when she's not around."

He took another sip. "What's she saying about me?"

"She told me not to talk to you. She said she'd call the police if you came to the house."

"I don't know where she gets these crazy ideas. She's an excitable woman. You never know what's going to set her off."

"She says she'll get a job at the town hall for seven dollars an hour."

"That's peanuts. That's not enough to pay the butcher."

"That's what I told her."

The Dad nodded. "How you fixed for cash? You need anything?"

I shrugged, and he said, "Here, take this," and reached into his pocket and handed me a portion of his Michigan bankroll. "Buy something for yourself. Some records that you like. Get something for your mother too. Some flowers. She likes lilies. Don't tell her where you got the money."

"Okay."

He picked up the newspaper and ruffled it. "You want some of this?"

I said, "Sports."

He handed me the sports page. Then he lifted the business page in front of his face. We read the newspaper as the rain came down. After a while he said with his face behind the newspaper, "I could've bought IBM when it was ten dollars a share. Look at it now. Calio was smart. He bought a thousand shares."

I said, "Huh."

"Now American Home Products. That's another one. Pretty much anything you buy in a grocery store, there's a good chance they make it."

"Pecan rolls?"

"Anything like that."

He turned the page. After a while he said, "I'll take you back when the rain stops. No sense getting soaked all over again."

"I don't mind riding."

"Too late to be out on that bike."

The rain beat on the overhang and windows and pavement behind the building.

"Listen to that rain," said The Dad.

We listened. The rain came down for a long time. We read the newspaper and periodically The Dad talked about stocks he should have bought and others he shouldn't have sold. The newspaper was three days old.

The rain stopped as suddenly as it had started, like someone turning off a faucet. The Dad and I went outside, which was cool and moist. The clock above Mechanics Savings Bank flashed the time. It was 10:52 P.M.

The Dad loaded my bike into the trunk of the Mark IV, and I sank down into the leather passenger seat, yawning as we drove through the rain-covered streets with the tires making a hissing sound. When The Dad used the turn signal I felt my eyes closing. There was something about the clicking sound of the turn signal that hypnotized me, causing an irresistible urge to fall asleep.

When we reached the bottom of our street, The Dad pulled over and shook my arm. "Get out here," he said. "That way your mother won't have a conniption fit."

I said, "Are you coming home soon?"

The Dad took the silver flask out from under the seat and had a swig. He pursed his lips. "Pretty soon, I think."

"Albert's coming back next week. He'll be done with camp then."

"Good. Exercise is good for a boy."

I got out. "I'll let you know if Mom says anything else."

The Dad nodded. He said, "Make sure and change out of those clothes. That's how Roosevelt got polio, by sitting around in wet clothes."

"Okay."

I got my bike out of the back and slammed the trunk. The Dad accelerated down the street. I watched the rear red lights fade out of view.

39.
LIGHT ON HIS FEET

The ambulance arrived early in the morning. I saw the red light reflecting on the ceiling of my room, flashing on and off. I got out of bed and looked out the window.

The ambulance was parked in the Cosgroves' driveway. Two guys wearing white got out and opened the front door and went inside the house. A few minutes later a police car showed up, followed by another. The police cars parked in the street. You could hear the engines running.

People came out of their houses like sleepwalkers, wearing housecoats or robes. They kept their distance, watching from driveways, stoops and porches. A policeman walked to the Cosgroves' garage and bent down and opened the garage door. He took out a handkerchief and covered his nose. After a while another car arrived and parked on the street, and a man with a camera went inside the garage and took flashbulb photographs.

Mik Cosgrove walked out of the house. He stood on the lawn, looking down. After a while a cop ruffled his hair and patted him on the back, and then they got into one of the police cars and drove away. After some time the ambulance workers wheeled a stretcher out of the garage. The stretcher was carrying a body with a sheet pulled over the head. They inserted the stretcher into the back of the ambulance and closed the double doors. The ambulance drove away, followed by the police car and photographer's car.

Everything was quiet again.

"He was stark naked," said The Myra. "Blue, like a fish."

She and The Mom were sitting on the back porch. They were too excited to keep their voices down. Sometimes they talked at the same time, like birds chattering in treetops.

"The poor boy," said The Mom. "To find your father like that."

"Something happens when you hang yourself," said The Myra. "The body releases. You lose control."

"What's to control if you're dead?"

"You make a mess."

"At least he didn't do it inside the house. That nice white carpet. So clean. At least he didn't use a gun."

"What's the difference? Dead is dead."

"Guns are dangerous. The boy could've gotten hold of it."

The Myra sighed. She said, "I remember the day they first moved in. He wasn't overweight then. He looked like Glen Campbell. Handsome, I thought. Remember? The children had those round freckled faces, running around. They looked so healthy and happy. He went door to door introducing himself. He was a sociable man. Before."

"He didn't come to my door."

"Every Wednesday night they went to Frank's Restaurant, he, John Wentworth and John Powers. The three of them, like clockwork. One night Leonard and I were there and he asked me to dance. His hands were all over me. It was like getting a massage. Meanwhile he was talking a blue streak in my ear. The dirtiest talk. I didn't know what to think."

"Buddy Cosgrove was a very troubled man. That's all I'll say."

"He was a lovely dancer. Very light on his feet. I always thought he was charming in the way that big men have."

"It was too much for him. Losing his job. His wife leaving, taking the daughter. What man wouldn't take that hard?"

"He's lucky he didn't end up in jail for embezzlement, from what I've heard."

"What about the boy?"

"Vanya's coming back for him. She's selling the house. It's on the market already. You could buy it for a song."

"No one wants to live in a death house."

"Something like this happens, it makes you think. One day you're here, the next you're gone. What does it matter?"

"The children matter."

"If not for the children, sometimes I think I'd just get in the car and go."

"Myra, that's crazy talk. Where would you go?"

"Just go."

"Go like Vanya Cosgrove? To Tucson? Be a cocktail waitress? Work for tips? Is that where you want to go?"

As they talked, crows flapped overhead, going from tree to tree, high in the branches. Bluejays screeched. Cardinals chirped. A sole mourning dove made its sad sound.

40.
FLIPPING

Stev came home from camp.

We went up to my room. I got out his birthday present, which was gift wrapped. The birthday present was *Friends* by Elton John. I bought the album at Caldor for ninety-nine cents in the bargain bin. It was the only copy left. I tried to find another at The Lodge, but nobody had even heard of the record. I wanted to keep the record for myself and give Stev some other present, but he liked Elton John more than anyone in the world.

I handed it to him. I said, "I know it's a week late but I couldn't send it to camp or it might've gotten wrecked or melted."

Stev said, "An album. Cool."

He tore away the wrapping paper and looked at the record and turned it over.

I said, "It's a movie sound track he made before he got famous. He wrote all the songs with Bernie."

Stev said, "I never heard of it before."

"Me neither. It's rare."

Stev fingered the top right corner of the album cover, which was cut off. Some of the cellophane was missing. He said, "Who cut the corner?"

"It was like that when I bought it."

We put *Friends* on the record player and started listening. Elton sang, "Picking friends for the whole world to see." Stev liked that song but got bored during the others on side one. He said, "Let's try the other side."

We turned the record over. Side two was mostly violins and cellos and flutes whistling like little birds. The orchestra kept going, five minutes and counting. We waited for the guitar and drums to come in, like in "Funeral for a Friend," but it didn't happen. Stev switched off the record halfway through.

He said, "Thanks. I should have it because it's Elton but I don't think I'll listen to it very much."

I said, "I could get you something else if you want."

"No. This is good. It's rare. That makes it good."

"I didn't know it was classical music. I thought there'd be more Elton songs. It says so on the cover. 'Songs by Elton John'."

"Yeah. That's a rip-off."

Stev put the record back in the sleeve and placed the album on the bed next to him. He looked at me and quickly looked away. He looked a lot different. He had a dark tan and his hair was long and curly. Also, he had a necklace made of wooden beads around his neck.

I said, "I can't believe you're fifteen."

He said, "I know. You're only twelve."

"I got a birthday coming next week."

"I know. But it still sounds weird."

"Did you get my letters?"

"Yeah. They were good. I meant to write back."

"You were busy, huh?"

"Yeah."

"Even at night?"

"At night we snuck out of the cabin after the counselors went to sleep. There was this guy Graham. He came from California. He's sixteen but they put him in our cabin because it was his first year. We went down to the lake and smoked and stuff. No one ever caught us. One of the counselors was cool. He gave us some pot."

"Really? You smoked it?"

"Yeah. It was pretty cool."

"Huh."

"The girls were crazy for Graham. You should have seen it. He'd give the signal during dinner period. He'd walk up to some girls and tell them: 'Midnight. The dock. Be there. Aloha.' Then later on they'd show up at the lake and we'd make out."

"Were they pretty?"

"A couple were."

"Was he good at sports?"

"Who, Graham? He didn't like sports. He was okay at riflery but that was about it."

"Was he a spaz?"

"Nah. He just didn't like sports. He's got really long hair."

"What else happened?"

"That's about it."

"Will you write it up for me?"

"Why? I just told you."

"I know. But if you wrote it I could put the pages with your other letters."

"What for?"

"Just to have."

"It's better if I just tell you."

"Want to listen to another record?"

"Not really," said Stev.

I opened the desk drawer and took out "The TV Testament." During the time Stev was away at camp, I had made several entries, including "The Top Ten Greatest Shows of the Week" for each of the four weeks that he was absent and a new list entitled "The Top Twenty-Five Foxes (TV Only)," which began with Audra Barkley and ended with Colonel Klink's secretary, Fraulein Hilda. I had also made up several quizzes. Stev liked taking TV quizzes. We kept track of his marks, just like teachers with their blue booklets.

I said, "I got a couple of quizzes for you. Are you ready?"

Stev said, "I'm not in the mood."

"Really?"

Stev shrugged.

I said, "Try anyway. I'll give you an easy one to start. The *Wild Wild West*. Here goes."

I read the following questions: "What is the name of Artemis Gordon's twin brother? Does this twin brother actually exist or is he one of

Arty's disguises? Who replaced Artemis Gordon as Jim West's sidekick when Arty was on assignment in Washington, D.C., for multiple episodes? Name one item that Jim West keeps in his shoe. What is Jim West's number-one rule of fighting?"

Stev looked at me and didn't say anything.

I said, "Well?"

He said, "I don't know."

"Which question?"

"I haven't seen that show for a long time. He always had a knife in his shoe. I know that much."

"Correct. Do you want to know the other answers?"

"Not really."

I said, "The answers are as follows: Adolphis. He's a disguise. Jeremy Pike. A short knife to cut ropes or a bomb made out of putty that blows doors off jail cells. Always get higher than your opponent."

Stev said, "So what?"

"What do you mean, so what?"

"I mean, who cares?"

"You're just mad because you missed every question except one."

"I'm not mad. I just don't care. Let's do something else."

"Still, the results must be recorded."

"Write down whatever you want."

I recorded the results of the *Wild Wild West* quiz in "The TV Testament" and put the notebook in the desk drawer.

Stev said, "Let's go flipping. There's some guys that want to."

"Which guys?"

"Shinebottom and Pearlman."

"Those guys are older than us."

"So what? They like flipping. They flip all the time."

"Shinebottom drives a car," I said.

"Big deal. I'll have a car next year too. Come on. Bring some cards."

I opened the shoe box and grabbed two big handfuls of baseball cards, and we took off.

Stev and I possessed nearly every Boston Red Sox baseball card since 1968, including players no one ever heard of, like Joe Lahoud. We traded and flipped with kids at school to increase our collection. We played Topsies, Closest to the Wall, Farthest, Knock Down the Leaner and games of our own invention, like Bounce Back. As a result of all the flipping, many of the cards got nicked and scratched and bumped around the edges, but not the Boston Red Sox. We did not risk our Boston Red Sox cards. We left our Boston Red Sox cards at home in the shoe box and flipped San Diego Padres and Milwaukee Brewers and players with lifetime batting averages of .099 or less.

Shinebottom lived two streets over. Instead of riding our bikes, we cut through the backyards. Behind Stev's house there was an empty lot overgrown with grass and bushes and fallen trees. We followed the path through the empty lot and emerged on Juniper Lane, then cut through someone's yard and stepped across the brook on some rocks without getting our feet wet and entered Shinebottom's backyard. We cupped our hands against Shinebottom's garage windows and looked inside. There were four kids in Shinebottom's garage. They were Shinebottom, Pearlman, Franky DiLorenzo and Scully.

I said to Stev, "There's Scully. Let's get out of here."

Stev said, "Why?"

"He's the kid that beat you up. He punched you in the forehead eight times."

"That was a joke."

"No, it wasn't. You cried."

"I mean, it hurt and everything. But he was just joking around."

"I don't think so."

"Anyway, it doesn't matter."

"Are you sure?"

"Yeah," said Stev. "Follow me."

He opened the side door and we went into the garage.

Everyone looked up.

Shinebottom said, "Hey, Steve. You made it. Good. Come on in."

Scully said, "Look who's here. It's Mandelbaum. Hi ya, Mandelbaum."

Stev said, "Hey, Scully. What's going on?"

"What's it look like?"

"Looks like you're winning."

"Correct-a-mundo."

It was the middle of a sunny day but Shinebottom's garage was dark and cold. The only light was shadow light coming from the two small windows in the garage door. There were no cars in the garage, just tools, brooms, oil cans, empty boxes and other junk.

Franky DiLorenzo came over next to me and took off my baseball cap and knocked his knuckles on top of my head, making a wooden sound. He said, "I'm still waiting. Did you find it yet?"

I said, "Find what?"

"My turkey leg. Where's my turkey leg?"

Pearlman said, "What are you talking about? What turkey leg? Is that a type of bourbon?"

Franky DiLorenzo said, "No, it's not a type of bourbon, you dumb fuck. It's a fucking turkey leg that you eat. He was supposed to bring me food one night when I was hiding out from the cops. Fucking left me hanging."

Scully said, "That's low."

I said, "I got busted. There was nothing I could do."

"Who busted you?"

"My mother."

"Oooh. Your mommy. That must've been rough."

"She would've called the cops if she saw you."

"What is she, some kind of narc?"

"No. She's just . . . I don't know. Maybe she wouldn't have."

"She better not."

"Are you still hiding out?"

Franky DiLorenzo scratched his ear and said, "Nah. She took me back. She always takes me back."

Shinebottom said, "That's all very interesting but are we flipping or are we flipping?"

Pearlman said, "We're flipping. We're flipping."

They were playing Closest to the Wall. Stev and I watched. Each player had his own particular flipping technique. Shinebottom was a leaner. He arranged his front foot at the edge of the fault line, which was a chalk mark across the garage floor, and leaned forward, way out over the line, extending his hand like a first baseman stretching for a throw. Pearlman made a stiff, spastic motion when he flipped, like a tennis player hitting a backhand. He kept a special stash of waxed cards in his back pocket, which he used sparingly, at critical moments. Franky DiLorenzo licked his fingers when picking out a card. Before flipping, he made three or four practice motions, rocking back and forth like a dancer without a partner. Scully made a pronouncement at the moment he released a card. He said, "Fuck you," or "One time," or "Eat me," or "Take that," or "Your mother," or "Game's over," or "Suck my dick," or "Up your ass," or "Douchebag."

After a few rounds of Closest to the Wall, Shinebottom nodded toward Stev and me. He said, "You guys bring cards? You want in, right?"

Stev said, "Sure."

"We got six guys so we might as well play Topsies. Everyone agreed?"

"Sure. Topsies."

"Topsies is good."

Topsies was played in the following manner. Each player, in turn, flipped a baseball card toward the opposite wall. You left the cards scattered across the floor until someone landed his card on top of another card. That was a topsy, which entitled the winner to collect whatever cards had been pitched.

In Shinebottom's garage, the distance from the fault line to the wall on the opposite side of the garage was approximately twenty feet. Twenty feet was a long flip, much longer than usual for your typical game of Topsies. At a distance of twenty feet, landing a topsy was primarily a matter of luck.

We began the game.

Pearlman won the first pot. He said, "Bingo," and adjusted his glasses and shuffled across the garage and collected approximately twenty-five cards.

Franky DiLorenzo said, "Fuck you."

Pearlman said, "I'm feeling lucky."

"But you're looking ugly."

Everyone laughed.

Shinebottom won the next three pots. Pearlman said, "No wonder he's winning. It's his garage. He knows the angles. We should find a different place. Some place neutral."

Scully said, "He doesn't know shit for angles. He's lucky, that's all."

We played approximately fifteen games of Topsies, and I lost each one. Every card I flipped landed on concrete, miss after miss. The pile in my hand dwindled to almost nothing. It was uncertain how many cards I lost, exactly. The cards were flying so fast, I couldn't keep track. Nearly one hundred, I estimated, which constituted nearly my entire 1974 Topps collection. There was no way to replace the lost cards. The drugstore no longer sold that series. To make matters worse, many of the cards were Boston Red Sox cards, which I had mistakenly grabbed out of the shoe box.

Shinebottom said, "I'm up eighty. Wait. Eighty-two."

Pearlman said, "I'm up forty-five."

Franky DiLorenzo said, "Stop counting your cards and flip already."

I said to Stev, "I better quit."

Stev said, "What for?"

"I'm down a lot. I only got a couple cards left."

Franky DiLorenzo lit a cigarette and held the smoke in his lungs for approximately ten seconds. Then he made a fish mouth and released perfect circles that floated into the air and slowly dissolved into nothing. He said, "You can't quit. That's bush league. You gotta give us a chance to win some cards."

Scully said, "Yeah. Don't be a fag."

I said, "I haven't won anything."

Franky DiLorenzo said, "Fuck you, you haven't."

Pearlman said, "He hasn't. He lost every pot."

Stev counted out some baseball cards. He said, "Here's twenty-five cards. Give them back to me later."

Shinebottom flipped a card across the garage.

I went next, and topped it.

Pearlman said, "Unbelievable. He topped it. A single card and he topped it. I've never seen that before. That's one for the record books."

Shinebottom laughed and handed me a card and said, "Here. Take this. You just doubled your winnings."

Everyone laughed.

I went across the garage and retrieved the two cards and came back.

Shinebottom said, "Winner starts. Go."

I flipped a card, and the big game began.

One by one, we flipped and missed, throw after throw. It didn't take long. The cards spread like a rash, multiplying across the floor. Everyone got excited. Everyone yelled after each miss. In his haste, Franky DiLorenzo stopped making practice motions. Pearlman used every waxed card he had. The cards landed on bare concrete, drawn like magnets. You hoped the player before you missed, because there was no way, absolutely no way, that you would get another chance. The pot could not grow any bigger.

But somehow it did.

Shinebottom said, "It's unbelievable."

Pearlman said, "It's the biggest pot I've ever seen. There must be two hundred cards."

Stev missed.

Pearlman missed.

Franky DiLorenzo missed.

Shinebottom missed.

It was my turn.

The garage floor looked like a giant jigsaw puzzle with only a couple pieces missing.

Pearlman took off his glasses, shined them against his shirt, put them back on his nose and said, "This is it. There's no way he can miss."

Scully said, "He'll miss. He better miss. It's my turn next."

I flipped. The card flew across the garage and hit the opposite wall and fluttered end over end to the floor.

"Topsy," I said.

Everyone rushed across the garage to look.

Pearlman said, "Watch the cards. Watch where you're stepping."

Shinebottom said, "It's close. But not a topsy."

I said, "Of course it's a topsy."

Scully said, "Topsy my ass."

Shinebottom said, "It didn't break the border. It's got to break the border."

Shinebottom got down on his hands and knees and examined the cards. I got down next to him. My card was lying across the bottom corner of another card. I said, "Look. It's a half inch on top of the card. And it's touching the border. See?"

Shinebottom said, "It has to break the plane. Not touch."

I said, "What plane?"

"The line. It has to cross the border line around the player's picture to be a topsy."

"You're making up rules just because you don't want me to win."

"Bullshit. Those are the rules. We always go by the rules."

"A topsy is a topsy. There's no such rule."

Scully said, "The fuck there isn't. Ask Pearlman. Pearlman knows the rules."

We looked at Pearlman.

Pearlman said, "I'm not saying anything either way."

Scully said, "What does that mean?"

"It means I'm neutral."

"He's neutral. That's fucking great. That solves everything."

Shinebottom said, "Ask Mandelbaum then. He's your friend. You can trust what he says. Right?"

I said, "Sure. Tell 'em, Stev."

Scully said, "Stev? Why do you call him Stev? That's stupid."

I said, "It's his name."

Scully said, "Is that your name, Mandelbaum? Is your name Stev? Is that what they call you at school?"

Stev said, "No."

"Your name's Steven, right? Steven Fucking Mandelbaum."

"Yeah. I guess."

"Steven," said Scully. "Even Steven."

Shinebottom said, "Forget about his stupid name. What about the rules?"

Everyone looked at Stev. Stev blinked several times, like he had something stuck in his eye.

Shinebottom said, "Well?"

Stev said, "I don't know."

Scully said, "Don't know what? What the fuck don't you know? Are you neutral like Pearlman? Is that what you're fucking saying, you little twerp?"

Stev said, "No."

"Well then?"

"Maybe he should take it over."

"No way. There's no takeovers. It's either a topsy or not. What's your vote?"

Stev looked down. He said, "Not, I guess."

Shinebottom said, "Good. That settles it."

Scully said, "Stand back, suckers. It's my turn."

I looked at Stev as Scully crossed the garage. Stev smiled his liar's smile and looked at me and quickly looked away.

Scully said, "Eat shit," and flipped.

No one said anything when the card landed. I had one card left in my hand. The card was Bill Freehan. I turned the card over and looked at Bill Freehan's lifetime batting statistics but I could not read the numbers. I saw the numbers clearly but they did not make sense. It was like trying to read a book reflected in a mirror.

We walked home. Stev was walking behind me. I heard his sneakers flapping on the grass and crunching twigs. After a while he said, "Hey." I turned around.

He said, "You don't have to give back those cards."

I said, "What cards?"

"The twenty-five I loaned you."

"I lost them. They're gone. How can I give them back?"

"I meant other cards. You don't have to replace them even though I loaned them to you."

We came to the brook. I crossed to the other side. Instead of crossing, Stev bent over and crept along the opposite bank.

I said, "Are you coming?"

"Wait a minute."

Stev stood perfectly still. Then he jumped into the brook and lunged forward, making a splash, and grabbed a frog out of the shallow water.

I said, "How come you said that?"

"What?"

"You know."

Stev didn't look at me. He looked at the frog in his hand, which he raised over his head, like the Olympic torch. The frog puffed out his neck and squirmed and bulged his eyes. Stev said, "Those guys got different rules."

"They made it up to cheat me."

"I know."

"I should've won the big pot. I should've gotten all my cards back plus more."

"I know."

"So why didn't you tell them?"

"Watch. Watch this," said Stev, and he reared back and hurled the frog into the sky. The frog went up, legs kicking, climbing sunward like the air force jet in *High Flight*, up the long delirious burning blue to hover high in the sunlit silence. The frog did not hover long. The frog did not touch the face of God. The frog came down with a splat on top of a big rock and oozed red and blue guts.

Stev said, "Whoa. What a shot. Did you see that? Did you see it?"

I said, "I saw it."

"Wasn't that cool?"

I shrugged.

Stev said, "It's just a frog. What do you care about a frog?"

"It's stupid."

"You're just mad because you lost all your cards."

"They tricked me."

"They always trick kids. They like doing that."

"So why did we go there?"

"Why not? It's just a stupid game. What else do you wanna do?"

I started walking toward home.

Stev said, "Wait up. I want to catch one more frog."

I didn't wait, and Stev didn't catch up.

41.
CROWS

Black was the only color of crow. There was no such thing as a brown crow or a red crow. The crow was the first bird in the morning to open its beak and shriek. The crow was loud. The crow did not make a musical, birdlike noise. There was nothing you could do to kill a crow. The crow was harder to kill than a groundhog. The crow was too smart and flew too high. The crow saw you coming at him with a slingshot and bolted before you could release. A BB gun could perhaps kill a crow but we did not own a BB gun. A bow and arrow could perhaps kill a crow but we did not own a bow and arrow.

The crows attacked the cherry tree in the morning. I heard a tremendous squawking and looked out the window. There were at least ten crows sitting on the branches, pecking, and more on the grass, strutting back and forth, plucking the cherries that had fallen. I ran outside and grabbed a handful of white pebbles from the garden and threw the pebbles at the crows. The crows flapped their wings and flew away without injury.

The cherry tree was bald.

42.
HOT AIR

The Dad wheeled into the driveway in the Mark IV. I was sitting in the kitchen, waiting for the mailman, when I saw his car. I stood and watched from the window as he got out of the car and straightened his belt. His hair was combed to the side, pasted down with Brylcreem. He was wearing a white button-down shirt, tucked neatly into his bright yellow slacks. He walked up the steps and came into the kitchen.

He said, "Where's your mother?"

I said, "Upstairs."

"Go get her. Tell her I'm here."

The Mom called from the top of the stairs, "There's no need for that. What do you want?"

The Dad turned toward the stairs. He said, "I got something to show you."

"You're not allowed to come here. I could call the police."

"Five minutes is all I'm asking. You owe me that much."

"I don't owe you anything."

"Just take a look at what I brought."

The Mom came down the stairs. She was wearing her housecoat, and she pulled it tightly around herself and said, "Go outside, Timmy."

The Dad said, "He can stay right here. I want him to see this too."

The Mom said, "See what, for God's sake? What's the big mystery?"

The Dad took a piece of paper out of his back pocket and laid it on the kitchen table. "What does that say?"

The Mom and I leaned over the piece of paper. The piece of paper was a bank check that said "Fifty thousand dollars." It was made out to The Mom.

The Dad said, "That's the first of two. That's your money, no matter what. That's for you and the kids. Do anything you like with it. I don't want anyone saying I don't take care of my family."

"What did you do? Take a second mortgage on this house?"

"I didn't take any second mortgage. What gives you that idea?"

"Because if you did, so help me."

"We sold the Cott Building. Sal and I got two hundred grand for it. Twice what it's worth."

"You sold it? The only property you own worth anything?"

"That's right. And it was the smart thing to do. Locust Street is going to the dogs. That whole side of town will be a slum within a couple of years."

The Mom adjusted her housecoat. She said, "What about income? Where will the money come from when this runs out?"

"Sal and I got that all planned out. We got six or seven prime lots picked out in Avon. We're going to build private homes on spec. There's a fortune to be made. Joe Bologna's in on it too."

"Another Italian."

"He's the best real estate developer in the state."

"I'm sure that's an exaggeration."

"You should see his house in Farmington. Like a palace. Timmy's seen it. Tell her."

I said, "It's got columns out front. We drove him home one day when he drank too many beers at the club and couldn't stand up straight."

The Mom picked up the check and examined it and placed it back on the table. She said, "So you think you can just buy us off? Clear your conscience?"

"You got it wrong," said The Dad. "I want to make it up to you and the kids. This is my house and my family."

"That's a lot of hot air."

"Look at that check. Is that hot air?"

The Mom said, "How do I know you won't be out gallivanting on the golf course or worse every time I turn my back?"

The Dad said, "You have my word."

"What good is that? I don't trust you as far as I can throw you."

"You think I like living out of a suitcase? Sleeping on a couch?"

"What do I care what you like or don't like? My concern is for the children."

"That's what I'm saying, for Christsake. They got to have what's best. I don't want any goddamn court order coming between me and my family."

The Mom picked up the check and put it into the pocket of her housecoat. She said, "I've heard just about enough hot air for one day. Your five minutes are up."

She turned and went up the stairs and closed the door to her bedroom.

The Dad winked at me. He took a pack of baseball cards out of his back pocket and slid it across the table. "Here's to you, jellybean," he said.

43.
TROPHY

Albert came home from camp.

We went up to our room and unpacked his trunk. He took out two lamps that he made in arts and crafts. One lamp was made out of a Schweppes ginger ale can and the other was made out of a Coca-Cola can. He handed me the Coca-Cola lamp and said, "This one's yours. It's not a birthday present or anything. It's just something I made in arts and crafts."

I examined the lamp. The Coca-Cola can was glued to a wooden base with a metal pole sticking through it. The electrical cord went through the bottom of the wooden base into the can and out the top, where the lightbulb fixture was attached to the metal pole. I plugged the cord into the wall and pushed the switch. The lightbulb came on.

Albert said, "You can put it on top of your desk and write your lists and stuff."

"Adequate," I said. "Very adequate."

"They wouldn't let me make one out of a beer can. I asked but they said no."

"What else did you do?"

"Sailing. Tennis. All that stuff."

"What happened at night? Did you make out with girls?"

"At night the counselors played guitar at sing-alongs. 'Puff the Magic Dragon' and 'Kumbaya' and queer stuff like that."

"Mom wants me to go next year."

"The worst part was they play reveille on a trumpet over a loudspeaker at six in the morning and everyone has to get out of bed or the counselors will yell at you and throw cold water on you. And they make you wear white clothes for Sunday dinner and line up and salute the flag."

"What about the girls?"

"The girls were in the girls' camp about a mile down the beach. We only saw them a couple times. We met them once at a hot dog place called Cobies and one girl ate so many ice cream sundaes she threw up in the parking lot like a hose. All over her T-shirt and sneakers."

Albert unpacked his camp clothes, which said "Camp Monomoy" across the front, and put them into the dresser. He took out the trophies he'd won and lined them up on top of the bookcase. The largest trophy was shaped like a man holding a cup over his head with both hands.

I reached into my pocket and took out the blue marble and dropped it into the trophy cup. The blue marble rattled to a stop and reflected on the sides of the cup, which were gold.

I said, "You see this marble? Monty had it inside him. He barfed it up the day before he got run over."

"Really?"

"Yup."

"You saw the whole thing, huh?"

"Yeah," I said. "The tire rolled over his stomach."

"What did the cop say?"

" 'Goddamnit. Goddamnit.' Stuff like that. He was driving too fast."

"What a jerk."

"Yeah."

"It's going to be lonely without Monty," said Albert.

"I know."

"We'll keep the marble in the trophy."

"Okay."

"Don't lose it."

"I won't."

We went across the street and rang Stev's doorbell. Approximately thirty seconds later The Myra opened the front door wearing a tight, fuzzy sweater. She was smoking a cigarette and holding a glass in her hand containing brown liquid that looked like Seagrams V.O.

I said, "Is Stev home?"

She said, "How did I know you were going to ask that question?"

"I don't know."

"Because it's the same question you always ask. No, he's not home."

"Where is he?"

"He's out with someone named Shinebomb who drove into the driveway in a big black Buick. A little boy, driving such a big car, as big as a hearse. They went to The Lodge."

"You mean Shinebottom?"

"What did I say?"

"Shinebomb."

"What's the difference?"

"It's his name. Shinebottom. There's no such person as Shinebomb."

The Myra looked at me and exhaled a cloud of smoke, which slowly wafted in my direction and encircled me. She said, "Do you have a girlfriend yet?"

"No. Why?"

"Because someday you will and you'll think about her instead of all the things you think about now."

"What do you mean?"

"It doesn't matter what the boy's name is. You know who I'm talking about. You don't have to be so precise about everything. If you had a girlfriend you wouldn't be so precise."

"You mean precious?"

"Did I say precious?"

"That's the word you usually call me. Precious."

"I'm calling you precise. That's a different word. Do you know what it means? It means asking the questions you ask. That's being precise. It means writing things down in notebooks when you should be outside doing something else. It means always calling things by their exact names."

"All I told you was the kid's name. Shinebottom. What does that have to do with liking girls?"

"Absolutely nothing. But someday you'll know what I mean."

The Myra took a sip from her drink.

She said, "Hello, Albert."

Albert said, "Hello, Mrs. Mandelbaum."

"How was camp?"

"Good."

"Good," said The Myra, and she went inside and closed the door.

Albert said, "Nice mammaries."

"Pointy," said I.

"Was that the glass?"

"Might have been. Or one just like it."

"All around the rim, huh?"

"Everywhere," said I.

Albert took off his baseball hat and scratched his head. He said, "I can't believe Stev went to The Lodge with Shinebottom."

"It's his new thing. He thinks he's cool 'cause he hangs around with older guys."

"Shinebottom's a dickhead."

"No kidding."

"It's practically his title. Shinebottom, dickhead."

We walked into the middle of the street and looked around. The street was quiet. The sun was bright and shining high overhead. A lawn mower buzzed a few backyards away, the sound rising and fading as someone pushed it closer, then farther away.

Albert said, "Where is everyone?"

"Like who?"

"Like everyone."

"I don't know. Gone somewhere, I guess."

"Where's Tiger?"

"Tiger won't come out. Ever since the time we held him down and you farted on him."

"Really?"

"He won't say a word. Won't even look at me. He runs the other way when he sees me."

"Let's go get him."

"I can't. His mother told me not to knock on the door anymore."

"I'll knock."

Albert and I walked to Tiger's house. He went up the driveway and knocked, and almost instantly Tiger opened the door.

Albert said, "Hi, Tiger."

Tiger looked at Albert. Then he looked at me, standing behind Albert. Then he took one step backward and slowly closed the door. A moment later came the sound of the lock being locked.

I said, "See what I mean?"

Albert banged on the door with his fist. You could hear the door rattling and the metal mail flap clanking back and forth. Albert said, "Come out, Tiger. Come out and play. Here, Tiger. Here, Tiger Tiger Tiger. Where are you, Tiger?"

I said, "He's not coming out."

Albert said, "He'll break down. No one can keep up the silent treatment for long."

I said, "You don't know Tiger. He sets his mind on something and that's it."

We walked into the street and turned toward the Cosgroves' house.

"Look at all that crap," said Albert.

There were piles of junk on the Cosgroves' lawn, lined up alongside the street. There was a pyramid pile of black garbage bags. There were boxes of old magazines, such as *Life* and *National Geographic* and *Redbook* and *Good Housekeeping,* damp and curling at the corners. There was a fan with rusty blades. A torn lamp shade. A mattress with the stuffing coming out and a big brown stain in the middle. A box of *World Book* encyclopedias. A box of canceled checks. A batch of curtain rods, tied together with a string. A door with broken slats. A cracked mirror. An old TV, the antenna bent in half. A mound of brown shopping bags with a brick sitting on top of them. Mildewed books, such as *Jaws, Jonathan Livingston Seagull, Love Story* and *The Winds of War.* A metal pail filled with forks, knives, spoons, wooden spoons, bottle openers, rolling pins, spatulas. A bean bag, torn in the side, spilling white beads. There were boxes of loose papers, some scattered on the grass.

I picked up an envelope and took out the letter from inside. The letter read:

Dear Reader:

Thank you for your interest in Tempo Books. You will find that our spring 1972 catalogue has much to offer. New this season is *Barons of the Bullpen* by Dan Schlossberg. In recent history no team has won a pennant or a series without a crackerjack relief pitcher. Here is the first book on the Firemen of Baseball since World War II, Mike Marshall, Roy Face, Hoyt Wilhelm, Jim Konstanty and many more. $1.25.

Albert handed me Mik Cosgrove's report card from the seventh grade. The highest mark was a B-minus in math. The other grades were C's and D's. The teacher wrote, "Michael is easily distracted. If he learns to concentrate his energies he will be a better student."

"What a dummy," I said.

Albert took the report card and scrunched it into a ball and tossed it onto the garbage pile.

"Hey," I said. "Look at this."

I plucked Mik Cosgrove's catcher's mitt out of a garbage can. The web had a couple strands missing but otherwise it was in good condition. Mik Cosgrove was the only kid in the neighborhood with a catcher's mitt. No one wanted to play catcher except for Mik Cosgrove. Mik Cosgrove liked playing catcher. Like most fat kids, Mik Cosgrove was no good at any position except catcher. He didn't have to run. He didn't have to chase grounders or pop-ups or fly balls. He just squatted behind the plate and smacked his fist into his mitt and said, "Hey batter batter batter he's no batter he's no batter batter batter swing batter batter swing."

I said, "Do you think we should take it?"

Albert stuck his hand into the catcher's mitt and punched the pocket a few times. He said, "Why not? Who's going to know?"

"Maybe they'll come back."

"They're not coming back. They're gone for good."

"I wonder why he left his catcher's mitt."

"Who knows," said Albert.

We looked through the rest of the trash. Albert found twelve *Playboys* and a framed black-and-white picture of the USS *Constitution* firing its cannons. I found a miniature wooden elephant. We took the stuff and headed home, our arms full.

44.
SILENT TREATMENT

The Dad moved back into his room.

I came home from the center of town one afternoon, and there he was, making his bed. The Mom explained that he was staying with us on a trial basis. "I might change my mind tomorrow," she said.

The Dad went around the house, like always, smoking in the bathroom, watching TV in the den, but The Mom refused to talk to him. At mealtime we sat down at the kitchen table and passed the food back and forth and talked, except The Mom wouldn't answer The Dad. If he asked for the green beans, she would look the other way and say, "Daphne, where did you get that blouse? It's an exquisite shade of yellow." Or she would turn to me and say something like "Tell your father to wash his dirty hands. I won't sit down to the dinner table with someone with dirty hands."

Meanwhile The Dad was on his best behavior. He painted the garage, trimmed the hedges, replaced the broken slats under the back porch and pulled the weeds from the garden. He did these things without being asked. You'd hear him go out the screen door, which squeaked and slammed, then a few moments later you'd hear the sound of digging or mowing or sawing. The Mom would stop at the kitchen window and watch him. Once I heard her say to herself, "This place is finally starting to look presentable."

We had two TVs, the RCA color console and the Magnavox twelve-inch black-and-white. The Magnavox was The Mom's TV, located on the kitchen counter for soap opera viewing in the afternoons while she cooked and cleaned. The Magnavox got one channel, a blurry version of CBS. The only way to get a clear picture was to hold the antenna in your hand while you watched.

As part of the Silent Treatment, The Mom refused to watch TV in the den with The Dad. So each night she carried the Magnavox up to her bedroom and closed the door and watched the shows she liked to watch, such as *The Brady Bunch* and *The Waltons.* Sometimes Daphne watched along with her. They'd sit side by side on the bed, propped up against some pillows.

One night, when *Sonny and Cher* came on, The Dad said to me, "Go upstairs and ask your mother if she wants to watch."

I said, "Why?"

The Dad said, "She likes this show. No sense in her watching that little screen. She'll give herself eyestrain that way."

I said, "Okay," and went upstairs.

The Mom and Daphne were sitting up in bed, smiling, watching TV. Sonny and Cher were teasing each other, which was what they did every week at the start of the show. Neither Daphne nor The Mom was holding on to the antenna, so the screen was hazy like a snowstorm, and every couple of seconds Sonny and Cher would rise like people on an elevator to the top of the screen, only to be replaced by identical versions of themselves.

I grabbed the antenna, and the picture became clear.

Daphne said, "That's better. Stay like that."

I said, "Dad wants to know if you want to watch TV in the den."

The Mom said, "Tell your father we're perfectly happy where we are."

"He said you'll get eyestrain."

"You tell him not to worry about us. Right, Daphne?"

Daphne said, "Actually my eyes are getting a little sore."

The Mom said, "I prefer eyestrain to sitting in the same room with that man."

"Why?"

"Why? Because I can't stand the sight of him, that's why."

I said, "You better hold the antenna at least."

I handed the antenna to Daphne and went back downstairs.

The Dad said, "Well?"

I shook my head.

He said, "Just as well. I hate that skinny Cher. Let's see what else is on," and he got up and changed the channel.

45.
FIRE AND WATER

The Dad said, "Phew. It's hot. I'm sweating bullets here."

He and I were sweeping the driveway. We swept up crab apples and pine needles and fallen leaves and stray paper and dirt. The Mom insisted that we keep a clean driveway. A spotless driveway was very important to The Mom. She would look out the front window and say, "Who put that junk in the driveway? Go out there and clean that up. What will the neighbors think of us, looking like some Front Street hovel." She always used those three words, "Front Street hovel," to describe any place that looked dirty or sloppy or low-class. Front Street was the neighborhood in the City of Hartford where The Dad grew up in the 1920s. Front Street was where the Italians and Irish and other immigrants used to live in tenement houses, which no longer existed. All the tenement houses were torn down to make room for office buildings made out of blue glass and a place called Constitution Plaza, where people went once per year to watch Christmas lights. The Mom learned about Front Street from black-and-white pictures in The Dad's photo album. In the pictures, everyone hung their laundry out the windows and grew tomato plants in planters on balconies and leaned out of upper-story windows when it got hot. In the pictures, men wearing hats and short-sleeved shirts and black pants stood with their arms folded across their chests, looking directly at the camera without smiling. Beneath each picture The Dad had written the person's name. The names were: Uncle Rock, Cousin Vito, Pop Kelly, Tot Grady, Mushy Cohen, Label Cohen. The Mom called the people in the pictures "peasants." She would point to a picture and say, "Look at this peasant. Poor uneducated soul. He looks mildly retarded." The Dad said, "That's Uncle George. He was a stonemason. He was as bald as a bat and he had a flap of skin on the top of his head that stuck up like a thumb. Grandpop called it his doorbell. We'd sneak up behind

Uncle George and push down the flap and say, 'Bing Bong,' and Uncle George would say, 'No one's a home, you come a back later.' " Uncle George was dead. Uncle Rock was dead. Most of the people in The Dad's photo album were dead. The Mom talked about Front Street as if it still existed, but Front Street was no place you could go. It was only a memory in The Dad's photo album.

After sweeping up, we watered down the driveway with the garden hose. Then we sat in the shade of the crab apple tree admiring our work.

The Dad said, "I'm not like your mother. I don't give a damn what the neighbors think. I just like a job done right."

I said, "What job?"

"Any job. That's one of the things your grandfather always said. If you're going to do a job, do it right."

"What else did he say?"

"Fire and water, fire and water."

"What does that mean?"

"It means beware the power of nature. Man's nothing compared to nature."

I said, "Fire and water, fire and water."

"That's right. Never forget it. You can drown in a coffee cup. Takes less than a minute."

"How can you fit your head inside a coffee cup?"

"You know what I mean. Two inches of water, that's all it takes."

"What else did Grandpop say?"

"He said, Expect the unexpected."

"How can you expect something that's unexpected? That doesn't make sense."

"It makes sense if you think different than the next guy. Everyone thinks one way, you think the other."

"Then you'd be a weirdo like Mik Cosgrove."

"You're missing the point. You have to be ready. You have to be on guard at all times. That's what it means."

I said, "Stev has a lot of rules like that. He'll say, 'Rule number one. Never use the word "tranny." ' Or, 'Rule number one. Never follow the purser.' "

"That's nonsense," said The Dad.

"It's a line from a movie."

"I'm telling you things Grandpop learned over the course of a lifetime. He was a smart man. He came to this country without a penny and died in a big house on Prospect Avenue. How many people can say that?"

"I don't know."

"You want to hear more?"

"Sure."

"Friends come and go. But your family's forever."

"I've heard that one before."

"Grandpop said that all the time. That's the most important rule. That's rule number one."

A moving truck rumbled up the street and backed into the Cosgroves' driveway. Two men wearing blue overalls got out of the truck and went into the house. A few minutes later they came out, carrying pieces of furniture, which they loaded into the back of the truck. They took the coffee table. They took the bar stools. They took the world's longest white vinyl couch, broken up into three sections. They took mattresses and bed frames and box springs and chairs and tables and lamps and dressers and framed pictures and rolled-up rugs and bookcases and a birdcage and curtains and mirrors and a kitchen table and a stereo console and a television and a stuffed owl and an artificial Christmas tree and an upright piano. They took box after box, maybe fifty boxes. It didn't take long. The movers worked fast.

The Dad said, "Look at those sons of bitches work. On a day as hot as this."

The movers slammed the furniture and boxes into the back of the truck. They made a lot of noise. They were wearing work gloves and heavy boots. Their footsteps reverberated when they walked into the back of the truck, making a metal clang. It seemed impossible that they could fit any more furniture or boxes into the back of the truck. But they kept going in and out of the house, getting more.

The Dad said, "You see all that? All those chairs and tables? That's just stuff. Something you pack up and take away. It doesn't mean anything. That's what Grandpop meant."

I said, "About what?"

"About family. Everything else can be replaced. But not your family. If you lose your family, that's the end of you. *Basta.*"

"What does *basta* mean?"

"*Basta* means the end. Finished."

"Oh."

"You remember that."

"What?"

"What I just said. What Grandpop said. Your mother, Albert, Daphne and me, that's your family. That's forever."

"Don't be queer, Dad."

"I'm serious. You remember that."

Finally the movers loaded the last box. They pulled down the back door of the truck like a window shade and slammed the bolt into place. They wiped their gloves off and climbed into the front of the truck. Then they started the engine, rumbled out of the Cosgroves' driveway and drove down the street.

46.
EVEL KNIEVEL

The Evel Knievel ramp was Albert's idea. He got the idea watching TV footage of Evel Knievel's famous motorcycle jumps. Albert had an Evel Knievel lunch box and thermos. I had an Evel Knievel action figure manufactured by the Ideal Toy Company. We knew everything about Evel Knievel, whose real name was Robert Craig Knievel, born in Butte, Montana. Evel Knievel jumped his motorcycle over all kinds of stuff. He jumped over a rattlesnake pit, a water tank filled with man-eating sharks, a row of double-decker buses. In Las Vegas, Nevada, he jumped over the fountain at Caesar's Palace and crashed on the landing ramp and broke every bone in his body and didn't wake up for a month. The best part about watching Evel Knievel was the moment he went airborne. At that moment, anything was possible. He might just do it. He might just clear the double-decker buses or cars or man-eating sharks and soar to the other side, touching down safely. You cheered for him to make it but secretly hoped for and simultaneously dreaded the coming crash, when the motorcycle landed on the handlebars and flipped over and Evel Knievel went twisting through the air like a rag doll, bouncing and skidding on the pavement, rebreaking every bone in his body.

Evel Knievel was everywhere, on every newspaper, magazine cover and TV show. The networks played footage of his old jumps, over and over. They played the movie, *Evel Knievel,* starring George Hamilton as Evel Knievel and costarring Vic Tayback, Sue Lyon, Dub Taylor and Cheryl Rainbeaux Smith, filmed on location in Butte, Montana, and told in a series of flashbacks. The TV stations replayed the movie in anticipation of the big jump.

The big jump was Sunday, September 8, 1974. Every person in the United States of America was waiting for it. Tomorrow, Evel Knievel would attempt to make history by jumping over the Snake River

Canyon in his Skycycle X-2 rocket. Evel Knievel had originally intended to jump over the Grand Canyon but certain unnamed United States government officials refused to grant permission for him to do so because there was a high likelihood that he would kill himself trying. Normal TV programs, like the *Wide World of Sports*, were not allowed to telecast the big jump. The big jump would be available only on closed-circuit TV. Closed-circuit TV was special TV that played on a big screen in local auditoriums, where they charged you money to get in. I had never seen closed-circuit TV because the price was too steep. The Dad always refused to pay. But in addition to being the day of the big jump, September 8, 1974, was my birthday. For my birthday, I had asked for two tickets, one for Albert and one for me, to watch Evel Knievel jump the Snake River Canyon on closed-circuit TV.

The Mom said, "Wouldn't you rather have some nice new clothes that you can wear to school on Monday?"

"No," said I. "I wouldn't rather have some nice new clothes to wear to school on Monday. I don't care about school on Monday. I want to watch the big jump."

"Well, you're getting them anyway. We're going to Caldor later today. If you want tickets to the movie, you'll have to ask your father."

"It's not a movie, Mom. It's real. It's Evel Knievel on live TV."

"I never liked that man. He's uncouth."

"But it's my birthday. Dad promised."

"Then you'll have to talk to him, won't you?"

Albert and I went outside and began working on the Evel Knievel ramp. We took the following items out of the garage: cement blocks, a crowbar, a yardstick and some paint cans. We split the old Ping-Pong table in half and placed it against two cement blocks. The old Ping-Pong table was the takeoff ramp. The takeoff ramp was not high enough to jump a garbage can, which was what we wanted to do, so we lined up two paint cans instead. Albert got on the Banana and pedaled to full speed with his knees pumping high and yelled, "Viva Knievel," and wheeled onto the takeoff ramp, which immediately collapsed.

The Dad came outside and said, "What's going on? What's all that junk?"

We said, "We're making a takeoff ramp."

"A what?"

"A takeoff ramp, like Evel Knievel. To jump our bikes."

"That won't work. I'll show you how to do it. Put that junk back in the garage before your mother sees."

The Dad went around the side of the house and came back approximately two minutes later with a sawhorse under one arm and a wooden door under the other. He arranged the sawhorse in the middle of the driveway, leaned the door against the sawhorse and banged four nails at an angle through the door into the sawhorse, four bangs per nail, bang bang bang bang.

"Now there's a ramp," he said.

We began with one garbage can.

I went first. I hopped on the World's Greatest Bicycle otherwise known as the Chopper otherwise known as the Green Machine. I licked my index finger and tested the wind, then gave the thumbs-up signal. I accelerated to full speed and nearly chickened out approaching the ramp, which looked high, but instead pedaled harder and went up the takeoff ramp and flew in dead silence over the garbage can for approximately one second that seemed a lot longer and touched down in a perfect two-wheel landing and skidded to a stop in a skid shaped like a fishhook, so that I ended up pointing back toward where I started from.

Albert said, "Cool."

The Dad said, "Better put on the batting helmet if you're going to do that."

"What for?"

"Trust me. Get the hockey gloves and knee pads and elbow pads too."

The Dad was right. The batting helmet and hockey pads were necessary equipment. Albert wiped out on his first attempt at two garbage cans and landed on his elbows and knees. He did not suffer injuries. The pads cushioned the fall. He got to his feet and picked up the Banana and straightened out the front wheel and got back on the seat and tried again and made the jump successfully. Wearing the batting helmet and hockey pads, you felt twenty pounds heavier but you could wipe out with impunity. You were close to being invincible. Albert cleared two garbage cans twice. I cleared two garbage cans once.

Franky DiLorenzo walked into the driveway and looked at the Evel Knievel ramp and said, "I can do four cans."

We said, "Two's the record."

Franky DiLorenzo said, "Four. Get the cans. I'll show you how it's done."

Albert and I carried the garbage cans out of the garage and lined them in a row in front of the ramp. We stepped back and studied the situation. Four garbage cans looked insurmountable. Four garbage cans looked farther than the Snake River Canyon.

Franky DiLorenzo said, "Give me your bike."

I said, "No way."

"Why not?"

"It's too far. You're going to crash."

Albert said, "You can have mine. I wiped out twice already. The Banana is indestructible."

I said, "You better put on the hockey pads."

Franky DiLorenzo said, "What for?"

"You're not going to make it."

"You think so, huh?"

"I know so."

"Fat chance," said Franky DiLorenzo.

He got on the Banana and began riding around the driveway, popping wheelies. As he warmed up, I pretended to be Frank Gifford. I held my fist in front of my face like a microphone and said,"Spanning the globe to bring you the constant variety of sport. The thrill of victory and the agony of defeat. The human drama of athletic competition. This is ABC's *Wide*

World of Sports. Hi, I'm Frank Gifford and I have bad breath. We're here today in scenic Snake River, Connecticut, to witness history. We're here to see Evel DiLorenzo, world-renowned daredevil and all-around A-hole extraordinaire, go for the world record. The world record is two garbage cans. Evel DiLorenzo is going for four. That's right, folks. You heard right. Four garbage cans. Here he comes now, the man of the hour. Can we have a word, Evel? Can you tell us your secret?"

Franky DiLorenzo said, "Fuck you."

I said, "The ambulance is standing by. The hospitals are on full alert. The Hells Angels are holding back the crowd. The crowd is going crazy. It's pandemonium here in Snake River, Connecticut. Wait. He's beginning his final approach. A hush comes over the crowd. Here he comes. He's on his way."

To attain the proper speed, Franky DiLorenzo started pedaling from the far end of Stev's driveway. He picked up speed and crossed the road and rolled onto our driveway with his knees pumping furiously and steadied himself before zooming up the ramp, which made a sound like paper being ripped, and went airborne and yelled, "Aaaagh," and he almost made it. He cleared three garbage cans but the fourth was too far. The Banana came down like a javelin inside the fourth garbage can, sending Franky DiLorenzo over the handlebars. He landed forearm-first on the driveway and skidded onto the lawn.

Franky DiLorenzo groveled on the grass and said, "Ow. My arm. I broke my fucking arm."

I said, "I told you so."

"Ow. Ow. I can't feel my arm."

"It's probably fractured."

"Go tell my mother. Quick."

"Not me."

"Do it or I'll kick your ass."

I ran down the street and turned up the DiLorenzos' pathway and rang the doorbell. I waited approximately thirty seconds. Then Mrs. DiLorenzo opened the door and said, "Yes?"

I said, "Franky fell off the bike and hurt himself. He wants you to come. He's this way."

"Oh my," said Mrs. DiLorenzo.

She followed me down the pathway. We took one step into the street and saw Franky DiLorenzo limping toward us, holding his arm, which was bloody and hanging down at a strange angle. At least one layer of skin was burned away from his forearm.

Mrs. DiLorenzo said, "Franky, are you hurt?"

Franky DiLorenzo said, "Nah."

"That's a terrible scrape. Let me see."

"It's all right. I hit my funny bone, that's all."

"You should have worn the pads," I said. "Now you got a broken arm."

"It's not broken," he said. "It's fine."

Mrs. DiLorenzo said, "Are you sure, Franky? It looks twisted."

"It felt tingly for a minute, but now it's better."

I said, "Why don't you let go of your arm if it's not broken? Why are you holding it like that?"

Franky DiLorenzo said, "It's sore, that's why."

Mrs. DiLorenzo said, "Can I touch it, Franky? Just for a second?"

"Not now. I wanna let it sit for a minute."

Mrs. DiLorenzo said, "I'll be gentle, Franky. I won't hurt you."

Franky DiLorenzo tried to lift his arm but winced and brought it closer to his chest instead.

I said, "You better go to the doctor. Your arm's busted."

Franky DiLorenzo said, "Busted, my ass."

Mrs. DiLorenzo said, "Don't get upset, Franky. Come into the house. I'll take care of you. We'll look at it together."

"Okay."

"Come, Franky."

"I'm coming, Mom."

Franky DiLorenzo went up the pathway, cradling his broken arm, and Mrs. DiLorenzo followed him into the house.

47.
SHOPPING SPREE

The Mom and I went to the Youth Center, located in the center of town, which sold every type of clothing you could possibly wear. We went to the boys' department. The Mom always picked out clothes for me that were at least one size too small. Most of my clothes felt like I was being squeezed on my neck or waist or some other body part. The Mom never believed me when I told her my size. She always thought I was smaller. Her mistake was understandable with Albert because Albert grew three inches in one summer. But I did not grow as fast. I changed sizes at a normal pace. Still, The Mom could not keep up. She always picked out clothes for me that were *S* for Small. I did not like clothes in that size. I was five feet two inches tall. I weighed one hundred and five pounds. I was *M* for Medium.

The Mom handed me short-sleeved shirts, windbreakers, corduroy pants, button-down shirts, a blue blazer for dress-up, shoes, sneakers, Fruit of the Looms. Trying on clothes was more exhausting than playing a game of badminton to 500. The Mom made me model each article of clothing except underwear. I went back and forth to the dressing room approximately twenty times. I changed out of the former clothes and put on the new clothes and walked in front of the full-length three-sided mirror and showed The Mom what I looked like and The Mom said, "Oh yes, that's perfect," or she pursed her lips and asked the clerk, "What do you think? Too big?"

Finally, I rebelled and refused to try on any more clothes.

The Mom and I carried three big shopping bags to the car. She said, "Are you excited about your new clothes?"

I said, "No."

"It's your birthday tomorrow. You can't wear anything until then."

"They aren't real presents. I already know what they look like."

"Of course they're real presents. These are expensive clothes. Any boy would be ecstatic to go around dressed like this."

"Who cares?"

"You need clothes for school. You can't show up looking like a ragamuffin."

"All I asked for was two tickets to Evel Knievel. That's all I wanted for my birthday."

"We can't always have everything we want, can we?"

"I didn't ask for stupid clothes. That's not what I wanted."

"You're acting like a brat. One would think you were spoiled rotten." The Mom put the clothes into the backseat. She said, "Meet me back here in a half hour. I've got some more shopping to do."

I nearly complained because I was tired from trying on clothes and wanted to go home, but then I thought better of it, since there was a high probability that any further shopping on her part was probably for my birthday.

I went into The Lodge. The sign on the door said "Big Labor Day Sale." I nodded to Tom Majusiak, who was sitting at the stool behind the counter reading a copy of *Circus* magazine, and he said, "Hey."

I said, "Hey."

"How'd you like the Triumvirate?"

"It was excellent."

The Big D Sound Surveys had arrived. Every week WDRC offered multicolored copies of the survey. There were stacks of them on the counter. I took one copy of each. I took an orange one, a blue one, a yellow one, a red one, a green one, a purple one and a brown one. In addition, I took two copies each of the weekly surveys published by WCCC and WPOP. I compared the surveys. There were slight variations. For instance, WDRC listed "Radar Love" as the number-one song, as compared with "I Shot the Sheriff" on WPOP and WCCC.

Tom Majusiak said, “All those came in today. Take whatever you want.”

“Cool,” I said.

I noticed two kids I knew from school, J.C. and Chuck. They were thumbing through the record bins in the rear of the store. Chuck was second-string running back on last year’s team. J.C. was defensive end. I hadn’t seen them since the end of school. During that time, J.C. had grown approximately two inches. Chuck looked about the same height but his hair was much longer and parted in the middle, rather than neatly on the side.

They came to the counter.

J.C. said, “You ready for football?”

I said, “I guess.”

“We’re gonna have some new cheerleaders this year. That’s what I heard.”

“Really?”

J.C. nodded. “Maybe some will have big mamma tits.”

“Maybe, but I doubt it. It’ll probably be the same old girls.”

Chuck looked at the stack of surveys in my hand. He said, “What’re all those colored papers?”

I said, “Just some stuff I need.”

“What for? To do drawings?”

“Drawings?”

“Yeah. My little sister likes to draw on colored paper. Is that what you do?”

“No. These are lists of the best songs.”

“Lemme see.”

I handed over the stack of surveys. Chuck thumbed through the pages, creasing some of the corners. He said, “What do you need them for?”

“I just want to look at them.”

“Then why are you taking them home?”

J.C. said, “I bet you’re right. I bet he wants to draw on them.”

I said, "I was just looking, okay?" I took the surveys from Chuck and put them back on the counter.

Tom Majusiak looked up. "Don't you want those?"

I shook my head.

Tom Majusiak said, "They're all out of order now."

"Sorry."

He said, "You might as well keep them. We're trying to get rid of them anyway. Every week they dump off that junk. It's a waste of paper. Go ahead. Take them."

I folded the surveys and stuffed them into my back pocket.

Tom Majusiak said, "You buying anything? There's a sale on, you know."

Chuck said, "Nah. You don't even have eight-tracks. All you got is old crap."

Tom Majusiak said, "Records sound better, man."

We opened the door and went outside. The Lodge always smelled like incense. The incense got inside your lungs, a sweet smell. After a while you got dizzy from breathing that air. You didn't know how sweet the air was until you went back outside and breathed the real air and took a deep breath and cleared your lungs.

We stood on the sidewalk in front of the store. J.C. looked from side to side. Then he reached under his shirt and pulled something out. He said, "Check this out." He held up a yo-yo, still in its plastic wrapper.

I said, "Where did you get that?"

J.C. said, "I lifted it off the counter while you were talking to the tall guy. Pretty cool, huh?"

I looked over my shoulder at the plate-glass window of The Lodge but all I could see was our own reflections. J.C. took the yo-yo out of its wrapper. He warmed up with a few tosses, snapping the yo-yo into his palm. He said, "I'll let you try in a minute."

Chuck said, "Don't bother. He doesn't like yo-yos. He likes drawing."

There was a trash can by the side of the road. I took the surveys out of my back pocket and crunched them up and dropped them into the can. The can was full, so I mashed the surveys down into the pile of trash among banana peels and soda bottles and old newspapers.

Chuck said, "Now what are you gonna draw on?"

I said, "Your face."

He said, "What do you mean?"

I said, "It wouldn't be hard. You got a nose as big as a potato."

He said, "Says who?"

"Says me."

"Shut up already."

"You shut up."

J.C. said, "Come on. Let's go."

We went down the sidewalk, side by side. Chuck and I stuffed our hands into our hip pockets. J.C. was Walking the Dog. The yo-yo scooted along the sidewalk next to him.

Outside Plimpton's we came up behind three girls. The girls were wearing tight cutoffs. One of them was Jill Polanski, the prettiest girl in our class. She and the other girls crossed the street, and we followed. They window-shopped and made jokes to each other. Chuck moved his hips from side to side, imitating the way Jill Polanski walked. We followed them to the end of the shopping district and all the way back to The Lodge. They opened the door and went inside, and we did too.

Tom Majusiak said, "You guys back already?"

J.C. said, "Yeah. We forgot to look at something."

We stood near the poster display, flipping posters and watching the girls browsing through the record bins. After a while Jill Polanski said something, and the girls glanced in our direction and broke out laughing.

J.C. said, "They saw us. They know we're watching."

Chuck said, "Go over and say something."

J.C. said, "Like what?"

Chuck said, "I don't know. Anything."

"Why don't you?"

"Why should I? I asked first."

"Gimme a minute. Lemme think."

"You're chicken shit."

"I'm thinking. Shut up while I'm thinking."

The girls glanced at us and giggled.

I said, "Stop talking so loud. They can hear you."

Chuck said, "Oh yeah? Then why don't you do something? You're the big talker. Let's see you do something besides talk."

I said, "Watch and learn."

I put my hands in my pockets and went down the aisle between the record bins. I pulled out a couple of records at random and pretended to study the covers. Then I put the records back in the bin, moved closer to the girls and pulled out another record.

Jill Polanski glanced up and said, "Oh. Hi."

I said, "Hey. What are you doing?"

"Looking at records."

"Cool."

She said, "Do you like David Cassidy?"

"Who?"

"David Cassidy," she said, pointing.

I looked down. I was holding a David Cassidy album. On the cover was a close-up picture of David Cassidy making dreamy eyes. His shirt was unbuttoned, showing chest hair.

She said, "I used to like him when I was a kid."

I said, "I was just looking."

I quickly put the record back in the bin. After approximately one minute of silence, I said, "So do you like music?"

She said, "Oh yes."

I said, "What's your favorite band?"

"I don't know. Lots. I don't have any one favorite."

"I like Elton John. He's the best. He's my all-time favorite."

She said, "I like him too."

I said, "Cool."

One of the girls whispered something to Jill Polanski, and she shook her head. After another minute of silence I said, "So I guess I'll see you in school."

She said, "I guess."

I walked back to the poster display, aware that all three girls were watching me, which made it difficult to move my arms and legs naturally. I walked very stiffly. My arms moved like mechanical arms. It felt like I was a robot and there was someone controlling the way I walked by remote control. Before I reached the poster display, the girls broke out laughing and ran out of the store, making the bell ring.

48.
THE GROUNDHOG DEPARTS

Dogs were barking when The Mom and I returned home.

We went to the rear kitchen window and looked out. Two big dogs were running around the backyard, one black, the other one brown. I had never seen these dogs before. They may have been stray dogs or wild dogs or dogs from some other neighborhood that had gotten loose and ran into our neighborhood looking for something to do. The dogs were chasing an animal. The animal was scurrying around furiously, trying to get away. The animal was short and fat and had a long furry tail.

I said, "Dad, come quick. Alert. Alert."

The Dad said, "What's going on?"

We looked out the window, crowded together.

The Mom said, "What kind of creature is that?"

The Dad said, "It's the groundhog. They got him out in the open. They're trapping him."

The groundhog ran from side to side, weaving and cutting like a punt returner, but the dogs cut him off wherever he went. The dogs worked as a team. They stayed on opposite sides, with the groundhog in the middle. Whenever the groundhog ran one way, one of the dogs cut him off and chased him the other way. The groundhog stumbled and rolled onto his back, kicking his stubby little legs, and the black dog pounced. He picked up the groundhog and growled and swung his snout from side to side and hurled the groundhog into the air. The groundhog fell back to the ground, and before he could get up, the brown dog grabbed him in his mouth and stepped on him. After a while the brown dog tossed the groundhog to the black dog, who barked and snatched him out of the air.

The Dad said, "They're throwing him around like a football."

The Mom said, "It's terrible. I can't watch."

The dogs barked and drooled and growled. They tossed the groundhog back and forth. The groundhog landed on the ground and tried to get up. He moved slower and slower. He crawled. He squirmed. Only his mouth kept moving, his buckteeth reaching for dirt. He lay on the grass, twitching.

The Dad said, "That's it. He can't take any more."

The black dog stood over the groundhog, poking with his paw. The brown dog leaned over and sniffed. The dogs looked at each other, panting. Finally the black dog picked up the groundhog and went trotting proudly into the woods, his mouth full, the groundhog's big tail hanging to the side. The brown dog followed.

The Dad said, "Good thing they carried him off. Otherwise I'd have to bury him."

The Mom said, "I can't say I'm sorry. Look at what he did to our yard. Look at the marks he made. He made holes everywhere. I'm glad they got him. Horrible creature."

49.
BLASTOFF

One of the best things about having a birthday was the night before. You were permitted to stay up until midnight and witness the first minute of your birthday. Albert and Daphne had to go to sleep at their normal bedtimes. Only I, the birthday boy, was allowed to stay up late. The Mom and The Dad stayed up too. We watched TV together, waiting for the tolling of midnight. At midnight you received one present, no more. The real celebration came the next day, along with the rest of your presents.

The eleven o'clock news came on. I yawned.

The Mom said, "Someone's tired."

I said, "That was only one yawn. The first yawn doesn't count."

The newscaster said, "Sources report that tomorrow Gerald Ford will grant a full and unconditional pardon to Richard Milhaus Nixon for all federal crimes committed against the people of the United States of America. The pardon will be absolute. The pardon may not be contested."

The Dad said, "That goddamn Nixon. He's getting off with a slap on the wrist. After all the lying and scheming. They're letting him off scot-free. A full pardon."

The Mom said, "It's just as well. We don't need any more trials. I couldn't take any more of that."

"The man was guilty as sin."

"He was our president. He thought he was doing what was best."

"He's a crook."

"It's over now. We can get back to normal. It's for the best."

"I suppose," said The Dad.

I yawned twice during the news and once during the first part of the late movie. Finally the moment arrived. The clock struck midnight. The Mom and The Dad cheered and clapped and sang a perfectly on-key rendition of "Happy Birthday to You."

The Dad said, "You're thirteen. You're a teenager now."

The Mom said, "He's no such thing. He's my baby boy. He'll always be my baby boy."

I said, "Don't be queer, Mom."

The Dad took an envelope out of his back pocket and handed it to me and said, "Here's to you, jellybean. Happy birthday."

I ripped open the envelope.

Inside were two tickets that read, "Admit Bearer."

That was all I needed to see. I raised the tickets above my head and said, "Excellent."

The Dad said, "You're welcome."

"You got them," I said. "I can't believe you got them. This is going to be great. You're going to drive us, right, Dad?

"Sure will."

"I'll tell Albert. He's not going to believe it."

The Mom said, "Wait a minute. Don't go anywhere yet. I've got something to show everyone. Timmy got it for me. Didn't you, Timmy?"

"I did?"

"Yes. You did."

The Dad said, "What is it?"

The Mom said, "Wait here." She left the den and went upstairs.

The Dad said, "What'd you get her? Some lilies like I told you?"

"No."

"What then?"

I shrugged.

He said, "That was nice of you to get a present for your mother. That was thoughtful of you."

"I guess."

We heard The Mom coming down the stairs. She said, "Here I come. Close your eyes."

The Dad and I did not close our eyes. We sat on the couch, watching the doorway.

The Mom appeared in a full-length mink coat. She sashayed into the room and turned on one foot and walked back in the opposite direction, eyes forward, back straight.

A mink is a nasty little mammal that resembles a weasel. But when you shaved a couple hundred minks and sewed their fur into a full-length coat and draped the coat around The Mom, a transformation took place. The Mom glowed. She shone. She was tall and thin and had dark red hair that she wore in a curly fashion. Her hair fell onto the black fur, which glimmered.

She said, "Well? How do I look?"

The Dad had his mouth open. He said, "Well, goddamn it."

The Mom stopped sashaying. She looked at The Dad, frowning. He said, "Timmy bought this?"

The Mom nodded.

He said, "How much did you pay for that coat, Timmy?"

I said, "A couple thou."

"A couple thou?"

"Yeah."

"You got a bargain. It's worth every penny. I've never seen a more beautiful coat."

The Mom said, "Do you like it? Does it look good?"

"It looks beautiful. You look beautiful."

"I do, don't I?"

"Beautiful," repeated The Dad.

Then he did something strange. He got up and went over to The Mom and placed his hands on her shoulders and kissed her on the forehead. Then he wrapped his arms around her and hugged her. The Mom patted him once on the back and looked at me and shrugged and patted him once more.

The Dad stepped back and looked at The Mom. He said, "Model it. Walk around for me."

The Mom said, "It's bedtime, Timmy. You've got a big day tomorrow. It's your birthday."

I said, "I'm not tired."

"Go ahead. Go up to bed."

"Okay. Good night."

"Good night."

"Good night, son."

I went upstairs and opened the bedroom door and listened to Albert breathing deep-sleep breath. I walked quietly to my desk, so as not to wake him, and put the two tickets on the desktop, then took off my clothes and put on my pajamas and got into bed.

Tomorrow was the big day. Tomorrow Evel Knievel would attempt to make history by jumping over the Snake River Canyon in his Skycycle X-2 rocket. People gave him a fifty-fifty chance. All kinds of things could go wrong. The rocket was untested. Evel Knievel might crash into the side of the cliff and kill himself. The rocket might explode or break apart in midair. No one knew what would happen. But we would be there to see it, live on closed-circuit TV. Albert and me. We would see the rocket wheeled onto the takeoff ramp. We would see Evel Knievel give the thumbs-up signal from the cockpit. We would see the flames shoot out of the back of the rocket on the way up the takeoff ramp. That was the best moment, the moment of blastoff. At that moment, anything was possible. He might just do it. He might just soar for miles and miles, as far as anyone could see, as high as the clouds. He might just clear the canyon and land safely on the other side.

Anything was possible.